A Vacancy for a Village Vet

Joanne Boden

Choc Lit

Where heroes are like chocolate – irresistible!

Published 2022 by Choc Lit Limited
Penrose House, Crawley Drive, Camberley, Surrey GU15 2AB, UK
www.choc-lit.com

EPUB: 978-1-78189-005-9
PRINT: 978-1-78189-013-4

Printed and bound by Amazon.

To my husband, Andrew. This one's for you.

Acknowledgements

I would like to thank all the team at Choc Lit for bringing *A Vacancy for a Village Vet* to life. This still feels like a dream come true.

To my editor, who once again provided me with insight and guidance and wise words. This book is stronger because of you. Thank you for your patience and kindness. I loved working with you!

I would like to thank the Choc Lit family for their ongoing support and encouragement. It means a lot to me. Thank you to the cover designer for the gorgeous cover. I would like to thank the Tasting Panel readers who read my manuscript and saw its potential and who made publication possible: Kate Avetoomyan, Donna Morgan, Bee Master, Laura Sumner, Samantha May-Emberson, Alma Hough, Hilary Brown, Ruth Nägele, Anne Eckersley, Fran Stevens, Yvonne Greene, Jo Osborne, Lorna Baker and Gill Leivers.

Thank you to my boys, Stephen and Tom, who came up with the names of Sammy and Daisy!

And thank you Andrew for just being there. I love you.

Prologue

Fifteen years ago ...

'You'll come back, won't you?'

Daniel pulled Hannah towards him and closed his eyes. He couldn't look at her, couldn't bear to look into those smokey grey eyes and see nothing but sadness and hurt. He inhaled her strawberry shampoo, felt her breath on his neck. She couldn't see his face. He wouldn't cause her pain by allowing her to see the lie that lay beneath the surface.

'I'll be back,' he said, unable now to stop those words, his throat tight and dry. He stroked her flyaway blonde waves that could never be tamed and rested his hand on the back of her head.

'And you'll write to me every day?' she asked.

He heard the uncertainty in the shaking of her words.

He wanted to slow time. To stay in this moment forever. They'd agreed to write proper letters, not quick texts or emails, although of course they could. "Handwritten letters are much more romantic" she said. They reminded her of the olden days. Of "Elizabeth and Mr Darcy".

'I'll write to you,' he said. His fingers twisted in her hair.

He wanted to believe that he would.

A car horn sounded. His mother popped her head out of the half-lowered window, followed by a plume of cigarette smoke. 'Daniel,' she hollered, 'we need to get going.'

He exhaled slowly, felt Hannah's shoulders slip away from him as she stepped back. She swiped a finger across her eyes. A smear of black mascara followed in its wake. She gave him a slow, sad smile.

He reclosed the gap between them and his fingers traced her cheekbones as he dipped his head to give her one last, tender kiss on the lips.

Eyes were on them. He wished with every breath in his body that they were alone.

"You're only kids" his mum had told him, when she announced she'd be moving to London with her shiny new husband, although none of this was David Brewer's fault. Daniel liked him. He hadn't pretended to be a substitute father. After all, he had a grandfather for that. David had made that perfectly clear.

But they were all wrong. Yes, he was only fifteen, nearly sixteen, but he knew his own mind and heart, knew what he felt in his bones and blood and muscles. And he loved Hannah. His mother had laughed when he shared that bit of news with her, his cheeks flaming and his heart pounding with this shared intimacy. "You'll fall in love a dozen times – it's part of growing up." And then more forcefully when he'd told her Hannah was important to him – "*You don't know what love is at your age!*"

She told him with a faraway look in her eyes that she had fallen in love at sixteen, and look where that had landed her – almost as an afterthought she'd quickly added she wouldn't have changed having him for the world. But he'd seen the stark truth in those words. She'd have changed things in a heartbeat. Back then at least, maybe not now. That boy she had loved was long gone, married twice since then, and with four kids to his name, not including Daniel. He had never been a part of his life.

“Stay or go” his mother told him, giving him a choice. The decision was his, and his alone. Go to London, or stay here in Middlefern with Gerald. “It’s up to you. You’re nearly sixteen, old enough to make up your own mind”. But apparently not old enough to know if he was in love with a girl he had loved all of his short life.

There was no choice. There had never been a choice.

He couldn’t stay in Middlefern, not under the same roof as Gerald. He’d briefly toyed with the idea of asking Kathy, Hannah’s mum, if he could stay with them, but that, he knew, would only lead to more questions, none of which he could answer. The main one being, why couldn’t he stay with Gerald?

If he left he knew he could never come back, not while Gerald lived and worked in the village. He could never return.

So he did what he had to do. He lied and told Hannah he would do all of those things. His final act of kindness before breaking her heart.

‘It’s time to go, son.’ Gerald stood on the threshold to his veterinary practice, arms folded across his broad chest, a slight sneer spread across his face. Daniel’s hands curled into tight fists. He refused to turn around. He would not look at him. He’d never have to look at him again.

Gerald sauntered past them and stopped at the side of the car. He peered in through the passenger window. ‘You got everything, Samantha?’ he asked.

She nodded. ‘Yes, and thank you, for everything.’

‘Take care of yourself, and phone me when you get there.’

Gerald opened the passenger door. ‘Time to go now, son,’ he shouted in Daniel’s direction.

Daniel's jaw tensed as he reached for Hannah's hand. 'I'll write soon,' he said. Another lie.

'Promise.'

'Promise.' He very nearly choked on the word. His final act of betrayal.

He turned to go, but she grabbed his arm and pressed something cold and hard into the palm of his hand.

'Don't look now,' she whispered. 'Look later, in the car.'

He nodded, unable to formulate any words.

He turned towards the car, averting his eyes so he wouldn't see Gerald.

Kathy placed her arm around her daughter's shoulder. The two of them like statues, silently watching him go.

'Bye, son,' Gerald said as he grabbed Daniel's arm, forcing him to stop.

Daniel looked at his shoes, taking solace in this small victory.

'Look after your mum for me,' Gerald growled.

Daniel shook his arm free and unfolded his long, lean body into the car. He shut the door without turning to face the old man. Instead he looked at his mother.

'Ready love?' she asked.

'Yeah.'

'She'll be okay, you know. So will you.'

'I hope so,' he said. He had a chance at a brand new start. Away from Middlefern and away from *him*. He just wished Hannah could be a part of that new start. Maybe in time she could join him. Travel to London. She could go to university there, as they'd planned. Maybe they could buy a flat. Move in together. It was possible. Anything was possible, wasn't it?

But even as he had these fleeting thoughts he knew it was a fantasy.

This was the end.

Time to move on.

He would forget and so would she. Given time.

The car pulled away from the kerbside.

Hannah lifted a hand to wave, but it slowly dropped as she hugged her arms around her body. He saw Kathy raise her hand to stroke her daughter's hair. The image became smaller and smaller in the rear-view mirror. He observed the whispering of words that he could not hear.

His fingers unfurled and in his palm he found half a heart. A locket made of sterling silver. He turned it over. There was no engraving, just smooth metal, the size of a ten pence piece. It took several seconds before it hit him like a punch to the gut. He had half, Hannah the other. Two halves of one heart, forever broken.

Chapter One

Present Day

The sleepy village of Middlefern was nestled in a dip. On one side of the valley was a large working farm and on the other, sprawling countryside stretched for miles before you reached the nearest town. Although small, the village had a post office counter in the friendly corner shop, a fruit and veg shop, a bakers, butchers, small village school, GP surgery, pharmacy, a friendly pub called The Middlefern Arms and a small parish church. A home care agency was housed in a flat above the village shop and in the centre of everything stood a stone cottage attached to the Jackson Veterinary Practice.

Dr Daniel Jackson leaned against his ancient Land Rover, the bonnet still warm to the touch, and surveyed the land around him, basking in the warmth of the summer sunshine while breathing in the fresh air of cows and grass. How could he have forgotten how green it was here? And not just one green, but a kaleidoscope of different hues and tones that drew the eye in.

He hadn't set foot in the village for fifteen years and although it felt strange to be back, a part of him felt like he'd never left.

Sammy, his black and white Border collie, ran round him in circles, kicking up bits of gravel and dust, enjoying the feeling of freedom after being cooped up inside the vehicle for the past three hours.

It had been a long journey from London, with only one motorway stop along the way. He raised his arms above his head and stretched out his tight, aching muscles, feeling the knots in his shoulders loosen and the crick in his neck slowly fade.

He looked over towards the corner shop and remembered. How they always called in for sweets and cans of pop after school. Jelly babies had been her favourite, and she always gave him the orange ones.

Over time the memories of the village and of her had slowly faded. Did she still live here? Or had she moved away just like he had done? She'd been ambitious, full of dreams.

He sighed softly. He hoped Hannah Kennedy had followed her heart and lived in a big city with a high-profile job in publishing or the creative arts, with a couple of kids.

Leaving Middlefern had been one of the hardest things he'd ever done.

He reached into the passenger side and pulled out a green bulging rucksack which he swung onto his shoulder. He couldn't put it off any longer.

Although still early, at just seven in the morning, the day was already warm and his red-checked shirt stuck to his back. He'd need a quick shower and a bite to eat before heading into the veterinary practice. His stomach churned at the thought. How would he be greeted? The prodigal grandson returns and with all the accompanying baggage.

He called for Sammy to follow him into the cottage. How they reacted to him wasn't his problem. He wouldn't be around long enough to care. Digging the keys out of his jeans back pocket he placed the key into the lock and opened the door.

The Old Cottage wasn't really a cottage, but rather a large extension that had been built onto the back of the Jackson Veterinary Practice a little over a hundred years ago. Daniel stood in the small hallway, the air still and oppressive. He decided to leave the door open to allow fresh air in. He absorbed the enormity of the space. It felt huge and probably bigger than it actually was because he'd been cooped up in a one bedroom flat for the better part of six months.

Dumping his rucksack by the door he padded through to the kitchen, Sammy at his heels, switching on lights as he went. Even on the sunniest of days the cottage had remained stubbornly dark. As a child, the kitchen had been his favourite room. A place of warmth and cooking and filled with his mother's laughter.

The cleaning firm he'd hired to gut the cottage had done a fantastic job. The kitchen sparkled and shone, thanks to the aid of cleaning fluids and elbow grease. The cupboards and countertops were dated, and not to his taste, but he noticed that there were new cupboard doors. They would do for now. More importantly, the cottage held absolutely no trace of *him*. Gerald couldn't be found anywhere, although a smell lingered in the air, a lived-in smell that always takes a while to fade. He could live with that. Memories posed the biggest problem.

First thing first, he needed to find the boiler so he'd have hot water. He'd open a few windows to air the cottage and he'd make a brew. He'd brought bread, coffee and butter with him, plus a box of dog biscuits. It would do for now, until he had time to do a big shop.

He opened and closed several cupboards before finding a large bowl that he filled with water for Sammy.

He located the boiler and switched it on, praying there would be no problems. It lurked in a cupboard by the larder door and looked to be fairly new, which was a good sign. Gerald had done some alterations to both cottage and practice in recent years, including installing new windows and radiators.

In the fifteen years since leaving Middlefern, his mother had only visited Gerald a handful of times, but she'd phoned him every Sunday afternoon, regular as clockwork.

He opened the kitchen window, creating a through draft and gazed around the room, taking in the situation. The cottage and practice were both his. This reality still hadn't quite sunk in.

He ran a hand over his face, feeling the rough stubble and yawned. He'd need to clean himself up before meeting his employees, first impressions and all that. Dr Jeffries, a locum vet, had been covering the practice for the past couple of months, following Gerald's death. He'd come out of retirement on the understanding that he could only do three months at most. *And not a day more.* Today was his last day.

Daniel retraced his steps to fetch his rucksack. He poked his head into the living room, the room on the left side of the hallway. He sucked in the dry air, steadying himself against the open door. He felt like the little boy he had once been. He pictured himself sitting on the floor surrounded by toy cars, Gerald working in the surgery or in the study, his mother baking in the kitchen; the smell of freshly baked biscuits wafting into the room. Standing there now, looking into the room, he shuddered. It hadn't changed at all. Not one bit.

The walls were still lined with brown striped wallpaper, peeling near the skirting board. The familiar threadbare red carpet, a rust red, the colour of dried blood, but it was clean as he'd asked the cleaners to steam clean it. Wooden bookshelves lined two walls and the brown leather three piece suite with matching armchair and footstool dominated the space. He'd imagined the furniture would be long gone, replaced by new and modern pieces. But here they were.

He'd have to get rid of them, redecorate. He didn't want to be reminded of his past. He preferred light and airy rooms. But as quickly as the thought entered his head he dismissed it. What was the point? In six short months he'd be gone. He had no intention of staying here. He was going to sell up, both the cottage and the business. He had a plan and he was going to stick to it.

He strode into the room and opened the window wide. He'd do the same in the small study, located on the right of the hallway. He opened the door and stepped into the room.

The only two pieces of furniture that remained were a large wooden desk and chair. On the desk was a cardboard box, the kind used by removal companies and for a second he wondered if it was one of his. But no, it couldn't be, as all his boxes were in storage and wouldn't be arriving until tomorrow. This had *not* been the original plan, as the removal company had been booked to deliver his belongings on moving day, not the day after. They'd apologised, blaming the mix-up on a computer error. More like human error, Daniel scoffed when he'd been told. Another day wouldn't make much difference as he didn't own that much stuff, not after the divorce. They'd offered him a discount because of the inconvenience and probably to avoid a bad review, to which he'd agreed.

What was inside the box? The cleaning firm hadn't mentioned finding any boxes. Unless it was from one of his neighbours? A welcome gift? A food parcel? But then why leave it in the study and not the kitchen? Sammy bounded into the room, her tail wagging. She sniffed at the box.

'I know, girl, I know,' he said. 'Let's take a look.'

His palm rested on top of the box. He checked the sides for any clues. On the back someone had written, "For the attention of Samantha Brewers".

Not for him then.

Why leave a parcel for his mother here? And more importantly, who was it from? Gerald? He didn't recognize the handwriting. Surely Gerald's handwriting hadn't changed that much over the years? More likely he'd got someone to write it out for him. Daniel leaned against the desk. It didn't make any sense. If the parcel was for his mother then why hadn't she taken it with her after the funeral? Unless she'd missed it in packing up stuff. Who'd found it? Whatever the reason he would have to post it. He'd do it later on before he went shopping.

After a hot shower, a change of clothes and two cups of strong, black coffee, Daniel found himself hovering outside the surgery's main entrance with Sammy. He bent down and stroked her head, taking a few more moments to collect his thoughts. His stomach churned at the thought of what they would see when they looked at him. Would they see a man who had come crawling back to inherit his deceased grandfather's fortune and business? Would they see a man who simply had no choice? Did they even know what happened to him in London? He assumed they might. Gerald would have delighted in telling them all about his grandson's failings.

Muttering under his breath he reminded himself once again he didn't need to be best friends with these people. He was here as their boss, as a vet. It was a job and a place to live until he could sell up and move on with his life. He raked a hand through his short wavy dark brown hair that now had a few lighter strands thanks to the sun, and pushed old memories aside.

He sensed his failure; it oozed from every pore. Would others pick up on that? At the age of thirty-one he'd achieved a lot in life. He was a trained vet, and a good one. Throughout his childhood and teenage years he'd pushed against his instincts, his need to become a vet, because Gerald had wanted him to take over the family business one day. Daniel had dreamed of becoming a vet, but he refused to acknowledge this to his mother, to his grandfather and even to Hannah, instead pretending to hate the idea because being a vet meant validating Gerald's own dreams and wishes about his grandson's future. In Daniel's heart he knew that becoming a vet was his only path in life though, what he was meant to be, no matter how hard he rebelled.

But despite his successes and hard work, studying without a scrap of help from Gerald, he now found himself reliant upon Gerald's inheritance and home. It shouldn't be this way. He didn't want to live this way, to rely on *him* or anyone. He hadn't done so for the past fifteen years, but now he had no choice. Not after the messy and painful divorce.

With a deep sigh and a final silent prayer he pushed the heavy oak door open and stepped inside.

The woman sitting behind the reception desk looked up and beamed at him. How could he not notice her? He guessed her age to be around sixty. She wore her bright purple hair in a bun. Large pink glasses framed her face. He walked towards her with an introduction on the tip of his tongue, but before he could utter a word a tall man with a shock of silver hair strode towards him with an outstretched hand. He wore a starched white lab coat, the crisp folds evident on the sleeves, under which were a navy blue tie, a navy blue jacket, white shirt and tailored grey trousers. Daniel thought the man must be very hot with all those layers.

'Dr Jackson, I presume,' the man said. 'I'm Doctor Jeffries.' His eyes lowered towards Sammy who sat at Daniel's feet, before swooping upwards, dismissing her, just as he had dismissed the receptionist.

Daniel recoiled from the man's nasal twang. He hadn't imagined the emphasis that had been placed on the word, *doctor*, but he let it slide, raising an eyebrow before shaking his hand.

Daniel turned his attention toward the receptionist and offered her a wide and warm smile which she matched with one of her own.

'Well, I'll give you a quick handover and then let the nurses give you a tour before you take over,' Dr Jeffries interrupted, his voice booming over Daniel's shoulder.

Daniel exhaled a long held breath and slowly folded his arms as he eyeballed the older man. He wasn't intimidated by him, just simply ticked off. Who the hell was in charge here?

This obnoxious man had all but dismissed the nurses, almost as if they were of little importance. Daniel had worked with the likes of him before; vets with a superiority complex. Often they were older and full of their own importance. 'I assumed you'd be working until the end of the day?' Daniel asked, in that slow, drawn out way of his. He had all the time in the world. After all, he was paying this man's wages.

'God, no, now that you're here I must get going as soon as possible. I promised my wife we'd go out for a pub lunch today.'

Daniel swore the receptionist suppressed a grin, her lips tight with the effort. He gave Jeffries one last, long, lingering stare before opening his mouth.

'Okay then,' he said, unfolding his arms. 'Talk me through what we have before you go.' He didn't have the energy to start an argument.

Jeffries didn't need telling twice and scurried away from the reception desk, gesturing wildly with his arms for Daniel to follow. Daniel sucked in another breath while telling himself that this man would soon be gone.

'*Wait* there girl,' he told Sammy. He followed Jeffries – not missing the receptionist pulling an exasperated face at Jeffries' retreating back while mouthing, "and good riddance". He saw her bend over and stroke Sammy's head. Perhaps the staff here would warm to him after all?

The two men passed through the waiting area and along a long corridor, off which were several rooms, including the staffroom slash kitchen, which is where they were now headed. A young woman with mousy brown hair pulled back into a high ponytail, poured boiling water into a brown teapot. She turned her head towards the door when it swung open. Jeffries spoke first. 'This is, erm – Becky, a trainee nurse.' His words were rushed. He never even looked at her. Becky's mouth hung open.

Daniel had seen and heard enough. The young girl looked terrified and he wasn't sure if it was because of him being the new boss, or this idiot.

He smiled his slow smile, the one that made his eyes crinkle, and held out his hand to the young woman. 'Hi Becky, my name is Daniel Jackson. I'm the new owner, and your new boss. My grandfather owned this practice. It's nice to meet you.'

She shook his hand, relief written all over her face as she smiled back at him.

'Is there another nurse?' he asked. The question was aimed pointedly towards her.

She nodded. 'Yes, Emily, she's in with Phyllis's rabbit.'

'O-kay,' he said in that slow way of his, 'well I'll go and say hello to her then.'

He shot Becky a wide grin before leaving the staffroom and entering the corridor once more. The other rooms included a consulting room, a nurse consulting room, operating room, a small lab and a storeroom. There was also a room for animals who needed to stay overnight that they called the hospital. He didn't need Dr "I-am-too-good-for-this-place" to show him where to go. This time Jeffries followed him with an audible huff.

'It's fairly quiet at the moment,' Jeffries wheezed as he tried to keep pace with Daniel's long strides. We have a rabbit in for observation. He'd not been eating but is now doing much better.' Daniel pushed open the hospital door.

'Flopsy has passed some droppings this morning, and is now munching on some lettuce leaves, so I think she's okay.' A young woman with unruly red curly hair piled up on top of her head thrust a hand towards Daniel as she spoke.

He shook it. 'Hi I'm Daniel Jackson,' he said. 'The new vet.'

'Hello.' She smiled at him, unfazed by his sudden appearance. She didn't look at Jeffries as she spoke. 'Other than that there's not much else going on.'

'Am I needed?' Jeffries interrupted, his voice now a high-pitched squeak. Every word sounded clipped and short.

Daniel turned to face him, sighed and then paused a beat before speaking. 'I think I can take it from here.'

Five minutes later in the cosy staffroom, Emily ran through the morning routine for him and told him what patients had been booked in. Flopsy the rabbit, he learned, belonged to Phyllis, the purple-haired receptionist.

'That man,' Phyllis uttered with an exasperated sounding sigh. 'I know I shouldn't say this, but I'm glad to see the back of him. Mind you, I can't begrudge the fact he's a good vet. He looked after Flopsy for me, and he did a grand job.'

Daniel suppressed a smile as he lifted his mug of black coffee to his lips. He'd only known the man for less than ten minutes but that had been ten minutes too long.

'Must be strange for you, Dr Jackson, being back here, in the village I mean, after all these years,' Phyllis said, as she dumped her cup into the sink.

Daniel's arm froze mid-air, before placing his cup down. He should have been prepared for this type of question. Of course they'd ask him about his grandfather; it was only natural. They'd also want to know why he'd left, why he hadn't set foot in the village, not even to visit his grandfather. Or to attend his funeral. People would be curious. He couldn't blame them for that.

He joined Phyllis at the sink. 'It's a little strange, but I'll get used to it,' he said.

'You don't look like him.' She took the empty cup from his hand and dumped it in the soapy water. 'I'd never had guessed you were Gerald's grandson.'

Please don't ask me anything else.

'Well, it's good that you're here Dr Jackson. If you need anything, you only need to ask.'

'Thank you, and it's Daniel. Call me Daniel,' he said.

'Right, I'll go and open up. No one's due in until ten, but it's open surgery this morning so you might have a few visitors.'

'Okay. I'll come out with you.'

'Oh, you don't need to do that,' Phyllis said, all flustered, 'I'll call you if anyone pops in.'

'No, it's okay. I always used to hang around the reception desk if it was quiet, in my old practice,' he added. It was true, he had done that. Mainly out of curiosity, but also because he met people on neutral ground, not in the formal consulting room, and that gave him an advantage as he often got a truer picture.

'Right then,' Phyllis said, with a flash of a smile.

Daniel rolled up the sleeves of his checked blue shirt and leaned against the reception desk waiting to see who would arrive. He heard the hum of the air conditioning, but the room remained warm. His neck prickled with sweat.

It didn't take long for the first person to arrive.

An elderly lady opened the door with one hand, a cat carrier and a walking stick swinging from the other.

Daniel rushed over to her and gently took the cat carrier from her outstretched arm. She smiled at him with relief shimmering in her eyes. 'Thank you, young man,' she said.

'Mrs Barlow, whatever's the matter?' Phyllis asked, now at Daniel's side. She took the old woman's arm to lead her towards a chair.

Mrs Barlow's eyes flitted between Phyllis and Daniel as she spoke. Phyllis squeezed her hand. Daniel placed the carrier on the floor and crouched down, peering at the cat who lay on its side.

'Ted's off his food, and it's not like him. He's always eating, he has a hearty appetite.' Mrs Barlow's voice cracked with every word.

'Hello boy,' Daniel said gently, eyeing the cat through the bars of the door. 'Should we go and take a look at you?' He turned his attention to Mrs Barlow. 'My name is Daniel Jackson, I'm the new vet. Is it okay if I take him in the back, take some blood and just have a feel of his tummy?'

The poor woman looked terrified. She pulled a tissue out of her coat sleeve. 'Can I come with you?'

'Sure you can,' Daniel said. 'How old is Ted?' he asked, although he guessed he was around twelve or thirteen years old.

'He's just turned fifteen. He's an old man now,' she said.

‘I’ll come with you, Mrs Barlow,’ Phyllis said as she helped the older woman to her feet. ‘Then I’ll go get Emily,’ she added.

‘Come on Ted, let’s see how I can help you.’ Daniel pushed the nagging feeling in his chest back down. He had a feeling Ted was one poorly cat.

Chapter Two

Hannah Kennedy swung the door shut behind her and tucked the hem of her trouser legs into her socks. She pulled a small key from the front zip of her rucksack and unchained her bike from the railings. A bike that had seen better days. The deep blue paintwork had faded over the years and there were rust patches all over the frame which, over time, had joined together so that not much paint remained. On the whole though it still served its purpose in getting her around the village and to the people she cared for on a daily basis. She loved her job as a home carer. She took great pride in her work. Her life had a purpose, a daily goal and that was important – vital even – for her survival, following the death of her mother.

She tucked a loose strand of blonde curls back into a bobby pin as she looked over the road towards the two bedroom house that had once been her childhood home. She had so many fond memories of living in that house, but when her mother passed away from cancer eighteen months ago, she could no longer live in those four walls. She needed somewhere new, somewhere she could make new memories, more happy ones, leaving the unhappy ones behind.

So she had compromised, seizing the opportunity to rent out the ground-floor flat on the opposite side of the road. She lived close to her roots and work, with the constant reminder of what had once been before illness. The perfect solution. She felt as if she'd made a change, a new start, that she could get on with the rest of her life.

This is what she told herself, but the stark reality was very different. Her life had been put on hold, and she had no idea of how to move forward. For over ten years her life had revolved around looking after her mother, and now that she was gone, Hannah needed to find a new way of living, of being; she just wasn't sure how to go about it.

She checked the rucksack straps were tight on her shoulders and mounted the bike. Another busy day stretched ahead of her.

She cycled slowly down the hill and continued along the high street, past the corner shop and then on towards the vets. As she passed the car park she noticed that the shiny BMW was no longer there. It had been replaced with a battered old green Land Rover. She couldn't imagine old man Jeffries driving a beat-up Land Rover. The thought made her giggle. Then she remembered a conversation she'd had with Emily only a week before. Emily told her Jeffries would be leaving soon and a new vet would be taking over. There was a lot of mystery surrounding the new vet. The only thing the team had been told was that he would be relocating from London and had bought the business and cottage.

Hannah assumed the man must have money as the cottage alone was worth a fortune. The new vet would most likely be one of those city slicker types who wanted to relocate to the country. Live the *All Creatures Great and Small* life. A quieter life. Away from the noise and smoke. Hannah laughed as she puffed out her cheeks. He'd last five minutes in a village like Middlefern.

Hannah cycled past the surgery and wondered who he could be and why he'd chosen to leave London to come to this tiny, relatively unknown part of England. She'd ask

Emily for the gossip later on after work. Surely he couldn't be any worse than Jeffries. That man didn't even like dogs.

She tore her gaze away from the vets and looked at the road ahead. She thought about Daniel Jackson, just as she did every time she cycled past the vets. She tried not to think about him, but she couldn't help herself. She often thought about Gerald Jackson and of how he'd devoted his life to that practice, the village and community as a whole, and then inevitably her mind wandered to Dan and what he was doing now.

Had he ever stopped in the middle of the street because a woman passing by wore her perfume or resembled the girl she used to be? Had he ever thought about her at all? Those thoughts and whims had faded over the years. But she found herself thinking about him. His memory etched into the village streets. She liked to think that perhaps he thought about her every now and again. She hoped he was happy, even though he had broken her heart.

She'd told herself again and again that they'd been kids, just kids. It was a long time ago, but the sight of that cottage always brought back the memories of what could have been. With a bitter laugh she carried on her way. She had her job, her friends, her flat and most importantly, Daisy the tabby cat in her life. What more did she need? She had no place, nor time for a man, despite Emily's attempts at playing matchmaker. She'd been told on many occasions by her so-called best friend that she would die alone surrounded by cats. Hannah actually thought this wasn't such a bad way to go in the grand scheme of things.

Her first port of call was with Mrs Jones. Her duties involved helping her in and out of the shower, and assisting with her medication. She'd known Mrs Jones for five years and the two of them had quickly become friends. Then, next on the list was Mr Bakewell who needed a little bit of help to check his blood sugars. She also changed his dressings twice a week. She'd only known him a matter of months because his daughter had had to return to work on a part-time basis. They needed a little bit of extra support when she wasn't at home. He was a nice man, always polite, no bother. In years gone-by he'd have been called a proper gentleman. Mr and Mrs Billings required her to do a little light housework, and the last call of the morning would be to see Mrs Barlow. She'd known Mrs Barlow for ten years. She'd visited her during her first week at the home-care agency. Even when Mrs Barlow wasn't on her books for that day's duties, she usually popped in to check on her anyway. Sometimes she'd even pay her a visit on her day off.

Picking up speed now, she cycled along the lanes. She didn't want to be late.

'It's so lovely to see you, love.' Mrs Barlow ushered Hannah into her flat with a huge smile and a wave of her hand. 'Would you like a cup of tea?'

Hannah shrugged off her rucksack. The flat was always stifling, the thermostat set to high, despite the warmth of the June sunshine. 'I'll make you a cup of tea, and you can tell me anything else you need doing,' Hannah said, already filling the kettle.

'Oh, you're a good girl.' Mrs Barlow sat at the kitchen table. 'Make sure to make yourself peppermint tea. I think you left a few bags here last time. Now you come to mention it, there are a few things you could do for me, love.'

Hannah found the teabags and mugs and rooted inside her rucksack for the digestive biscuits she had brought with her from home. She also pulled out a box of cat biscuits, not wanting to leave Ted out.

'Where's Ted?' Hannah asked, suddenly realising he hadn't brushed up against her leg like he usually did. He had a sixth sense when it came to Hannah as she always brought treats with her. She glanced at his cat bed. It was empty.

'He's asleep on the couch, love. He's had a busy morning. Took him to the vets as he's been a bit off his food. That nice young vet took some blood and told me he'd be in touch when he got the results.' She paused. 'I have a feeling it's bad news. He didn't say anything, but I could tell from the look in his eyes.'

'Oh, I'm so sorry to hear that,' Hannah said as she placed a mug of tea on the kitchen table. 'But you never know, it might just be a bug or something.'

'Maybe,' Mrs Barlow said, reaching for a digestive biscuit. 'I don't know how you drink that stuff,' she said, pointing to Hannah's cup.

Hannah picked up her peppermint. tea. 'It's an acquired taste,' she said.

So the vet was young? She wanted to know more about him, but she couldn't ask, not now. She didn't want to cause any more upset when it came to Ted.

'I'll pop my head in and say goodbye to him before I go, check he's okay. I brought some of those cat biscuits he likes. Daisy loves them.' She smiled as she said this.

She'd be lost without Daisy. A rescue tabby she brought home from the animal shelter a week after her mum's passing. The house had felt cold and empty without her mother's smile and warmth. Too quiet. She'd needed someone else to care for, someone else to protect.

'Oh, you didn't need to do that, love. Those biscuits are expensive,' Mrs Barlow tutted.

'It's my treat. I like to buy them.' Hannah sipped her tea. 'What would you like me to do today? I have an hour before my lunch break.'

'Well, there's not much to do really. I suppose you could pop a wash on for me, and there's a bit of ironing that needs doing.'

'Do you want me to run a hoover over the living room for you?'

Mrs Barlow pondered this for a moment before shaking her head. 'No, love, leave it for today. Best let Ted sleep. It can wait a day or two.'

'Okay, well I'll finish my tea then get to work.'

Every time she visited Mrs Barlow it was the same old routine, but she loved it. They'd sit and drink tea, have a chat, then she'd get to work. The conversation was more important than the cleaning or the cooking. There were no other visitors. Only Hannah, and she knew the importance of making time. Time was everything. She couldn't rush, she needed to listen. That was how you learned things about people, how you really got to know them. Mrs Barlow needed to be listened to.

'Oh, and if you wouldn't mind I have a parcel that needs to be posted, but that means going to the post office.'

Hannah smiled. 'That's no bother at all, it's on my way back home for lunch anyway.'

'Well, if you don't mind that'd be a great help. Hard for me to carry a box, what with my stick and all. Had to get a taxi to the vets this morning, but luckily that nice young nurse gave me a lift back. Not Emily, the other one, I forget her name.'

'That'd be Becky. She's a trainee veterinary nurse. Very quiet apparently, but Emily told me she's a good worker and will do well. I've only met her a couple of times.'

'She was lovely to me, as was the vet.' Mrs Barlow sighed with a faraway look in her eye. 'I know Ted's in good hands.'

Hannah nodded then drained her cup. 'Right, I'd best get on with my jobs and then I'll take that parcel to the post office for you.'

'Thank you love, you're an angel.'

Hannah balanced the large cardboard box on her hip as she pushed her bike down the hill, her mind full of thoughts about Ted and Mrs Barlow being all alone in the world. She also knew she needed to talk to her boss, Claire about her concerns. She'd call into the office at the end of the day.

She stopped to catch her breath at the bottom of the hill, the straps of her rucksack cutting into her back. Her skin felt sticky and her stomach rumbled. The cardboard box became heavier with every step she took. She would post the parcel, have a quick sandwich at home, and then it would be back out for her afternoon rounds. She shifted the parcel onto her other hip and continued on her way.

She wondered what was inside the box. Mrs Barlow hadn't told her. She knew it was a birthday gift for her niece who lived down south. Hannah wondered if it was a stack of books? Thinking about it now, she should have asked because Pat would need to know if it contained anything valuable. She pushed her bike, her arm now aching with the effort.

She leaned the bike against the railings outside the corner shop, glad to have the use of both hands again and pushed open the door with her hip, the old bell tinkling as she did so. The post office counter was situated at the front of the shop, next to the till. Pat was busy serving a customer, so Hannah waited patiently for her turn, gripping the box with both hands.

'Hello, love, that looks heavy.' Pat took the box from Hannah's outstretched arms.

'It is heavy,' Hannah grunted, 'and before you ask, I have no idea what's inside'—she shrugged apologetically—'I should have asked Mrs Barlow.'

'You never carried this all the way here did you?' Pat craned her neck to look through the window, spotting the bike against the railings. 'You carried that while pushing your bike!'

Hannah nodded.

'Feels like a ton of bricks in here, but my guess is they're books. She sends books every birthday, without fail.' Pat placed the box on the scales. 'These are particularly heavy. It'll cost twenty-two pounds to send first class, or nineteen pounds fifty second class.'

Hannah jiggled her shoulders, releasing her rucksack so she could retrieve her purse from the front pocket. 'She told me she wanted it sent as quickly as possible, but she only gave me ten pounds.' She emptied the contents of her purse onto the counter and coins scattered in all directions. Pat slapped her palm down to catch them.

'You've only got one fifty in change here,' Pat said as she picked up the coins and dropped them onto Hannah's palm.

Hannah sighed and dug out her debit card. 'I'll pay for it, then she can owe me back.' She knew full well she'd tell Mrs Barlow that it only cost ten pounds.

'First or second class?' Pat asked.

'First, please.'

'Machine's ready.'

Hannah pinged her card and popped her purse back into her rucksack.

'You're too soft, love,' Pat said, but she was smiling.

'I know, but she has no one else.'

'Is everything okay with you?' Pat leant over the counter, her eyes on Hannah's face.

The question took her by surprise. 'Yes, I'm fine.'

'Hmm-mm,' Pat said, smoothing her grey hair. 'Well, I'm glad to hear that love.' She bit her lip, her eyes darting to the floor before landing on Hannah's face once more. 'Your mum would be so proud of you.'

Hannah smiled. 'Thanks, see you soon.'

'That you will love, take care now, and be careful on that bike. You really need to wear a helmet you know,' she shouted as Hannah pulled on the door handle.

Her hands felt light without the weight of the box. She swung the door open to a man stood waiting outside with a huge cardboard box in his hands, obscuring his face. He stepped aside, wedging the door open with his foot, so she could get past him. She mumbled her thanks as she stepped out onto the pavement.

Her hand rested on the handlebar of her bike. And she froze … before then turning around to face the door once more. The man had gone.

Surely it couldn't be him? He'd severed all ties with this village, with her. The last she'd heard he was in London. He hadn't even made it back for his grandfather's funeral. That was the talk of the village for months. It couldn't possibly be him … could it?

Maybe he was back here checking on the cottage, or the business? There was no other reason for him to be in Middlefern. Could he be checking up on the new vet? It was a possibility. After all he might need to check they'd settled in.

But hadn't Emily told her the new vet had relocated from London? *London* ... No, surely not! Could *he* be the new vet? Emily knew nothing about their shared history, that they had dated. She'd moved to the village long after Dan had moved away and Hannah had never spoken about him. She wouldn't understand the significance of his return.

No. She was being silly. He never wanted to be a vet. He'd made that perfectly clear growing up.

Her hands shook. She hadn't seen his face because the cardboard box was in the way, but it had been the way he moved. A repressed memory floated to the surface … it *was* him. It had to be!

She hovered for a moment, unsure of what to do, her hands still on the handlebar. She made a split decision; she'd need to move otherwise he'd see her as soon as he walked out of the shop. She wasn't ready to see him.

She pushed the bike over the road, propped it against the railings and ducked behind a van. She'd be able to see him, but he wouldn't see her. She tried to steady her nerves, feeling suddenly wobbly on her feet. She placed her hand on the van's bonnet and forced her eyes to stay on the shop door. It only took another minute before he stepped through the door.

He lifted his head towards the sky and that's when Hannah's breath caught in her throat. All air was sucked from her body. She steadied herself against the sturdiness of the van as her vision blurred. Despite the blistering heat she felt stone cold.

He hadn't changed that much. He was no longer the gangly teenager he had once been; he had grown into that body. He had the same dark brown wavy hair that curled slightly towards the ends and his walk was the same, slow and measured. By God, she thought, he still looked good. Her mouth became dry and she couldn't take her eyes off him. He stood for a moment, hands in his pockets, before he turned to the left, away from Hannah and walked over to the railings. He bent down.

What was he doing?

She needed to follow him. She couldn't talk to him, not now, but she needed to see him; she couldn't quite let him go, not yet.

He stood up. In his hand was a lead, and on the end of it a beautiful black and white Border collie dog with the biggest brown eyes she had ever seen. Dan said something to the dog. She drew in a big breath and followed him from the safe distance of the other side of the road. Where was he going? And then it hit her. What if this was a fleeting visit and she'd never see him again? She couldn't let that happen; she had too many questions to ask. Why had he never written to her? Why had he never picked up the phone? Why come back here now? Why did he never come back to see her? Her head spun with so many unanswered questions. She'd be brave. She'd stop and confront him. He owed her an explanation. He owed her that much. Yes, they'd been young, but that still didn't excuse his actions. Why he'd tossed her aside once he'd got to London. The rejection still stung all these years later, even though she knew it shouldn't.

He carried on walking, past parked cars and then the only place left to go to was the veterinary surgery.

Her heart pounded in her chest as she stopped dead still to watch him.

He walked to the battered Land Rover, opened the passenger door and pulled out a green bag. Then he dug out a bunch of keys and headed into the surgery.

Dan Jackson was the new vet. And he wasn't going anywhere quite yet.

Chapter Three

The following day, Hannah waved goodbye to Mr Bennett, closed the door behind her, and made sure she heard the click of the lock. It had been one long and busy day. It had just turned six o'clock in the evening. During the summer months this was her favourite time of the day, when she'd finished work and could relax, knowing she'd done her best to help people. She liked helping people, which was why she finished late most days.

Her working day officially ended at five-thirty, but she almost always ran over, finishing nearer to six, even six-thirty on some days. She didn't mind, especially when her last call of the day was to Mr Bennett who lived out by Chris's farm. There weren't many jobs that'd give you such a breathtaking view of the natural world. Apart from the farm and farmhouse, Mr Bennett had no other neighbours for several miles. Hannah always felt like she'd been dropped into the middle of nowhere and that sense of freedom and space never grew old; it exhilarated her, while helping to soothe any worries or niggles she might have.

This evening the fields and the feeling of space were helping her to suppress the growing niggle that Daniel Jackson created. She did a few arm circles to loosen up her tight shoulders and ease the crick in her neck before adjusting the straps on her rucksack and hopping on the bike to cycle to the farm. She'd say a quick hello to the cows and sheep before cycling off home. She couldn't wait to give Daisy the cat a big cuddle, but before that she just needed five minutes to clear her mind, enjoy the light and the fresh air before being cooped up inside her flat for the evening.

She cycled slowly down the dirt track until she heard the cows mooing on the breeze. It'd soon be time for them to head back into the shed. She unfurled her legs from the bike and strode over to the pen, rucksack banging against her back, breathing in the fresh air and smell of cows. Her mother always used to laugh at her, not quite understanding why she liked the smell so much. *Who on earth likes the smell of cows?* Maybe that was why she liked to visit the cows every time she was near the farm. They provided a link back to her mum and although she hated to admit it – a link to Dan. She remembered many a summer evening when they'd sat on a scratchy haystack drinking cheap wine, and then giddy on life and love, had shared a kiss or two before slowly making their way back to her house.

A cow with wide chocolate-brown eyes pushed its nose through the bars of the fence, wanting to say hello. Hannah laughed. 'Hello girl, and how's your day been? As good as mine, eh,' she said when the cow appeared to shake its head before walking away.

Hannah pulled her hair free from the constraints of the bobby pins. Why had he chosen to come back here to Middlefern? Something must have happened for him to come crawling back. To uproot and move away from the place that had been his home for the past fifteen years. There had to be more to his story than him simply coming back home to rescue his grandfather's business. Surely he could have done that from a distance? He hadn't even come back for the funeral. Middlfern was far too remote for most people. But sometimes, wasn't that the point? She tilted her head up towards the sky and felt the gentle warmth of the sun on her face.

She couldn't quite wrap her head around the fact that Dan was actually a vet. All throughout school he'd been adamant that he wanted to be anything other than a vet and she hadn't quite understood why. He loved animals and enjoyed helping at Mr Heggarty's farm. She'd assumed it was some form of teenage rebellion, not doing what was expected of him, wanting to branch out on his own. She got that. But obviously, someone or something had changed his mind.

They'd been so young. Of course things changed. What sixteen-year-old knew what they'd be doing for the rest of their life? She'd wanted to go to university and study English literature, but those plans got dashed when her mother became ill, for the first time. Maybe something similar had happened to Dan? She should have chased after him. She should have been braver.

What could she say to him? He was a stranger now, a man, no longer a sixteen-year-old boy. Without really knowing why, she wanted to cry. She missed her mum. She'd know exactly what to say and do. She bit down on her bottom lip to stop the tears and sucked in a steadying breath. She'd give Emily a call once she got home, fill her in on bumping into Dan. Explain what had happened in their past.

A warm breeze blew towards her, lifting her hair up and over her eyes. She rubbed at her bare arms. She could stay here all evening, but she had stuff to do. Time to go.

She mounted the bike and set off down the lane in the direction of home.

As she approached the bottom road she began to slow down, but then without warning the bike shuddered and shook, making her wobble about violently from side to side. She clamped her teeth together. Something didn't feel right. She brought one foot to the ground and skidded to a halt, her heels digging into the dirt. With a sigh she swung her leg round, slid off the bike and examined the wheels.

Her heart sank.

Just as she thought. The front wheel was flat, the culprit a nail sticking out of the tread. She kicked the wheel in frustration. It was a two-mile walk back to the flat and she'd have to push the blasted bike with a heavy rucksack on her back. She swore under her breath. Why didn't she have a puncture repair kit? Then she remembered she hadn't replaced the last one she'd used a month ago. Mind you, not that a puncture repair kit would be of much use now, given the state of the tyre. She pulled her phone from her pocket and checked the signal. As she feared – no bars, no signal out here in the sticks, so calling Emily to ask for a lift was out of the question. Standing about on the side of the track wasn't going to get her anywhere, other than possibly death from dehydration or being mowed down as it was growing steadily darker. She'd better start moving if she wanted to make it back home in the next hour.

Daniel trampled across the familiar farmyard towards his Land Rover, Sammy at his heels, his boots now splattered with fresh mud and cow dung.

'Thanks for calling by, I really appreciate it,' Chris said, wiping his hands on his blue overalls before shaking

Daniel's hand. At six foot five, Daniel had to look up to meet Chris's eyes. Despite his height the man came across as a gentle giant with his curly black hair and easy-going nature. Daniel liked his no-nonsense style of talking and knew the farmer would be very easy to get along with. He also got the sense that Chris was extremely happy to have a new vet to help him maintain the health and wellbeing of his cattle.

After a busy morning surgery, followed by an afternoon of admin that couldn't be put off, no matter how hard he'd tried – thank God Phyllis had helped him – he'd thought it best to take a trip out to the farm and introduce himself. He'd be working closely with the local farmers and he wanted to get the lay of the land. It also created a good and lasting first impression if he made the first move.

The farm was just as he remembered it, back when old farmer Heggarty had owned the land. He'd done the odd job for him, had helped with the milking and the mucking out. He'd enjoyed the work. Heggarty had been a kind man. He'd learned about the old man's passing from his mum, via Gerald.

Standing in the farmyard now it was hard to forget about the time he'd spent here with Hannah. God, how he still missed those easy, lazy, summer evenings when they'd sat and watched the sunset together, her head on his shoulder. A part of him still longed to be that boy, the boy he had been when with her. He shook his head with a sigh. He couldn't let his thoughts drift to Hannah and what might have been. No good would come of that now.

'So, this is a permanent thing then?' Chris asked as Daniel unlocked the Land Rover after his visit.

'Is what a permanent thing?' Daniel asked, not quite understanding the question. 'You mean the practice providing you with veterinary services? Nothing's changed there, other than having me as your vet.'

Chris shook his head slightly and smiled. 'That's good to hear, but what I meant is, are *you* permanent? We've had a few different vets come up here, since Gerald's passing. All good, mind,' he quickly added, 'but it'd be nice to have someone more permanent.'

Daniel decided to ignore the remark about his grandfather's passing. He scratched his chin and opened the door for Sammy to jump inside. 'I'll be around for at least the next six months,' he said. Then he'd be gone. Hopefully it wouldn't take that long to find a new owner. People loved the countryside. The trouble would be finding a vet who wanted to stay. But he couldn't tell Chris any of that.

'Ah, well, that's good to know. And just between you and me, you're a lot friendlier than the previous guy. I don't even think he liked animals that much, didn't even have a dog!' He laughed.

'Is that so?' Daniel said, trying and failing not to smile.

'I've never known a vet not to own a dog,' Chris said.

Sammy poked her head out of the open window.

'She's a lovely dog. Had her long?' Chris asked.

'No, not really, only for a few months. She's a rescue dog.' He didn't tell Chris the dog had rescued him.

'You're beautiful, aren't you girl.' Chris gave her a final pat on the head before standing back to let Daniel jump in.

'Any problems, just give me a call,' Daniel said, closing the door.

'Will do, and thanks again. See you soon.'

Daniel waved through the open window and honked the horn before reversing out of the farmyard.

As far as the first two days went, they had been good ones. The staff seemed nice and friendly enough. He got the impression they'd be easy to work with and the two nurses were more than competent to handle things. He knew he was in safe hands. Phyllis, for some strange reason, reminded him of the grandmother he'd never had. She had that all-knowing look about her. She had probably seen and heard everything in life. Nothing would ever surprise her.

As he drove down the lane, Sammy riding shotgun with the window down so she could poke her head out, his thoughts turned to what microwave meal he should eat for tea.

He concentrated on the road ahead and thought of the interesting exchange he'd had with Pat. He'd fully expected her not to remember him, after all it had been fifteen years, but as soon as he walked through the door he'd been transported back in time to the fifteen-year-old boy he'd once been, all tongue-tied and awkward, minus the acne. She'd recognised him straight away and gave him a huge hug, right there from behind the counter, not caring who walked in.

'It's so lovely to see you again,' she told him. 'I hope you're staying a little while.'

He hadn't needed to do much talking, much to his relief, as Pat loved to talk. He'd simply nodded while handing over the cash. She knew all about him, that he was here working as the new vet and what a shame it had been when Gerald passed away. He hadn't commented on that, not quite trusting his own voice. He hadn't really paid much attention to what she said until it was time to go.

'Must have been a nice surprise to see Hannah again after all these years.'

He froze, he couldn't help it. Hannah was here in the village? He tried to move his mouth to articulate some kind of response, but he couldn't speak.

'Surely you saw her?' Pat asked, her eyebrows shooting up towards her fringe.

Daniel continued to stare at her.

Hannah was here. In the village.

Pat started to laugh. 'How could you have missed her? You practically walked slap bang into her as she left here, barely two minutes ago.'

'What! I did what?' His head swivelled to glance at the closed door. And then it hit him. He'd moved aside to let a woman out of the shop, but he hadn't been paying much attention. His mind was full of the cottage and its memories and what was inside the incredibly heavy cardboard box balancing on his hip. He hadn't looked at the woman. Hadn't she been wearing a uniform?

'I can't believe you didn't notice her. The two of you were thick as thieves when you were teenagers.' She laughed again.

Daniel didn't laugh and he wasn't laughing now as he steered the Land Rover towards his new home. What was he going to do? Had Hannah seen him? He couldn't ignore her. He didn't want to ignore her. But at the same time he didn't know what to say to her. He couldn't pick up from where they had left things, all up in the air.

Oh hello, how have you been these past fifteen years? No, I didn't bother calling you, or writing to you as we'd promised.

Maybe she'd forgotten? Anything was possible. But something told him that wouldn't be the case. After all, he hadn't forgotten a thing. Things would be so much easier if she'd moved away as he'd hoped. So much easier. Why hadn't she moved away?

Thinking about how he'd behaved towards her filled him with nothing but shame and guilt. He felt guilty then and he felt guilty now – nothing would ever change that. He had no other option at the time. Hell, he'd wanted nothing more than to turn back round and head back home and into her arms. But he couldn't return. His one last gift of kindness to her had been no letters, no phone calls. Nothing. She had to forget about him for his plan to work, for her to move on with her life, even though it had broken him. Leaving her had changed everything. It had ripped apart his heart and it had never fully healed. He had never got over her, which in hindsight was one of the reasons why his marriage had been one big fat failure.

He slowed down at the crossroads and indicated right, towards the village and the surgery. The sun was now low in the sky, the day still light and warm. He loved evenings like this. Up ahead he noticed a figure at the side of the road. They wore what looked like a nurse's uniform and a large rucksack slung across their back. He eased his foot off the accelerator.

Why on earth were they pushing a bike along this road, instead of riding it? He slowed to a crawl as he passed, but as he did so he turned his head to look more closely, just to check there wasn't some kind of problem.

That's when he noticed the shredded tyre. How could they even push the bike?

His eyes moved from the bike to … the woman. His gaze levelled with hers.

And time stood still. The past fifteen years disappeared in a puff of smoke and once again he was that stumbling, gangly teenager, madly in love with the prettiest girl in the village. He hadn't expected her to look the same, but she did. Everything about her sucked him back in time; the memory of her smell, her touch, were deep in his bones. He had to tear his eyes away from her face.

With his heart in his mouth he moved the Land Rover to the side of the road, hit the brake, cut the engine and pulled on the handbrake. He sat for a moment before slowly climbing out. 'Stay in the car, Sammy,' he said as he closed the door. He didn't recognise his own voice.

He stepped in front of her, did his best to smile. 'Hi Hannah,' he said. 'You need some help?'

Hannah watched the Land Rover slow to a crawl and stop at the side of the road. Part of her screamed for him to keep driving – she didn't need him or his help, while the other part felt nothing but relief. She really didn't want to walk home in this heat. She heard the slam of the door and then the heavy footsteps that followed.

'Hi Hannah, you need some help?'

She forced her gaze up from his brown scuffed boots, noticing the long lean legs covered in snug blue denim and the checked shirt, with the sleeves rolled up revealing muscular arms. She took in the pale blue eyes and the small dimple alongside his crooked smile. She wanted to throw her arms around him while fighting the urge to thump him on the chest for how he'd treated her.

We were kids, she reminded herself. People move on. People change. She pushed aside the memory of waiting for the phone to ring, the nights she'd spent with the phone in her hand so she wouldn't miss his call. The days, weeks and months she had waited for one of his letters to arrive. The countless nights she cried herself to sleep. She swallowed all these memories down along with the automatic, I'm fine, finding herself unable to take her eyes off his. My God, how could she have forgotten how handsome he was? 'I've got a flat tyre,' she managed to say.

His eyes swooped down to the punctured tyre, the nail sticking out. He crouched down, inspected it with his fingers. She watched him closely, reminding herself to breathe.

His arm twisted as he pulled the nail free, holding it up towards her. 'You want a lift then?'

She blinked several times. Was he smiling at her? Just like that, did he have nothing else to say? How about, *how have you been? Nice to see you again.* But no, nothing.

She nodded, unable to open her mouth.

'I'll pop it in the back for you. It'll fit.' He picked it up with one hand, as if it weighed no more than a bag of sugar. Once secured in the back he gave it another once over before turning back to her. 'If you like I can replace the tyre for you. I bet there's even a tin of anti-rust paint knocking about too if you want me to sort that out for you.'

She folded her arms across her chest and glared at him. 'No thanks. I'm perfectly capable of repairing a flat tyre.' The cheek of the man. *Anti-rust paint*? She'd accept a lift from him, because she had no other choice, but she didn't want anything else from him. She didn't want, nor need him in her life.

He studied her for a beat. 'Okay then, no problem.'

He walked round to the driver's side and opened the door. The black and white Border collie she'd seen outside the shop jumped out, tail wagging as it ran towards her.

She bent down to stroke the dog's back.

'This is Sammy. She was told to stay in the car,' he said, a laugh in his throat, as he instinctively reached out to touch Sammy's head.

They brushed hands. She jerked her hand away, not liking the bolt of electricity that shot up her arm. Her fingers tingled. She kept her eyes on the dog. 'Hello there Sammy, you're a beautiful dog,' she said.

'Yes she is,' Daniel agreed. 'Come on girl, you need to jump in the back. No more riding shotgun for you.'

Hannah watched in astonishment as the dog did exactly that.

'You getting in? Or are you going to walk home?' he asked, his head poking through the open window.

Hannah bit down on her lip. It was like that then was it? Pretend nothing had happened between them in the past. Well, two of them could play that game. She opened the passenger door. What choice did she have?

Chapter Four

Daniel tried his best to concentrate on the road ahead. Hannah angled herself away from him, her body twisted towards the door, eyes fixed on the passing landscape. Her blonde hair blew around on the breeze. He could smell strawberry shampoo. His stomach flipped, his body and mind transported back in time. She hadn't changed much. Obviously she looked older, they both did. Fifteen years created a few extra lines here and there, and in his case the first few stray grey hairs, although he told himself not to worry about it, but other than her hair being longer, she looked the same.

How could he forget those smokey grey eyes? He'd always been drawn to them, how they expressed every single thought and feeling. Now, instead of radiating warmth and compassion he imagined they were ice-cold slits, aimed directly at him. When he'd approached her at the side of the road, he couldn't get his tongue to work. Had to blink several times to clear his thoughts and his throat. What had he been thinking? *Hi, do you need some help?*

Was that the best he could come up with after all these years? No wonder she ignored him once settled into the passenger seat, cradling her rucksack on her lap like a protective shield. He told her to put it in the back with her bike, Sammy could guard it for her; a feeble joke in an attempt to break the ice. 'I'll hold on to it if it's all the same to you,' she snapped at him. Didn't even smile at his lame joke. Did she think he'd run off with it or something?

No, her reaction had nothing to do with the bag, but everything to do with how he had treated her. She hadn't forgiven him for abandoning the village and turning his back on her, and his heart ached because he knew he deserved it.

The silence unnerved him, but opening his mouth would be a huge mistake. He'd make matters worse. Best to say nothing and drive.

But he couldn't drive in silence.

He switched the radio on. Pop music blasted out. A song he hadn't heard before. Hannah tapped her foot to the beat. It made him smile. She'd always loved music. He remembered the way she used to dance around her bedroom, hairbrush in hand, using it as a microphone, not caring what people thought. His eyes flickered briefly to her face before focussing once more on the road ahead. She looked out of the window.

His fingers drummed the steering wheel. He had to say something. They couldn't sit together and not say a word to each other. He cleared his throat as he thought of what to say. 'So how's your mum doing?' he asked.

He wasn't sure if she'd heard him at first as she didn't reply.

The music was rather loud. He turned the dial down a notch and risked another look at her. She stared at him all wide-eyed. A horrible sinking feeling filled his chest.

'She passed away.' Her voice sounded so small. She turned back around to look out of the window. 'A year and a half ago. Cancer.'

'I'm so sorry,' he said, his eyes on the road. The words sounded hollow, meaningless. It wasn't enough. He knew it wasn't enough, but what else could he say?

She shrugged and hugged the rucksack.

'Is that why you're still here in Middlefern? Because you looked after your mum?' he asked. It made sense. There were no other family members. Well, none that he knew of anyway.

Her head whipped round so fast that it made him jump. He gripped the steering wheel, his knuckles turned white.

'Some of us can't run away,' she all but spat at him. 'Some of us don't have that luxury.'

What the hell did that mean? *Luxury*? She hadn't the faintest idea why he'd fled this village and it wasn't anything to do with luxury. It was a necessity. His jaw clenched with the effort of keeping his thoughts and words from tumbling out. Now wasn't the right time to tell her. Would there ever be a right time? 'It must have been a difficult time for you,' he said instead.

'She was my mother,' came her simple answer.

He considered her response, and wondered what she must have gone through while nursing her mum. He had no experience of caring for a loved one with cancer. 'And how are you, now?' he asked.

'How am I?' Her forehead furrowed, as if she didn't quite understand the question. Has no one ever asked how she felt?

'It's life changing, isn't it. I mean, after something like that, life will never be the same again,' he offered with a small sigh.

She stared at him, opening and closing her mouth before turning once more to gaze out of the window.

He indicated left onto the main road. Taking the hint, he turned the radio back up, letting the music wash over them.

'Why are you back?' she asked.

He'd been expecting the question, but had no idea how to answer it. Where to begin with that one, he thought. A version of the truth would be a good start. 'They needed a new vet after Gerald's passing, and seeing as I own the business it made sense that I come and fill in for a while.'

'Mm-hmm, so you're not staying then.' It wasn't really a question.

'I never said that,' he said. 'I'll just see what happens.' He couldn't bring himself to tell the truth. After his six months were up, he'd be gone, the cottage and business sold. By then he'd have a long-term plan. He'd know what he wanted to do with the rest of his life.

'Mm-hmm.'

Cursing under his breath he turned into her old road and parked.

She gaped at him. 'How do you know I live here?'

'He glanced at the houses, checked the street name. He was in the right place. 'My memory's not that bad,' he said. 'I remember where you live.' How could he ever forget. Did she really think he'd banished those memories of the past? The thought clawed at him.

She glared at him as she pulled the handle to release the door. 'I don't live there any more,' she said, pointing to her childhood home. 'I live there.' She swivelled around in her seat and pointed to the house on the opposite side of the road. 'I'm in the ground-floor flat.'

He looked to where she pointed. Why had she moved across the road? He opened his mouth to ask her when she wrenched the door open and decamped onto the pavement, swinging the rucksack onto her back in one sleek movement.

Sammy barked in excitement at the chance of being able to get some exercise. 'Not now, girl,' Daniel said, opening his car door. 'I'll take you for a walk when we get back home.' *Home*, the word still felt strange. It would never be a home for him. He stepped onto the pavement and shut the door, muffling Sammy's barks.

He opened the boot and lifted out the bike. He passed it to her.

'Thanks for the lift,' she said, her voice devoid of any sincerity.

'No problem.' He shoved his hands into his pockets. There was so much more he needed to say to her. So many questions. But she looked away, her eyes on the bike, not on him.

With a sigh he stepped back and placed his hand on the driver's door. 'Well, I'll probably see you around,' he said, forcing a smile. He wanted to carry the bike into the flat for her, and make her a cup of tea. Tell her everything. Tell her why he'd left. That leaving her behind was the hardest thing he'd ever done. That he'd never forgiven his fifteen-year-old self for how he'd behaved towards her. What a mess his life had become following the divorce. But he couldn't tell her a thing because she owed him nothing and he would be leaving again. He knew all of this to be true while every fibre of his being screamed to reach out and touch her. To tell her he hadn't forgotten a thing. That she was still beautiful and that even during his five year failure of a marriage he'd thought about her.

He pulled the door open. Sammy jumped into the passenger seat.

'Do you want to come in for a cup of coffee?'

'What?' he asked, stunned.

'Do you want a drink? It's the least I can do.' One hand was on her hip, the other on the handlebar of the bike.

He shook his head. He couldn't step foot in her flat. It wouldn't be fair to her. He needed to keep his distance. Keep things friendly and casual. He could cope with that. He tore his gaze away from those huge grey eyes.

'Oh, okay,' she said.

'I've got a few things to do, so maybe another time,' he quickly added when he saw a flash of disappointment in her eyes. There would be no other time, but it softened the blow.

'Bye then.'

'Bye.'

He watched her unlock the door and drag the bike in behind her. He climbed into the Land Rover, turned the ignition and pulled away. He didn't look back.

Hannah left the bike in the hallway, even though she should have chained it to the railing outside. It would mark the paintwork, but at this very moment in time she didn't care. She had no idea how she'd change the tyre. She didn't even think she had a spare and she'd have to order a puncture repair kit.

Why had she been so stubborn and refused to accept his help? The answer needed no psychoanalysis. She didn't want, nor need any help from him. The arrogance of the man. Thinking he could waltz back into the village like nothing had ever happened. As if he'd simply walked back into the village for a friendly chat and a catch up after a few days, not fifteen years of radio silence.

She kicked the bike's damaged wheel and dropped her rucksack onto the floor. Daisy rubbed against her leg. Good old Daisy, always there for her. She bent down and stroked her head, receiving a loud purr in response. 'It's so good to see you, Daisy. How's your day been eh? Better than mine,' she said as she kicked off her shoes and ran her fingers through her hair.

Shower then food, or food then shower? Her stomach grumbled, giving her the answer. She flicked on the kettle and opened the fridge, taking out the bowl of salad she'd prepared that morning. She chucked the cling film into the bin and made herself a cup of peppermint tea. She carried them into the living room, placed them on the coffee table, and switched on the TV.

She popped a lettuce leaf into her mouth. He'd asked how she was feeling. He made a good show of appearing as if he actually cared. She swallowed and speared a tomato. He had no right to ask her that question. No right at all. He lost that privilege the moment he left the village. And it had nothing to do with her holding a grudge. He didn't know her, not at all. He'd known the fifteen-year-old girl with hopes and dreams and ambitions. He didn't know this version. The woman who was a fighter and a carer and who would no longer be used as a doormat for any man. What did he care anyway? He probably didn't, it had just been a reflex question when she'd told him about her mother. She replayed their conversation over and over in her mind as she ate, not really tasting the food.

Chew, swallow, chew, swallow.

She pushed the empty plate away.

It slowly dawned on her, sitting with her feet up on the sofa and a cup of peppermint tea warming her hands. He hadn't told her much of anything really, but then again, she hadn't asked him any questions because she was so angry with him for upping and leaving her. They hadn't had a conversation at all. He'd done most of the talking. All she'd done was silently seethe and listen. She'd wanted to ask so many questions, but forced herself to remain silent. She hadn't wanted to hear how fabulous his life had been since leaving Middlefern. How he'd made the break, escaped, while she remained here, stuck, in this village. She hadn't wanted to hear him talk about his fantastic life, how he hadn't thought about her at all since leaving. The truth hurt too much.

Had he really thought that time would stand still? Why had he assumed she'd be living in the same house with her mother? Why assume her life couldn't evolve and change, just as his own? He'd actually thought he could carry on and pick up things from where he'd left them all those years ago. The cheek of the man! She remembered that day as if it were yesterday. Well, he could think again. Life didn't always work out the way you wanted. She was living and breathing proof of that.

She sipped her tea, inhaling the mint aroma. It always brought her comfort. Was she being too harsh on him? Anger masking what she really felt about him? Probably. But she couldn't change how she felt about him. He hadn't even denied running away. No flicker of emotion betrayed his real feelings. He was so difficult to read. Always had been. And he wasn't going to hang around for much longer by the sound of things. He'd all but hinted he was here to sort the business out. Hadn't he used the term, *filling in for a while.* That sounded temporary to Hannah's ears.

Daisy jumped up onto her knee and curled up in a ball, paws kneaded her thighs. She placed a hand onto Daisy's back, savouring the warmth, the deep rumble of pleasure that vibrated through Daisy's spine. He wasn't going to stay. It shouldn't hurt so much, not after all this time, but it did.

Why hadn't he written to her? What had stopped him? Another girl? She'd wanted to scream this question at him until her lungs ached and her throat stung. But instead she stared out of the window. It was best she didn't know. Better for both of them. What was the point? You couldn't go back in time and repair the damage.

She squeezed her eyes shut. Repeated his words over and over in her mind. Something had been off. She just needed to pinpoint it. *Think.* What was wrong? She was on the brink of giving up, preparing to jump in the shower and change into her cool, cotton pyjamas, when it came to her. When he spoke about Gerald's passing there had been no sadness. No catch in his voice. It had been a statement, merely expressing a point of view. They needed a vet and so he had stepped in. His decision to return hadn't been a personal one, but rather one born out of necessity. That's what had bothered her. He was here in the village because of the business, not because of the bond he'd had with his grandfather. His decision to return wasn't about family, or the love for his late grandfather, it was all about money.

Surely this couldn't be true. She thought she knew him better than that. Could people really change that much? She shook her head. This couldn't be true. He'd had a good heart and the way he'd acted towards her suggested he still had a good heart. When she'd looked at him, she'd seen the boy he used to be, the boy she'd fallen in love with. His hair slightly longer now and he still wore clothes for comfort, but his mannerisms, the way he spoke, were the same. Those cool blue eyes of his hadn't changed one little bit. She'd made a conscious effort to try and not look him directly in the eye. It would give too much away. But when she had she'd seen something in them, a sadness perhaps. The man was a mystery. What had happened to him in London?

Chapter Five

Hannah woke up bright and early and pushed aside the events of the previous day. She refused to think about the strange dream that involved driving with Dan in his Land Rover down narrow country lanes. She didn't want to go there. She wouldn't waste any of her time or energy thinking about Daniel Jackson.

She needed to call into the home-care agency office before starting her shifts for the day. It slowly dawned on her while enjoying her morning shower that she'd have a difficult time making it to some of her clients without the use of a bike. Most she could do on foot, but not poor Mr Bennett out by the farm. Thankfully he wasn't on her list today, but she wasn't sure how long it would take to repair her bike and so she'd need to rearrange her client list for at least the rest of the week.

Claire texted her back and told her not to worry. Could she call in and see her before starting work? She could juggle things around a little bit. The two other carers both had cars, so it wasn't such a big deal, but still, Hannah didn't like letting people down. She took pride in her work, and had never missed one single day, not even when nursing her mother. The only time she'd taken off was for her mother's funeral and the two weeks that followed.

She adjusted her rucksack straps and strode briskly down the street towards the corner shop. The agency office was based in the flat above. It consisted of one small room with a desk, two chairs and floor to ceiling bookshelves. Hannah had no idea how Claire sat in that stuffy office all day, but she seemed to like the confined space. She never complained. The small office always smelled of freshly brewed coffee and a tattered paperback could always be seen on the desk.

Hannah climbed the narrow staircase leading up to the agency and knocked on the door.

'Come in,' Claire shouted.

Hannah pushed open the door and as expected Claire greeted her with the warmest and widest smile to be found in Middlefern, along with the bitter aroma of fresh coffee.

'Hi Hannah, take a seat.' Claire looked up from her laptop screen. 'Bike trouble then, eh?'

'Yeah, a flat tyre.' Hannah removed her rucksack and sank onto the chair. 'I'll get round to repairing it, but I need to order a new tyre, so it'll take a few days to get one delivered.'

'Have you not got a puncture repair kit?' Claire asked, closing the laptop lid. She leaned back in her chair.

'No, but to be honest, that tyre is way beyond repair.'

'Okay, well, there's no problem on my part. I've changed your rota for the rest of the week, so you're only doing the local visits that can be managed on foot.' She ripped a piece of paper from a legal pad and passed it over the desk. 'When you've repaired the tyre I'll change you back to your normal duties.'

'Thank you,' Hannah said, 'that's really kind.'

Claire cocked her head to the side. 'It's fine, not a problem, these things happen. Is there anything else I can help you with?'

Hannah shook her head. 'No, I'm all good.'

'Okay then. I'll let you crack on.'

Hannah stood, grabbing her bag.

'It's such a shame you don't drink coffee,' Claire grumbled. 'I'd offer you a cup.'

Hannah wrinkled her nose. 'I love the smell, but can't stand the taste.'

Claire shook her head. 'As I said, such a shame.'

The doorbell rang just as Hannah sat down to binge on the latest Netflix box set. Muttering under her breath, she picked up a disgruntled looking Daisy from her lap, moved her onto the sofa, and padded to the front door. She peered through the glass before opening the door. 'What are you doing here?' she asked.

'Josh got off work early, so I thought I'd call round and drag you out for a drink,' Emily said. She moved into the hallway and eyed her friend up and down before her eyes landed on the bike. 'What's your bike doing in here?'

'The front tyre got attacked by a rusty nail. I'm waiting for a new tyre and inner tube,' Hannah mumbled.

Emily bent down to touch the ripped tyre. 'It'll mark the paintwork,' she warned. 'Do you want Josh to take a look at it for you?'

'No, it's fine. If I have any problems then I'll let you know.' She walked into the kitchen. Why did everyone feel the need to fix her problems? 'You want a coffee?'

'No,' Emily said, her red curls bouncing up and down as she shook her head. She placed her hands on her hips. 'I'm taking you out. You may not need a drink, but I most certainly do. The boys were full of mischief once they got back from school.'

Emily's smile betrayed her sound of annoyance. She loved those boys with an energy that took Hannah's breath away. Kaden and Harry were five years of age and a bundle of energy. They were the spitting image of their father, Josh who worked as a mechanic and had done ever since leaving school. Everyone knew Josh in Middlefern. Whenever anyone had a flat tyre or needed a jump start, they called on him for a lending hand and a friendly smile. The twins had Josh's straight blond hair, blue eyes and angelic looks that enabled them to get away with anything. But they had their mother's gritty spirit. They'd break some hearts when they were older.

Fully aware when she was fighting a losing battle, Hannah put the kettle back down. 'Well, I'll need to get changed. Just give me five minutes.'

'No problem,' Emily said, turning on the tap.

'You don't have to wash up!'

'I know, but I may as well do something useful while you're getting ready.' She added a generous squirt of washing-up liquid.

Hannah mumbled a thank you and retreated into the bedroom. She pulled out a pair of jeans and a clean tee shirt from the ironing pile.

'How'd you manage to work today without your bike?' Emily's voice drifted into the bedroom from the kitchen.

'Claire rearranged my client list so I could walk to all my appointments,' Hannah shouted, tugging the tee shirt over her head. She hadn't worn it for a few weeks and she noticed it felt a little looser than usual.

'She's so lovely,' Emily hollered above the clatter of cutlery landing in the drainer.

'Yeah, she's a great boss.' Hannah knew she was lucky to have such an understanding boss. She'd been so kind when her mother died, giving her extra time off.

She'd even arranged several counselling sessions free of charge. At first Hannah had refused, telling Claire she didn't need any help like that. But after a few months had passed, she'd taken up Claire's offer. The counselling had helped.

'Where did you get the puncture then?' Emily's face appeared around the door, making Hannah jump. 'That's a nice top,' she said.

'Yesterday evening, on the way back from Mr Bennett's. I'd stopped for a while at the farm. I think I picked it up there.'

'Oh my God, poor you.' Emily placed a hand on her hip. 'That's one hell of a trudge back home, and you had to push your bike. You should have called me. I'd have picked you up.'

'There's no signal up at the farm,' Hannah said. 'And I, erm, somebody gave me a lift.' She mumbled, hoping that would be the end of the conversation. 'Right, I just need to grab my trainers and we can go.' She slinked past Emily into the hallway.

'Who gave you a lift?' Emily asked, spinning on her heel.

Hannah gritted her teeth. Of course Emily wanted to know all the details. She shoved her feet into her trainers. She never untied the laces. 'Dan, I mean, Dr Jackson. He'd been to the farm and was heading back home.'

'Daniel gave you a lift?' Emily's face scrunched up. 'He never mentioned anything about giving you a lift.'

And why would he?

'What do you make of him?' Emily asked.

'Me?'

'Yeah. I mean, I like him. He seems like a nice guy. Kind, you know. He looked after Mrs Barlow when she came in with Ted.'

'She told me,' Hannah said, remembering how the old woman's face softened when talking about the nice young vet. 'He's all right I suppose.'

Emily arched a brow, suppressing what Hannah knew to be a scowl. 'All right? The man gave you a lift, and presumably brought the bike home too?'

'Yeah, he did.' Hannah snatched her keys from the hall table.

Emily's clear, no-nonsense gaze made Hannah flinch a little.

'Did something happen? What did he do?' Her voice rose an octave.

'Nothing,' Hannah said quickly. My God, she didn't want Emily to think he'd tried to attack her or something. 'Nothing happened. It's just … complicated – that's all. Me and him …'

'Whoa, stop right there Miss Kennedy!' She raised her hand, palm out. '*You and him?* What aren't you telling me?'

Hannah rolled her eyes. She'd have to tell her now. 'I grew up with him, here in the village. You know he used to live here, that he's Gerald Jackson's grandson.'

'Yes, I know that,' Emily said. 'I just never put two and two together. It's a small village isn't it?'

'It certainly is,' Hannah said, and it grew smaller with every passing second.

'So you must have gone to school together?'

Hannah nodded. 'He was my best friend. We even dated for a little while.' The words came out of her mouth before she could stop them.

'You and him? Wow! Was it serious?'

There was no point in denying it. Emily saw through every lie. 'At the time, yes, we were serious about each other. But, we were very young, only fifteen, so you know …'

'But it meant something then, and by the look on your face it means something now,' Emily said, her voice softening as she stepped forward to rest her hand on Hannah's arm.

Hannah shrugged her friend's arm free. She didn't need to be comforted or pitied. 'It was a long time ago. A lot has changed since then.'

'You still like him!' Emily gasped out loud.

'No, I do not,' Hannah said with steel in her voice.

'So, you still don't hold a torch for him? Listen, I get it, first love and all that. You were high school sweethearts.' She placed a hand on her chest, over her heart. The goofy grin on her face told Hannah everything she needed to know.

Hannah reached over Emily's shoulder for her handbag on the coat hook. She desperately needed to change the subject. It cut too close to the bone for her liking. 'It's complicated. What happened between us, and then him leaving.' She sighed. 'I'll tell you about it some other time, not now. It's a long story. Now I just want to go out and relax, have a drink and not think about the past or Daniel Jackson or my broken bike.'

'Okay, that's fine by me,' Emily said with a wink. 'Come on then.'

Hannah linked her arm with her best friend's, knowing she'd tell her everything that had happened, but not tonight. Tonight she just wanted to forget.

The Middlefern Arms was the sort of pub you snuggled up in by an open fire. They had real ale on tap, live music every Saturday and a choice of two flavours of crisps: salt and vinegar or cheese and onion. Every Wednesday the pub hosted the weekly general knowledge quiz and the knitting club met up on the last Saturday of every month. It was a place for the community to chat, drink and have fun, in a cosy and welcoming space with landlady, Brenda, at the helm. She'd been the Middlefern Arms landlady for the past thirty years and it didn't look like she was about to hand over the reins to anyone else anytime soon. She'd never married, had always lived alone. She'd often joke, telling the locals that she was married to the pub and that she didn't have time for a man in her life.

Emily and Hannah both nursed a glass of white wine in the nook by the open fireplace. It was their favourite spot to sit and while away a few hours.

'This is nice, isn't it.' Emily stretched out her legs and kicked off her heels.

'Yeah, it is,' Hannah agreed, glad she'd made the effort to get out of the flat. It was good for her. Not for the first time she thought of what her mother would say if she could see her lounging around the flat with Daisy in her pyjamas on a summer evening. She knew exactly what her mother would say and glugged a mouthful of wine to prevent herself from dwelling on that thought.

'I can't believe it's only Wednesday, but it's been an eventful week so far.' Emily laughed, placing her glass back down on the table. 'Feels more like a Friday night.'

'Well, we are in the pub,' Hannah said. 'And on a school night.'

'Mm-hmm, so we are, and it is so nice to be sitting with a glass of wine with no kids asking for something to eat or drink every five minutes.'

Hannah laughed, raised her glass and clinked it against Emily's. She sneaked a closer glance at her friend. She looked tired. It must be hard, working at the vets when you have five-year-old twins. She couldn't imagine what that must be like. She'd nursed her mother, so she had some idea, but being a parent was a different ball game. She couldn't see herself ever having kids. 'So Josh finished a bit early then?' Hannah asked.

Josh worked as a mechanic in the next village. He'd recently become a junior partner in the company. He loved his job, but it involved long hours and weekends, meaning Emily did most of the parenting while juggling part-time hours at the surgery. Hannah had the greatest respect for her friend – she had no idea how she did it.

'Yeah, it's been a quiet day for them, so they knocked off early. They're going to be busy tomorrow though. For some reason Thursday is always a hectic day, so it's another early start for him and then he probably won't be home until gone seven.'

'I'll babysit for you one day this week, you know, so the two of you can go out and have a drink or a meal or whatever.' Hannah often babysat. She loved her evenings with the boys that usually involved a tub of sweets and a movie. 'I like looking after them,' she added with a smile.

They were a joy to babysit. She'd looked after them on and off since they were babies. Less so when her mother became really ill and needed twenty-four-hour care, but even so, those boys felt like they were a part of her.

'Thanks, I'll take you up on that because it's our wedding anniversary on Sunday.'

'That's sorted then. You two go out and have some fun.' Hannah grinned.

'Are you sure? I asked Mum, but …'

'Of course it's fine,' Hannah interrupted. 'Book a table somewhere nice.'

Emily grinned back at her friend, said thank you again and drained her glass of wine. 'I should have got some crisps,' Emily mumbled, looking over towards the bar.

'I'll go grab you some. Cheese and onion?'

'I'll get them,' Emily began to protest, but Hannah shushed her with her hands.

'Sit and rest while you can. Won't be a minute.'

Brenda offered Hannah the broadest smile as she approached the bar, obviously pleased to see her out and about of an evening. 'You forgot the crisps, didn't you?' She reached for a family pack of cheese and onion, her bright bangles clanking against each other as she did so. A larger-than-life character, Brenda always wore huge hooped earrings, bangles, ruby-red lipstick and pale blue eyeliner with blue eyeshadow. She had such a good heart and had been there for Hannah through the dark days after her mother's death. Hannah respected the older woman immensely, and considered her a close friend. 'Here you go, love,' she said, handing her the crisps.

Hannah passed over the correct change. 'Thank you, Brenda.'

'No problem, love. Now, I've not seen you in here for a while.' She pursed her lips as she leaned over the bar. 'Don't be a stranger, eh.' She patted Hannah's hand.

Touched by the raw emotion that could be seen in Brenda's eyes, Hannah said, 'I won't, I promise.'

She was rewarded with a smile, before Brenda turned her attention to the next customer.

'Thanks,' Emily said, tearing the bag of crisps open with her teeth. 'Want one?'

Hannah shook her head. 'No thanks.'

Tutting, Emily popped a crisp into her mouth. 'I can never understand why you don't eat crisps. I mean, who doesn't like crisps?'

'Erm, me for starters.'

Emily laughed. 'Well, more for me then. Seriously, this is heaven – a whole packet of crisps to myself. Bliss.'

'Brenda decided to give you the family pack,' Hannah said.

'I love that woman.' Emily popped two crisps into her mouth, then crunched them, crumbs forming on her lips. 'Not good for my waistline, though.'

Hannah rested her head against the back of the chair. It was so warm she thought she might easily doze off. And the fire wasn't even lit.

Emily eased herself forward in her chair. Her eyes were wide as she looked over Hannah's shoulder. 'Look who's just walked in,' she said, her mouth full of crisps.

'Who?' Hannah peered over her shoulder, towards the entrance. Her stomach flipped as Daniel stepped through the door with Sammy by his feet, quickly followed by Chris the farmer. The two of them were deep in conversation as they ambled towards the bar.

'I should invite them over to sit with us.' Emily raised her hand without waiting for a reply.

'No!' Hannah managed to squeak out. 'Don't do that!'

'What?' Emily slowly lowered her hand. 'Why not? I just wanted to say hello.'

Hannah felt her cheeks growing warmer by the second and it had nothing to do with the warmth in the pub. She couldn't handle it if Dan came and sat with them, but by the looks of things it was already too late. Chris waved and offered them a beaming smile, then nudged Dan as he pointed towards their table. He too smiled and waved, but Hannah noticed the tightness of his jaw, how he looked away from her face as he waved.

Please don't sit with us. Please don't sit with us.

Emily gave them a thumbs-up sign. 'He's a nice guy and it must be hard for him, moving back here. After all those years away. It's bound to feel a bit strange.'

Hannah watched the two men at the bar. Brenda fetched their drinks. 'I only thought they might want to have a chat by themselves. They may feel a little awkward sitting with us,' Hannah stammered. *More like she'd feel awkward.* Surely Emily would see straight through her flimsy excuse.

Emily angled her head, and gave Hannah her "don't mess with me" face. 'Listen, I get that it may be a little awkward for you, you know, given your history, but it was a long time ago, and you can't ignore him in a village this small.'

You wanna bet, Hannah thought. But in a village this small, no way on earth could she avoid him for very long. Emily was right, she'd be seeing a lot of him from now on.

She would be polite, put on her professional face. Treat him as a newcomer, not a boy she'd once known.

'I think Chris has a thing for you.'

'What!' Hannah wanted to say more, but her words trailed away when Emily jumped up and waved. 'They're coming over,' she hissed. 'Be nice.'

Hannah's mind raced. Chris had a thing for her? Since when? Surely not. He was a lovely guy and everything, but why mention it now? Emily must have got that wrong. She'd known Chris for five years, and had never felt uncomfortable around him, had never picked up on those kind of vibes.

'Hello Daniel, hello Chris,' Emily said, shifting the weight of her chair towards Hannah, to make room for them to sit down.

Hannah bent down to stroke Sammy who'd chosen to sit by her feet, her tail wagging from side to side. The dog proved to be a great distraction.

Daniel chose the seat opposite Emily, while Chris pulled over a chair from the next table, sitting in that no-man's land between the two tables.

'She's taken a shine to you,' Chris said, pointing his pint glass at the dog.

Hannah ruffled Sammy's head and laughed.

'I think she remembers you from when we gave you a lift,' Daniel said, reaching down to ruffle Sammy's head.

Their fingers touched.

Hannah jerked her hand away and tilted her head upwards to look at him. He wasn't laughing at her, or looking all smug because he'd rescued the damsel in distress from the side of the road. She saw kindness and a softness in those pale eyes, something she hadn't noticed the other day. She dipped her head to concentrate on stroking Sammy's fur. 'She's a really good dog.'

'Yeah, she is,' Daniel said. He flexed his fingers.

'So, how are you adjusting to life back in the village? I bet it feels like you've never been away?' Emily asked.

Oh dear Lord above! Hannah wanted the ground to swallow her up.

'It feels a little strange but I'm getting there,' he said with a smile. 'It's not changed a lot in here and Brenda looks exactly the same.' He lifted his pint glass of coke and gulped down half the glass in one go.

Hannah remembered how they'd managed to sneak into the pub on busy nights. Brenda had obviously refused to serve them alcohol, but they'd soaked up the atmosphere and the odd drink that was brought for them by well-meaning locals. She watched him over the rim of her wine glass. His body language screamed discomfort. But a quick glance at Emily and Chris told her they hadn't noticed.

'You must come round for tea sometime,' Emily said to Daniel. 'The boys would love to have a chat with a real-life vet.'

Hannah shot her friend a look. They'd eat him alive.

Daniel stroked his chin. 'Yeah, I'd like that.' His eyes twinkled. Hannah got the feeling he knew exactly what was in store for him.

Hannah stifled a laugh. Like hell he would.

'Something funny?' he asked.

'No,' she said, wishing he'd ask someone else a question.

'Did you manage to get your bike fixed?' Daniel set his now empty glass back down on the table.

‘Yeah, all sorted,’ she answered without pausing for breath. She did not want to talk about her bike.

Emily opened her mouth to say something but Hannah kicked her under the table.

‘You two know each other then?’ Chris asked.

Hannah remained silent, having no idea how to answer that particular question.

Daniel cleared his throat. ‘We went to school together, but I moved to London with my mother when I was nearly sixteen.’

Chris angled his head to look at Hannah for confirmation, or maybe for her to add more to the story. She averted his gaze, saying nothing.

‘Well, it’s nice that you know someone, you know, that there’s a friendly face …’

‘I don’t think much has changed here,’ Daniel said with a shrug. ‘There are a lot of friendly faces, people I knew as a kid who still live here. Does Old Mr Bennett still live near the farm?’ he asked Chris. ‘I thought about calling round the other day when I passed by yours, but I didn’t want to call just in case he’d moved on.’

‘Yeah, still there, he’s a lovely old feller,’ Chris said with a warm smile. ‘I often pop over to check everything is okay.’

‘Hannah looks after him too, as part of her job,’ Emily piped up.

Daniel lifted a brow towards Hannah.

‘I’m a home carer.’ She hadn’t told him the reason she’d been out at the farm the other day. He hadn’t asked and it was really none of his business. ‘He’s not changed that much.’ *And neither have you.* What have you been up to with your life? she wondered. What had he been doing for the past fifteen years, other than training and working as a vet?

Daniel picked up his glass, realised it was empty, and placed it back down.

'What was he like then, as a boy?' Chris asked, grinning and his full attention now on Hannah's face.

She stared into her empty wine glass. 'I can't remember,' she lied. 'It was such a long time ago.' She tried to make it sound like a joke, but it sounded flat even to her own ears. No humour could be found in their backstory.

She remembered everything.

She remembered the way he'd held her hand on their walk home from school. How they'd sing songs in the kitchen while making hot chocolates with whipped cream and mini marshmallows. Their first kiss, shared after the school disco. She remembered it all.

The scraping of chair legs dragged her out of that particular memory. Daniel was on his feet, Sammy's lead in his tight fist. 'Right, well – we best be off.'

'Already? It's still early,' Chris said, holding up his pint glass. 'You've got time for another.'

Shaking his head, Daniel clipped the lead to Sammy's collar. 'No, I better be going. Still got some unpacking to do and I'm on call as well. I'll catch up with you all soon.'

Emily jumped to her feet and gave him a quick hug. Daniel, surprised, covered it with a laugh. Emily hugged everyone. 'I'll see you in the morning,' she said. 'Have a good night.'

'You too.' Daniel addressed the table, but his eyes lingered on Hannah's face before he turned and walked away.

‘I’m going to get another, same again for you ladies?’ Chris asked.

‘Please, Chris,’ Emily said. Hannah shook her head. ‘Not for me, thanks.’

‘What?’ Hannah asked in reaction to Emily’s cold hard stare once Chris had gone. ‘What have I gone and done now?’

Chapter Six

Sammy's tail wagged as she walked beside Daniel on the way home from the pub. Daniel's long strides thudded with impatience. He needed to get back home as quickly as possible, away from the pub and away from Hannah Kennedy. What had he been thinking? Why had he thought it such a good idea to go to the pub with Chris? He should have guessed he might bump into her in such a small village.

Sitting with her had been a mistake. When Chris waved and suggested they sit at their table, he should have said no, should have made up some kind of excuse about needing to ask him something personal. Just one brief look at Hannah's body language told him she didn't want to talk to him. It couldn't have been any more obvious than if she'd written "Go Away" on her forehead. And as predicted the night had gone from bad to worse.

'Am I that awful?' he asked Sammy.

She didn't respond, just wagged her tail with every step.

He couldn't make up for his past mistakes, what he'd done to her, but he was doing his best to be a decent human being. He'd tried to strike up a conversation with her, but she hadn't even pretended to be interested. She looked like Hannah, but there was very little of the girl he'd known left behind.

Was he partly responsible for that? Surely she still couldn't hold a grudge against him? He'd assumed she felt embarrassed when he'd helped her at the side of the road.

This evening, she hadn't been expecting to see him in the pub, maybe that's why things had been a little awkward between them. But if tonight was anything to go by, then past events were still very much relevant to her.

He mulled over their conversation from the other day, peeling away the layers. So what if her life hadn't gone exactly as she'd planned? Whose life ever did? He'd had to dodge his very own curveballs. Maybe the time had come to tell her the real reason he'd left? He huffed, knowing the answer. She wouldn't give him the time of day. But if he was going to be living here for the next six months then he needed to try and make amends, and the only way for that to happen was by being honest with her. Goodness knows he felt guilty enough about how it had all been left. He needed to explain his reasons for not writing or visiting. He needed to explain that none of it had anything to do with her and everything to do with his grandfather.

He pulled out his key and opened the cottage door, light and heat greeting him. He still couldn't bring himself to call this cottage home. The removals team had finally arrived though and he'd managed to unpack his books and DVDs, making the haunted space feel more like his own. He'd need a full weekend to fully unpack, but he had time; there was nothing else to do.

He unhooked Sammy's lead and she scampered into the kitchen towards her bowl in search of food. Daniel refilled her water and switched on the kettle. He shouldn't be drinking coffee so late at night, but he wouldn't sleep much anyway. Sally had always nagged him about drinking coffee late at night. One out of many things she'd had a go at him about towards the end of their short marriage. With hindsight he should have seen the signs.

He spooned instant coffee into the cup. He didn't want to think about Sally, or Jack, and what they had done to him. They wouldn't be wasting any of their precious time thinking about him. Thoughts of Sally would inevitably lead to anger and resentment that would leave him feeling low and not in control of his own actions. He'd learned that the hard way.

He took his cup of coffee into the living room, sunk down onto the sofa and propped his feet on the stool. He was on call tonight, but Phyllis had quietly informed him it was rare to be called out in the middle of the night. Most calls happened because the local farmers were dealing with an emergency. Very rarely had a vet been called out to a domestic emergency in the middle of the night.

He sipped his coffee, contemplating how different his life would be living here in the village. Back in the city, they'd mainly treated dogs and cats, with the odd rabbit or guinea pig thrown in for good measure. He'd enjoyed the work, but it hadn't challenged him in the way he thought it would. What he had found both challenging and enjoyable was the work at the local city farm. Ensuring the health and well-being of Barry and Harry, the farm's two alpacas, meant that there was never a dull moment when he visited the farm. He'd quickly fallen into the easy routine of being a city vet, but it had lacked something, and at the time he couldn't put his finger on what was missing. Living out here and having to deal with larger animals would be a challenge in itself, and he relished this change. He needed it. The problem would be giving it up and moving on, even though he knew this was something he had to do. He'd take the plunge and contact the estate agent in the morning, arrange a date for a viewing, get a valuation. It was best to be prepared for the future.

He drank his coffee. He should try and get some sleep. He padded into the kitchen, hovering for a moment by the sink as he looked out of the window to the garden beyond. It had once been home to a vast vegetable patch. He fondly remembered digging up potatoes and shelling peas on the step with his mother. Happy memories. So many of the cottage's memories were entangled with Gerald and their relationship. He needed to think more about the good times. How his mother had crocheted him a blanket one winter; a happy blanket she'd called it and all colours of the rainbow. How she'd read him a story every bedtime and the little notes she used to put in his lunch box during primary school. The cottage was full of those memories. He shouldn't think about Gerald, but the man's shadow could be sensed everywhere.

He switched off the kitchen light. Sammy was safely tucked up on her dog bed. He wished her good night and softly closed the door. He lingered for a moment by the cellar door. His hand touched the doorknob before grasping it. He needed to swallow his fear, go down there, into the dark and face what he should have faced up to years ago. Beads of sweat broke out across his forehead as his grip tightened. He turned the knob. The door creaked open. Cold, stale air escaped. He tasted dust and with it the memories flooded back.

He stumbled backwards.

The pounding of fists on the wooden door, the screams, the crying and then endless, hollow, silence. He reached blindly for the pull light, grabbed it, yanked it down, heard the click as the harsh yellow light illuminated the steps below. He should go down there. He needed to go down there to exorcise his demons, but his feet refused to budge. His hand clutched the light cord as he swayed ever so slightly. Gritting his teeth, he willed his feet to move but his muscles refused to do what his brain told them. With his mouth now dry as sandpaper, nausea swept over him.

Not today.

He couldn't go down there today.

He pulled the cord, the light snapped off. He stepped back, closed the door. Tomorrow. He'd try again tomorrow.

'You have to tell me what's going on.' Emily's words were fractured with the effort of trying to walk and talk at the same time. Her arm linked Hannah's, not for comfort, but for support in helping her to navigate the uneven paving slabs in her heels. She wasn't used to wearing them. She wore boots for work and trainers when at home with the boys. Sensible shoes. She only owned one pair of heels.

Hannah pouted, rolling her eyes, in the safe knowledge Emily couldn't see her. She was too busy looking at her feet, her mouth forming a thin, firm line.

'Something's going on,' Emily continued, as she tightly gripped Hannah's arm. 'You could've cut the air in there with a knife. Honestly, Han, I've never felt more uncomfortable in my life – and I've got to work with the man!'

Hannah cringed. She'd wrongly assumed it was only her who had felt that way. Chris seemed oblivious and Emily had happily glugged her wine while chatting away.

'Nothing's going on.'

Emily made a clicking sound with her tongue. 'I don't believe you.' She released her arm from Hannah's and pulled out her mobile from the back pocket of her jeans. Both thumbs began working the screen.

'Who are you texting?'

'Josh, just letting him know I'm going to be home a little later than expected, as you and me need to talk.' She hit send and grabbed hold of Hannah's arm. 'You have a lot of explaining to do.'

'It's a long story,' Hannah muttered, clutching her mug of peppermint tea. 'And to be honest, it's not that exciting.'

Emily gave her the side-eye, a mug of black coffee in her hand, her bare feet resting on the cool tiles. The high heels had been kicked off under the kitchen table.

'I don't believe you,' Emily said. 'You and him dated when you were in high school.'

'We did. For just under a year.'

Emily's eyebrows shot up to her fringe. 'A year! So what happened then? He broke up with you?'

'What! Why have you jumped to that conclusion?' Her tone was much sharper than she'd intended.

'I'm right – aren't I?' she said.

Hannah looked at her tea. 'He didn't dump me, he moved away.' It was important Emily knew that fact. There was a difference. She wanted to believe that if he'd stayed then things would have worked out differently. But who could say what would have happened? 'Him and his mum moved to London with her new husband. He'd just been promoted, had his own property.'

'So he did dump you!' Emily reached across and touched Hannah's hand.

Hannah snatched her hand away. She didn't want Emily's pity or kindness or even understanding. 'It wasn't like that.' She couldn't help her snarl. 'It wasn't meant to end.' She sounded stupid, pathetic, defending her younger self, but she couldn't stop her words. 'But he moved away. What else could we do? It had to end.' That's the story she'd told herself ever since. As a young girl she had believed that story, the romantic foolish version of events. It had been easier to swallow than the truth. She knew he must have met someone else in London, a prettier face, and had simply discarded her. 'It all sounds so silly now,' Hannah continued, trying to lighten the mood. 'I don't want to talk about this any more.' She was trying to resist the urge to sulk. 'It's just a bit weird, you know, seeing him after all this time. It was a shock to the system, that's all.'

'Hannah, you could barely look at the man, and then when you did, you wouldn't talk to him.'

'That obvious?'

'Yeah, well, it was to me and Daniel, probably not to Chris though.'

Hannah bristled at Chris's name, remembering what Emily had said about him liking her. She didn't want to talk about Chris. He was a nice feller and all, but she had no romantic feelings towards him whatsoever. He was more like a big brother.

'So-ooo?' Emily drew the word out in one long vowel, drawing Hannah back into the room. 'Even though he planned to move to London with his mother, he didn't want to end things with you? Have I got that right?'

Hannah nodded, suddenly weary with it all. What did any of this matter? It was all in the past. 'That was the plan, obviously things changed. We were going to carry on seeing each other. He planned to visit. To write to me. You know, proper letters, not emails.'

Mr Darcy and Elizabeth Bennett. What a fool she'd been.

'And he didn't?'

'No, he never phoned or wrote to me.

Once again the memories of sorrow and rejection hit her in the stomach. She'd phoned him once, but when it had gone straight to voicemail her mouth had dried and she hadn't known what to say, so she'd hung up. A tiny part of her hoped he'd phone back, but he never did. She wrote a letter to him every week for six months, in the hope that he'd write one back, but he never did. A part of her was still that sixteen-year-old girl waiting for a letter to drop through the letterbox. 'He moved away and I never saw him again until the other day when he helped me with my bike.'

'About that,' Emily said, pointing her finger at Hannah's chest while cradling the cup with the other. 'Why did you tell him you'd fixed the bike?'

'I don't know.' Hannah shrugged. 'It was just a reaction. I suppose I didn't want him to offer me any more help. I don't need his help.'

'Hannah, don't you think you need to let this'—she flung her arms wide—'whatever this is – just go? Move on. You're both adults now. You're not teenagers any more.'

Emily was right. She was being ridiculous. She knew that, but still she couldn't shake off the hurt and rejection she'd felt as a teenage girl, matters made worse by him waltzing back into her life as if he'd just popped to the shop only half an hour earlier. 'I saw him before my incident with the bike, you know, before he gave me a lift.'

'What do you mean?' Emily asked.

'I saw him when I left the post office the day before. It took me a few moments to realise it was him, but by then he'd already gone in so I didn't speak to him.' She couldn't admit to following him to make sure it really was him.

'Okay, well, I guess I'd have been shocked too,' Emily said, 'not having seen him after all these years. But Han, you really need to get past this. Middlefern is such a small village, so you're going to bump into him whether you like it or not. And'—she wagged her finger in Hannah's general direction—'I have to work with him, so it would be best all round if you just – you know – tried to get along with him.'

It all sounded so easy. It should be easy when Emily laid out those bare facts, but you couldn't erase over a decade of memories. Emily didn't know what they'd shared. The promises they'd made. Emily wouldn't understand and she didn't have the energy to try and explain it any more.

Emily rose and dropped her empty cup into the sink. 'I need to get going,' she said, 'early start and all that.'

'Yeah, same here.' Hannah hugged her friend. 'Thank you for the chat.'

Emily kissed her on the cheek. 'I worry about you.'

‘I know, but I’m fine. Really I am.’

‘Yeah well, you need to come round to ours at the weekend, and that’s an order. No wallowing in here by yourself.’

‘Okay,’ Hannah agreed. There was no use in arguing. ‘I’m going to babysit anyway. Remember? Your wedding anniversary meal.’

Emily let out a small giggle. ‘Forgot all about that. Must be the wine.’

Hannah walked Emily to the door, handing her a pair of trainers. ‘Wear these, you’ll get home quicker and give me a text so I know you’re back home.’

‘Yeah Mum,’ Emily grumbled, but she grinned as she snatched the shoes from her and shoved them on. The pair of high heels dangled from the middle finger of her left hand. She turned round to face Hannah once she’d stepped outside.

‘He didn’t want to stay?’ The question appeared to come out of nowhere, which was why for several beats Hannah couldn’t find the right words.

‘He didn’t really have a choice,’ she said. ‘His mother moved away and he went with her.’

Emily loitered on the step, the high heels swinging slightly from side to side from her fingertip. ‘But surely he must have had the option of staying with his grandfather. He was nearly sixteen wasn’t he?’

‘Well, yeah. I suppose so,’ Hannah murmured. ‘I just assumed …’ Her words trailed away.

‘He *could* have stayed then.’ It was a statement, not a question, and one that Hannah hadn’t fully explored.

He could have stayed.

‘What are you getting at?’ Hannah asked.

Emily shrugged her shoulders. 'Nothing. It's just, did he really want to leave? Did he really have a choice? By the sound of things he had feelings for you, but then he left and never came back. Doesn't that strike you as a bit odd?'

If he had been given a choice, then why hadn't he chosen to stay in the cottage with Gerald? Surely that could have happened? He'd never told her it was an option. He'd told her he had to relocate to London with his mother. Exhaustion washed over her and her head throbbed. 'Maybe,' she muttered.

'There's no maybe about it. Most sixteen-year-old lads who are madly in love with their girlfriend would fight tooth and nail to stay near her and their friends. So why did he choose to go?'

Hannah knew the answer. Because she obviously wasn't good enough to make him stay.

Chapter Seven

The heavens opened the moment Hannah crawled out of bed and they hadn't let up since. The weather matched her mood perfectly, both of which hadn't improved as the day went on. The bike tyre hadn't arrived, although it didn't matter very much. She hated cycling in the rain, afraid of being splashed by a car or veering into oncoming traffic, even though the chances of that happening in Middlefern were pretty slim. When she'd phoned Claire earlier that morning to explain she still couldn't use her bike, she'd been told not to worry and to just carry on with the rota she'd been given until the weekend.

Armed with a golfing umbrella, her sturdy summer waterproof and a pair of bright yellow wellies, she'd splashed and stomped her way to each home visit. Her last call of the day had been to Mrs Barlow. As usual they'd sat and had a brew together before Hannah started the cleaning and tidying up. She'd noticed Ted was quieter than usual. He hadn't moved from his cat basket during the hour and a half she'd been there. Mrs Barlow insisted he was on the mend now, that he just needed to eat a little bit more and he'd be as good as new, but Hannah had her doubts. She wondered if Mrs Barlow was in denial about Ted's condition. She needed to chat to Emily, find out the truth.

When five-thirty came and went and the work was done for the day, any sensible person would have headed home to have a refreshing shower, and a nice evening catching up with the soaps. But Hannah didn't want to do any of those things when she closed the door on Mrs Barlow with a cheery goodbye and the promise she'd call in to check on her and Ted the following day. She needed to speak to Emily before going home, not only about her worries concerning Ted, but about their last conversation that had been nagging at her all day. She'd tried to banish those negative thoughts of inadequacy but they'd crept in during those silent times while walking to the next client, when washing up the breakfast dishes or preparing lunch.

She hadn't been good enough to make him stay.

He chose to leave with his mother and start a new life in London. He hadn't chosen her. And his decision to abandon her still stung fifteen years later.

Why hadn't he stayed in the village? Had his mother made him leave? He'd told her he had no choice. Why had he promised to write when he'd no intention of doing so? Why not end things before he left? Why keep her hopes up, keep her dangling? That's what hurt the most. She hadn't even been worthy of the truth. It didn't add up.

She needed to talk to Emily. She needed to hear her friendly voice. More than anything she really needed a hug.

She tilted the umbrella when a gust of wind threatened to lift her up into the air, Mary Poppins style, and asked herself yet again if she had lost her mind? Why on earth pursue what had happened in the past? It shouldn't matter, but Dan had returned, making her question their history over and over and over again.

She dodged a torrent of rainwater gushing from a blocked gutter and hurried across the road, breathing in a sigh of relief when his Land Rover couldn't be seen in the car park. He must be out on his evening rounds, just as she'd predicted. She couldn't face seeing him today.

She ducked under the covered porch, quickly shook the raindrops off her umbrella, scattering water in all directions, and pushed open the surgery door. She wiped her wellington boots before approaching the reception desk. Phyllis waved a quick hello before shoving a Tupperware container and the biggest flask Hannah had ever seen into her bag. Phyllis didn't look best pleased to see Hannah standing there. Maybe because of the puddle forming at her feet. She unzipped her waterproof; her tunic top stuck to her damp skin.

'What on earth are you doing out in this weather?' Phyllis scolded, as she tore off several sheets of paper towel from a large roll. She handed them to Hannah. 'It's raining cats and dogs out there.' She erupted into a fit of giggles at her own joke.

Hannah blotted her face and neck with the paper towel, grateful she didn't wear make-up. At least she wouldn't have panda eyes.

'It's not safe out there love, you should be at home. These summer storms can be terrible, and this one's predicted to go on all night. Do you not know about the severe weather warning? It's been on the local news all day and there's even talk of a power cut too, you know.'

Hannah shook her head, scrunched the paper towel up into a ball and threw it in the waste paper bin. 'Not heard about it. I've been busy all day. Is it going to be a really bad one?' She tried to keep the tremble out of her voice. Storms were notoriously bad when they happened out here in the village. An old man had been killed a few years back when a tree fell onto his car. Maybe she should have gone straight home after all.

Phyllis nodded as she shrugged on her coat and shoved a rain cap on her head.

'You need to get home and stay safe, love. Come on now.' She started to usher Hannah towards the door.

'Is Emily here?' Hannah asked, doing her best to peer over Phyllis's shoulder into the back room. Had Emily gone home already?

'Emily's not here,' Phyllis tutted, 'no one is. Everyone's gone home because as luck would have it we have no animals in here at the moment. Thank goodness! Come on now love,' she said, with more urgency, giving Hannah another gentle shove. 'I want to lock up and get home myself.'

Hannah swallowed down her disappointment. She'd give Emily a phone later on, once the boys were in bed. 'I'm sorry I bothered you,' she said, feeling terrible because she'd now made Phyllis late.

Phyllis jangled her keys and switched off the lights by the main door. Taking the hint, Hannah prepared to go when the main door flung open wide and a bedraggled looking Sammy rushed in, spraying water everywhere as she ran past Hannah towards the waiting area.

'Sammy, come here girl,' Daniel shouted, looking equally as wet as he closed the door behind him. His eyes narrowed as they darted from Phyllis's shocked face to Hannah's, then back again. 'What are you still doing here?' He pushed his wet hair out of his eyes. He must have only walked from the car park, but he was soaked through.

‘What are you doing here, Daniel?’ Phyllis asked, tying the ends of her rain cap.

‘I saw the lights were on, so I came to tell you to get going. It’s getting bad out there.’

Hannah couldn’t take her eyes off him. He wore his shirt like a second skin. Where was his coat?

‘I’m going now. I was just talking to Hannah,’ Phyllis explained. She hoisted her bag up onto her shoulder.

Hannah leaned against the reception desk. Her eyes locked on Daniel’s face. His chestnut brown hair had formed slight curls at the nape of his neck. His jeans clung to his thighs. Her breath hitched.

‘You shouldn’t be here,’ he snarled, his eyes on Hannah. ‘You need to get home.’ He quickly dismissed her before walking over to Phyllis and lowering his voice. ‘You want a lift home?’

Phyllis shook her head. ‘No Daniel, it’s a two minute walk. I’m fine.’ She patted his arm. ‘You need to get back to the cottage and out of those wet clothes. You’re soaked through,’ she said. ‘I’ll see you tomorrow.’

‘Okay, be careful.’ Daniel held the door open for her, wished her a good evening and reminded her that the pavements were a little slippy.

Hannah watched Phyllis walk through the door, leaving them alone. She half expected him to keep the door open and push her through it, but he surprised her by closing the door and walking past the waiting area and into the back of the building. ‘I need to find Sammy, then I’ll give you a lift home,’ he shouted.

Hannah rushed after him. Her blood boiled. No man told her what to do. ‘I don’t want a lift,’ she shouted, not quite understanding why she ran after him instead of turning on her heels and leaving him alone with his anger and frustration and his dog. 'I have an umbrella,' she hollered, aware it sounded ridiculous.

He whirled around on her. A flash of anger in his eyes as he threw his arms up in the air. 'Whatever,' he huffed, sounding like a sullen child. 'I need to find my dog and then I'll take you home. You'll catch pneumonia if you walk home in this. It's not safe out there.' He stomped off, shouting Sammy's name. His voice bounced off the walls.

Pneumonia? He was the one soaked through, not her.

Hannah scurried after him, a slow fury building up inside her chest. She really should turn around and go home, but she needed to have the last word. 'I'm going now, I don't need any help from you!' Her words echoed off the white stone walls, louder than she intended.

'Sammy, come here girl! We need to go.' He stormed off down the corridor, hands balled into fists at his sides. 'Where the hell has she gone?' he muttered.

'I'll help you look for her,' Hannah said, following him down the corridor.

Daniel mumbled something incoherent before yelling for Sammy once more.

He flung open doors and peered inside darkened rooms before walking into where the hospital was located. 'She's not in here,' he said.

'Maybe she went back outside?' Hannah suggested.

Daniel gave her a "have you lost your mind?" look, his eyes wide and bright in the dimness. 'How could she open the door?' He flung his arms out in exasperation.

Hannah flinched – she'd not thought of that. 'Is there another way out?' she asked.

'No,' he snapped, pushing past her on his way back to the waiting area.

She turned back around, giving the hallway one last final look before admitting defeat and deciding to head home. She heard a noise. Where was it coming from? She walked back down the corridor. There it was again. A sort of scratching sound. She stopped so she could listen more clearly and that's when she heard the whimper coming from behind the closed door at the end of the corridor. 'Dan!' she hollered, running towards the door. It was a heavy fire door, the type that required you to press down numbers on a lock to open it. How had she managed to get in there? 'It's okay Sammy, we'll get you out,' she shouted through the door. 'Dan!' she screeched.

'What is it?' he asked, not bothering to hide his annoyance. He strode towards her, raking his hands through his hair.

They both heard the scratching sound coming from behind the door.

'How'd she get in there?' he asked. His fingers quickly tapped in the access code.

Hannah couldn't believe it. *1-2-3-4. Really?*

He opened the door.

'What's down there?' Hannah asked, peering into the darkness over his shoulder.

Daniel flicked the switch. The single bulb illuminated the concrete steps that led to the floor below.

'It's our storeroom. Someone must have left the door wedged open.' Just inside the door lay a wooden wedge. He kicked it with the toe of his boot. Directly in front of him were steep steps leading down into the basement. 'I'll be having words,' he growled, hovering just inside the door. ‘Sammy,’ he shouted, ‘come on girl, time to go now.’ His voice echoed, bouncing off the walls. More scraping sounded from the basement.

Hannah stepped forward, assuming Daniel was about to go down the steps, but instead of moving, he remained rooted to the spot. She stumbled into him. He whirled around on her, his face inches from her own. She expected to see anger, or frustration on his face, but what she observed could only be described as naked fear.

‘We need to go down there and find her. She must be frightened,’ she said, her eyes locked on his. He hadn’t blinked. ‘Dan,’ she said, more gently this time. ‘We need to go down there.’

He nodded, his Adam’s apple bobbing up and down. ‘Yeah, okay, I just need to check on something first.’ He stepped aside to let her pass.

Hannah wondered what he needed to check on.

He pulled his mobile from his pocket and the screen lit up his face, accenting the strong jaw and making his eyes shine.

Even though she didn’t understand this change in behaviour, she needed to go and check on his dog. Why hadn’t he run down the stairs? He’d been frantic a minute ago. Sammy could have hurt herself. Why hadn’t she come bouncing up towards the door when she heard it open? When she heard Dan shouting her name? Something didn’t feel right. With an audible huff, she removed her rucksack and gave it to Dan, before easing past him, on her way cautiously down the stairs. Her hand brushed the wall until she reached the bottom. The air was much cooler down there. ‘Sammy, where are you girl?’ she shouted.

There were boxes everywhere and rows of shelving that housed all kinds of medical equipment that she didn't know the names of. Where was Sammy? 'Sammy!' she shouted again.

There was renewed scraping. It appeared to be coming from the far corner. Nearly tripping over her feet in her hurry to find Sammy, she crouched in front of a large cardboard box that was surrounded by several larger boxes. The scraping came from inside the box. She realised Sammy must have jumped inside and somehow become stuck. She gently lifted up the flaps of the box and tilted it on its side. Sammy sprang out, her tail wagging and rewarded Hannah with a sharp bark and then a lick of the face. 'I've found your dog, she's fine,' Hannah yelled. She didn't try to keep the annoyance out of her voice. Daniel hadn't even followed her down the steps. It was his damn dog. She wasn't the hired help.

Sammy raced towards the steps, tail still wagging wildly as Hannah slowly stood, brushing the dust off her trousers. She couldn't wait to get home and stand under a warm shower.

Her foot touched the bottom step when the lights went out.

The room plunged into darkness.

Hannah couldn't see a thing. She forced herself to breathe, in and out, in and out, as she'd been taught to do when in therapy, and forced down her rising panic.

She would not panic.

'Hannah!' Daniel roared from the top of the stairs. 'You okay?'

‘I’m fine,’ she shouted back, feeling anything but fine as her body shook. Her eyes hadn’t adjusted to the blackness yet and she couldn’t see a thing.

‘Give me a minute. Stay where you are.’ She fumbled in her trouser pocket for her phone but was met with empty air. Then she remembered. She’d left it in her rucksack.

She had to move.

Her left hand brushed the cold, stone wall as she inched her way upwards, one step at a time. She couldn’t see Dan, but thought he was still standing by the open door. She heard Sammy bark. The torch app on his phone suddenly illuminated the steps. Her pulse slowed as she stopped a nervous laugh escaping from her throat.

‘It’s the storm. We have an emergency generator that should kick in soon,’ he said. Hannah detected something in his voice, but she couldn’t quite pinpoint what was bothering her. She pushed it aside. She needed to get out of there, out of this dark, confined space.

Halfway there.

She’d soon be on her way home.

Three more steps.

Then it happened.

Sammy jumped up in excitement, and in doing so knocked Daniel’s arm, making him lose his balance. He dropped the phone. The sound of it hitting the concrete steps was followed by the shattering of glass that plunged them once more into darkness.

Hannah felt the firm grasp of Daniel’s grip on her shoulder and then the heavy thud of the door as it slammed shut behind Sammy, who had dashed past Daniel, out into the empty corridor.

His grip was almost painful as he held her in place. She couldn't move because of the sheer strength of him.

'Dan, the door,' she shouted. 'Open the door.' She peered into the gloom, her eyes slowly adjusting to the lack of natural light. But he didn't move. She shoved his arm away, relieved when he let her go as she stumbled past him, tripping on the top step, her hands finding and then fumbling for the door's handle. It wouldn't turn. 'Something's wrong with the door,' she shrieked. 'Dan?' She sensed him beside her, felt his body heat. She grabbed his arm, shook him. 'You need to open the door,' she said, trying to keep her voice steady.

'I can't,' he said.

She barely heard him despite the suffocating stillness.

Unease prickled her spine. 'Don't mess about. I'm not in the mood for games.' This wasn't funny. Not at all. 'Open the door!' she yelled, thumping the door, but all she was met with was silence.

Chapter Eight

Daniel slumped onto the floor, his head in his hands. *Breathe*, he needed to breathe, otherwise he'd lose it and he couldn't do that, not here, not with Hannah by his side. She'd called him Dan. The only other person who called him Dan was his mother. He raked a shaking hand through his hair and thought about how his name sounded on her lips.

His phone lay battered and, no doubt, broken on the floor.

The demons awoke with vengeance.

A cold sweat broke out on his skin and his hands began to tremble. His heart felt as if it would jump right out of his chest.

Breathe, God damn it. Breathe.

He felt a hand on his arm and then the weight of her body as she sat down on the floor beside him. Both of their backs rested against the closed door.

'We're locked in.' Her voice was so quiet, almost a whisper and Daniel nearly missed what she said.

He nodded, trying to swallow but his tongue stuck to the roof of his mouth. He coughed, wishing he had water. 'Yeah,' he croaked.

'Why is it locked from the inside?' she asked.

He tilted his head back, sucked in the stale air and tasted the dust. He counted to five before releasing his breath. Was there enough air in here, enough oxygen? He wondered how long it would last. 'It's an electric door.'

He sucked in more air, counting five seconds in his mind. Slow and steady, that's what he remembered.

Don't think about anything else other than breathing.

'When there's a power cut it locks automatically. The generator should kick in soon.' He sucked in another deep breath through his nose. 'When it does, the door will open.'

'That's a really weird system,' she said. 'I mean, you'd think you'd be able to override it or something.' She paused, touching his arm. 'I think your phone broke.'

Daniel squeezed his eyes shut. If he did that it was only dark in his head. 'Where's *your* phone?' he asked. Why hadn't he thought to ask her this earlier?

'In my bag,' she said. 'Can you pass me my bag please? You must have dropped it on the floor.'

'I haven't got your bag.'

'I gave it to you, before going down *there* to rescue *your* dog.'

Daniel winced. She sounded angry. And then he remembered, dropping the bag by the open doorway. It was no longer there. He sighed.

'It's in the corridor, isn't it?'

'I'm sorry.'

He heard her mumble something under her breath. After a few seconds of silence she spoke. 'Will Sammy be okay?'

The question surprised him. Here they were trapped inside this room for God knows how long and she was worrying about his dog.

'She'll be fine. She'll be sitting on the other side of this door.' And despite the gnawing ache in his chest and his sweaty palms, he smiled.

It was easier with Hannah sitting beside him. Her warmth and words reminded him he wasn't alone.

There were a few beats before Hannah broke the silence with another question. 'Are you worried about Mrs Barlow?' she asked. 'I know I am.'

Mrs Barlow? He racked his brain trying to pinpoint the name. It rang a bell.

'Mrs Barlow, the old lady who has Ted, the tabby cat,' she added. 'I'm her carer.'

Ted, the tabby cat? Talking to Hannah made it easier to breathe. He needed to keep her talking. Then he remembered. Mrs Barlow had been the lady he'd met on his first day. The elderly woman who'd carried the cat carrier and a walking stick in the same hand. He'd run blood tests and was still waiting for the results. Hopefully he'd get them tomorrow, if not he'd chase them up. His gut told him it wouldn't be good news. He should have phoned her to let her know about the delay.

'Why are you worried about her?' he asked. It was becoming much easier to breathe now.

Don't think about the dark.

Don't think about being trapped.

Concentrate on talking and inhaling the scent of strawberry shampoo and her perfume that reminded him of cut summer flowers.

'She just seems a little sad. A little lost, you know?' She huffed out a breath of air. He felt it on his cheek as she turned to face him. 'I know it sounds silly, but I think she knows Ted is really poorly. He didn't move from his cat basket while I was there, and it's so unlike him. He usually starts meowing for cat biscuits the moment I step through the door.'

He thought it didn't sound silly at all. 'I should have the blood results back tomorrow and we'll know more then,' he said. 'But I also think he's a very ill cat.'

'Poor Mrs Barlow,' she said. 'She only has Ted. I don't know how she'll cope without him.'

'I'll be gentle with her, make sure Phyllis is with me if I need to give her any bad news. Apparently, she's known Phyllis for a long time.'

He sensed the hesitation in her breath. 'Oh, that's really kind of you. Do you—oh this probably sounds really stupid, but do you offer something like a counselling service for owners who've suffered a recent loss?' A nervous laugh escaped her throat before she added, 'I just think it would help her, you know, having people to talk to.'

By God, how could he have forgotten just how caring she was, how empathetic and how she cut to the core of any problem. 'I'm not too sure how things are done around here,' he admitted. They'd offered counselling to bereaved owners back in London. 'I'll ask Emily, she'll know. But I'll make sure Mrs Barlow's looked after.'

'I'll keep an eye on her too,' Hannah said. 'Between the two of us, she'll be okay.' She rested her head back against the wall. Their breathing was in sync with one another.

No longer sweating, Daniel's pulse had slowed and he felt much calmer. More in control. He could do this. He could get through this. He'd been through a lot worse.

Keep her talking. Don't think about the dark, about being trapped.

'I hate spiders,' Hannah said, followed by a nervous laugh.

He turned his head, searching out the white of her eyes. 'What?' Why had she never told him that?

'Mm-hmm. I hate spiders, always have,' she said. 'It's something to do with their thin, hairy legs that could break any minute. And they are *huge.'*

He felt the rumble of her laughter and smiled. 'I think you're pretty safe here. There are no spiders down here. Well, I don't think so anyway.'

He heard the catch in her breath.

'I hope not,' she said.

He closed his eyes. It became easier with every passing second. He needed to keep her talking. Stick to safe topics. He wouldn't mention anything about their past. 'So, you enjoy working as a carer then?' He grimaced at his forced joviality. Why was he trying so hard?

'Do I like being a carer? Why are you asking me that?'

He felt her shoulders tense through the cotton of his shirt sleeve.

Keep breathing.

'Just making conversation.' He shrugged. He wanted to ask her why she worked as a carer, instead of being a writer. She'd wanted to study English literature with the possibility of going into journalism. He didn't want to dredge up the past.

'I like my job. I'm good at it,' she said, her tone now defensive.

He hadn't meant to upset her. He'd obviously touched a raw nerve.

He waited for her to say more, but she remained silent. 'That's great to hear,' he said. 'I can see you being good at your job. You're a caring person.'

She shifted her weight away from him. He wished he could see her face.

'I don't need your affirmation, thanks,' she said.

'I know that, it's just …'

'Just nothing, okay. I don't want to hear what you think about my working as a carer.'

Why was she being so touchy? So much for sticking to safer topics of conversation. How much longer would they be stuck in here? He needed to get out to check on Sammy.

Don't think about the oxygen diminishing with every second. Don't think about that. Keep talking. 'So are you going anywhere nice this year?' he asked. He couldn't think of anything else to say.

Her sharp bark of laughter bounced off the stairwell. Maybe he shouldn't have asked that question. He stretched out his legs that were beginning to cramp. He didn't want to risk standing up. He felt safer on the ground.

'Are you going away this summer?' she asked.

'No,' he said. 'I have no plans to go on holiday.' He didn't have the money, thanks to the divorce, and he would be too tied up in the business, what with working long hours and then trying to find a buyer which he knew would be no easy task. Plus, he had no intention of holidaying alone.

Hannah's sigh reverberated around them.

Perhaps he should crawl down the steps, try and retrieve his phone? On second thoughts, probably not the best idea in the world when it was pitch black. He'd break his neck on those steps.

'So, now that I've shared my secret about being afraid of spiders, you need to share your secret. What are you afraid of? Come on'—she nudged his arm—'dig the dirt.'

The question appeared to come out of the blue. Where should he start? Sitting here in the dark, with you, he thought, with the air being consumed every time he opened his mouth, or took in a breath, or dry swallowed. He could feel the walls pushing in towards him. The ceiling bearing down, crushing his lungs. He sucked in air, or tried his best to as his hands trembled and beads of sweat prickled his neck. He couldn't lose his grip, not now, not when he'd been in control of everything. He heard the scratching mice below them, the sound of his grandfather—

'Are you okay?' Hannah's face was in front of his. He couldn't see her because it was so damn dark, but he could smell strawberries and feel her warm breath on his face. 'Yes, I'm fine,' he stuttered. He was far from fine, but her voice grounded him, brought him back to the here and now. His hands weren't shaking so much and the crushing pain had slowly faded.

'You don't like the dark, do you?'

'No, not much,' he said. He tried to laugh. Three words were the most he could articulate right now.

He sucked in another lungful of dry air through his nose and closed his eyes, willing her to keep talking.

'I never knew that,' she whispered. She touched his hand and the gesture felt so raw, so intimate that he grabbed her fingers as if they were an anchor. He felt her body stiffen. He loosened his grip. 'I'm sorry, I'm …'

'Why don't you like the dark?' she asked, interrupting him, still holding his hand. She tightened her grip.

He waited for her laughter, for her to mock him, about how a grown man shouldn't be afraid of the dark, but none came. He sucked in another breath, much calmer now, more able to talk. 'It's not the dark so much as confined spaces.' His voice sounded gruff so he cleared his throat. He needed a drink.

'I didn't know that,' she said. 'When did that start? I mean, you were fine when we were younger, so …'

When we were younger?

If only she knew. He must have hid it well.

'Did something happen to you? You were trapped somewhere?' Another gentle squeeze on his fingers.

He nodded, then realising she couldn't see him said, 'Yeah, but now's not a good time to talk about that.'

'No problem, let's talk about something else,' she quickly said.

His chest heaved with the relief of dodging that particular bullet. He didn't want to go down the rabbit hole. He had no intention of talking about Gerald. 'Thanks,' he heaved.

Please don't let go of my hand. Please keep talking.

'So, as we're stuck here, why don't you tell me the real reason you're back here in Middlefern?'

Hannah had to keep him talking, keep him engaged. She needed to take his mind off being locked inside this room. The look of sheer panic and then helplessness that flashed across his face before he dropped the phone had frightened her. She'd never seen him look that way before. She'd felt his body trembling as she knelt down beside him. Heard his shallow breathing, the change in his voice. He wasn't just afraid of the dark, or of being trapped inside this room, it was something much darker than that. She had almost smelt his fear. So she held his hand and prayed for the lights to come back on, while encouraging him to talk. She wanted to hear the real reason why he'd come back here to his childhood home.

She held her breath as she waited for his answer. She wanted to hear the truth. She didn't want to hear about how he'd come back to help out because they needed a vet, as that just didn't add up, not when they'd been using a locum vet for the past few months. Surely he could have found a replacement for Jeffries? Dan hadn't returned to work here in the village after Gerald's passing, so why return now? Why the sudden change? Something must have happened to him in London? Whatever had happened must be the reason he'd come back home to Middlefern, probably kicking and screaming.

She waited for his answer and when it came it didn't surprise her.

'I came back to help out. There was no one else.'

Liar, she thought. Coming back here surely wasn't a charitable act. The need to save the business was an act. The real reason must be money and she wanted him to admit that.

His fingers still gripped hers, a little too tightly. She wondered if her fingers would go numb, but she didn't dare let go. He gripped them as if she were a life raft. Despite everything that had happened since his departure, she felt the urge to protect him, to help him, not knowing if he'd do the same for her.

'Hmm, I don't think that's entirely true,' she said, trying to make her tone of voice sound light, 'because then you'd have come back after the funeral, to take over the practice, but you didn't.'

His grip slackened for a moment. 'I couldn't come back here, when he died, I …' He shook his head. 'Dr

Jeffries couldn't stay on any longer, and there was no one else to fill the role so I stepped in.' He let go of her hand.

She wanted to grab it again, but instead she placed her hands in her lap. Maybe he told the truth, but why hadn't he come back for the funeral? It had surprised everyone in the village when he hadn't shown up. She'd always thought he'd been close to Gerald, that he would have been back as quick as a flash once he'd heard about his illness, but he hadn't.

Once again she thought about his matter-of-fact manner when talking about his grandfather, his complete lack of emotion. It hadn't gone unnoticed that he'd referred to his grandfather without any affection. She didn't understand why he acted in this way. People dealt with grief in their own way she supposed, everyone behaved differently, but something didn't seem right. Her next question was on the tip of her tongue but she pressed her lips together, swallowing those words. Now wasn't the time to delve into his relationship with Gerald.

Keep talking. Keep him calm.

'So, who've you got waiting for you back in London, then?' she asked, not really expecting a reply. She heard an audible humph before he replied, 'No one is waiting for me.'

'Your mum's no longer there then?' she asked.

'Mum moved to Cornwall years ago. They moved because of David's job relocation, but it suits them. They much prefer the sea air.'

'Wow, that's amazing! I've always wanted to go there.'

'Yeah? I didn't know that.' He sounded genuinely surprised.

'Well, we didn't tell each other everything,' she said, before she could stop herself. 'Sorry, it was a long time ago. Forget I said that.'

He rewarded her with silence.

She didn't want to talk about the past. No good would come of it.

'We usually FaceTime once a month,' he said. 'She's happy.'

'That's so good to hear. I always liked your mum. You must miss her though.'

'Cornwall's not that far away. But yeah, I miss them.'

Hannah wondered what it must be like to move away to an area where you didn't know a soul. To uproot and start all over again. A clean slate. She'd thought about it, fleetingly, after her mother died, but then she'd wondered, where would she go? She'd only be taking her worries and anxieties and baggage along with her, no matter how many thousands of miles she moved away from Middlefern.

'There's no one else then?' she found herself asking. What had happened to her filter? She had no right to ask if he had a girlfriend back in London. 'Sorry, you don't have to answer that. None of my business,' she said. But surely there must be someone waiting for him in London?

'There's an ex-wife and an ex-best friend,' he said, his tone flat, but his voice wobbled slightly.

'Do you want to talk about it?' she asked, not liking the wobble in his voice.

'What's to tell?'

She felt his shoulders shrug, and heard a breath. 'Sally figured out she didn't love me any more. Told me she loved Jack, always had, so she left me for him.'

'Your ex-best friend?'

'Yeah, and partner.' He sighed.

'Partner?'

'We all worked together, set up the business from scratch.'

'No!' Hannah gasped. 'Oh my God, that's awful. I'm so sorry.'

'Don't be,' he mumbled. 'We should never have got married in the first place.

Hannah swore she saw a flicker of a smile in the gloom.

'Things had been a bit rocky for a while. It's just – I wish she hadn't left me for him.'

How should she reply to that comment? 'When did this all happen?' she decided to ask.

'Over a year ago now.'

'Were you married long?'

'Five years – we met at uni.'

The comment hung in the air between them. Five years, that was a long time. She'd never made it to university. She'd had commitments and no choice. But she regretted nothing.

'Things always work out though, don't they,' Daniel said. 'I mean things usually happen for a reason, don't you think?'

'No, things don't happen for a reason. I don't believe in any of that,' she said. 'That's the kind of remark people make when things haven't gone their own way. Shit happens and you have to cope with it as best you can.'

'I forgot how honest you are,' Daniel said. 'I just meant that if my marriage hadn't fallen apart then I wouldn't have been bought out of the business and I wouldn't be here now, sitting in the dark, with you.'

‘And that’s a good thing?’ Why was he joking? It wasn’t funny.

‘As I said, things happen for a reason.’

So, he viewed coming back to Middlefern as a good thing? He’d gained both a home and a business when he’d lost everything. Of course it was a good thing. But then he’d said he wouldn’t be sitting in the dark with her. A tingle ran down her spine. Memories of sitting in her bedroom with only a flickering candle for company. Did he remember too? She squeezed her eyes shut. Nope, couldn’t think about that right now. It really wasn’t the right time or place for those memories to resurface.

She wrapped her arms around her body. The damp clothes now cool against her skin.

‘You must be cold.’ He shifted closer towards her, wrapping an arm around her shoulder. She accepted his warmth, the kind gesture and leaned her head against his damp shoulder, devouring the warmth and solidness of his body.

‘Hopefully this won’t last much longer,’ he murmured into her hair.

Hannah wasn’t so sure about that. She remembered a storm from a few years ago when the lights had gone out and hadn’t come back on for another six hours. By God, she couldn’t sit trapped in here with Dan Jackson for six hours.

She closed her eyes. He smelled so good, but this one kind gesture did not make her forget what he’d done to her. This was about survival and she needed his body heat.

‘Why didn’t you write to me?’ The words tumbled out of her mouth before she could stop them, just like that.

It grew cooler by the second and she'd been lulled into a false sense of security with his arm wrapped around her, his breath on her hair. She felt the muscles in his arm tighten before he answered.

'It's such a long time ago. We were kids, Hannah. I can't remember,' he said.

Her eyes snapped open. He'd used that excuse before and Hannah didn't believe him this time either. 'Yeah, we were kids, but we both knew right from wrong,' she said.

'I did write to you.'

Hannah's heart thumped madly in her chest at those five simple words. 'What?' she managed to stutter. 'I never received a single letter from you.'

'That's because I never sent them.'

Hannah's thoughts were sent reeling. None of this made any sense. Why write letters and then not send them to her? 'Why?' The word came out as a whisper.

When he remained silent, she huffed out a breath, thinking he wasn't about to answer her.

'I had my reasons,' he eventually said. 'I'll tell you about them some other time.'

'Okay,' she said, trying her best to process this new piece of information. 'Did you get my letters? Did you read them?' She had to know, even if he told her that he hadn't. That he'd dumped them in the bin.

'Yes, all twenty-four of them.'

She gasped. He'd kept her letters. And he knew exactly how many she sent.

'I read every single one, I replied to every single one and I still have them.'

'You kept them?' *After all this time?*

‘I did,’ came his simple answer. ‘But I’m sorry I never posted those letters to you.’

‘It’s okay,’ she said. But it was far from okay. She’d accept his apology. What else could she do? But everything she had known, everything she’d assumed had been turned on its head. *He had kept all her letters?* Her hand found his and they stayed like that for a while, just the sound of their breathing audible in the cool, dark, silent stairway. Glad that he was here with her now. She knew that soon he would be gone again.

Chapter Nine

The flash of light that followed the hum of electricity from the overhead light made Daniel jump, and brought him back down to earth with a thud of reality. His heart pounded and his arm instinctively drew Hannah towards him before he worked out what was happening. He reluctantly released his grip from around her shoulder and blinked several times as his eyes adjusted to the bright light.

'Thank goodness for that,' Hannah said, echoing his own feelings of relief, as she shuffled awkwardly onto her feet. She brushed down her trousers that were covered in a fine layer of dust. Daniel did the same as he climbed down the steps, his eyes scanning the stairs for his broken phone. He found it and scooped it up. Yep it was broken all right; a huge chunk of glass was missing from the corner and an ominous spider's web of fractured glass splintered out from its centre. He pressed the power button and thankfully the screen lit up. He breathed a sigh of relief and shoved it into his back pocket. He'd deal with it later. At least it was working.

'Let's get out of here,' he said, retreating back up the steps to where Hannah stood. He pushed open the door. Another sigh of relief escaped his lips. He held it open for her as she ducked under his arm and stepped out into the brightly lit corridor.

'Freedom,' she said with a slight laugh.

He wasn't sure how long they'd been trapped in the dark, but it felt like hours. He tried his best to smile back at her, but if truth be told he still felt a little jittery, a bit unsettled after being trapped in the dark for so long. Their eyes locked, something unspoken passed between them, an emotion unsaid, but then Sammy barked and rubbed her head against his leg, breaking the spell. He ran a shaking hand through his damp hair. 'Sorry about – well – about what happened in there …'

'It's okay, no worries,' she interrupted, bending down to rub Sammy's head before picking up her rucksack. It still felt wet.

He tried to cover his embarrassment with words. What must she think of him? 'It's hard to explain what happens when I'm, when I find myself in confined spaces like that.' He shoved his hands deeper into his pockets. He was making a right mess of this. Had she noticed him shaking? She must have – she'd held his hand. He flexed his fingers, remembering her touch. But he couldn't quite remember if he'd grabbed her hand or if she'd reached for his. He thought he'd managed to hide his fear from her, but one look at her expression now, told him he hadn't got away with it.

'Really, don't worry about it.' She smiled again, a warm glow to her cheeks now. Had he embarrassed her? 'I'd best get going.' She hoisted the bag up and onto her shoulder.

'I'll give you a lift, who knows what it's like out there.' He was already halfway down the corridor, Sammy following. Hannah trailed behind them. The roads were bound to be flooded and who knew how long the electricity would stay on?

'It's okay, really, I'll walk …' Hannah began to protest, but her words trailed away when they reached the reception area. They peered through the main door observing the pitch black sky. No lights were on anywhere. The only light came from the lightning that lit up the sky and the surrounding hills. The generator must have finally kicked in. He turned around to face her, his eyebrow raised. 'You can't go walking home in this weather, and especially not in the dark.' He needed to make sure she got home safely. 'Come on, let's call it a thank you for keeping me company,' he said.

She walked to the door and opened it to peer outside. Her shoulders slumped. She turned around and faced him with a frown on her face. 'Thank you, that'd be great.'

Daniel suppressed his grin. He'd expected an argument, or for her to ignore his concern and walk through the door. She didn't need to listen to him, or do anything he suggested. He couldn't stop her. 'Wait here until I get to the Landy and open the door for you,' he instructed. 'Come on Sammy,' he shouted over his shoulder as he headed out. The sky lit up and another crack of thunder sounded. He pulled the keys from his pocket. Hannah opened her mouth to protest, but he'd already gone. He couldn't hear her anyway because of the thunder and the torrential rain that bounced up from the pavement, soaking his already damp jeans. His boots squelched. The water ran in rivulets down the street. Another flash of lightning speared the sky, followed quickly by a boom that rumbled and echoed off the hills.

He flung open the passenger door, before running round the front to jump in himself. Sammy leapt up through the passenger side, then hopped onto the back seat, as if she knew that Hannah was about to get in. He watched in amusement as Hannah half walked, half ran towards them. 'Oh my God,' she said, her teeth chattering. 'This is awful weather. It's not rained like this in a long time. And it's summer.'

'Growing up we often got bad storms in the summer.' He leant forward and cranked up the heater.

'I haven't locked the door,' she said. Small worry lines formed on her brow. He wanted to place his finger on them, smooth them away.

'It'll be fine, nobody'll be out in this weather,' he said. 'Let's get you home safely, eh.' He started the ignition and the window wipers squeaked across the windscreen. They made no difference – he couldn't see a damn thing.

'It's not safe, is it?' Hannah said, echoing his thoughts.

He peered through the rain-splattered windscreen. They weren't going anywhere. With a sigh he unclipped his seat belt. 'I think it's safer if you stay here …' He stopped when he saw the flash of panic in her eyes. 'What I mean is, just until the rain eases off and I can drive you home. It's not safe to go out walking in this.' He didn't want to have a fight on his hands, but if she set off on foot, right now, he'd worry about her. It was his fault she was stuck here with him, because if he hadn't frozen, if he'd been the one to go in and find Sammy, then she wouldn't have been locked in the storeroom with him.

She unclipped her seat belt. 'Okay, but I need to get home to feed Daisy, so I'll stay, but only until the rain stops.'

Daniel ushered Hannah into the kitchen, telling her she could kick off her wellies if she wanted to, then he grabbed two towels from the airing cupboard in the hallway. Sammy jumped into her dog basket and curled up, head on paws. Not only was the kitchen the warmest room in the cottage, but somehow it felt less formal than sitting in the living room. Hannah gratefully took the towel and began to towel dry her hair. She'd removed her wellies and he noticed with amusement that she wore bright pink socks.

The moment they stepped through the front door the power came back on. All the street lights snapped back to life. Daniel took it as a sign that the evening could only get better.

Hannah's gaze swept the room, taking in the subtle changes that had been made. The new kitchen cupboards and the window looked new. The only sound to be heard was the rain hitting the window pane.

'You want a coffee?' he asked, quickly changing the subject. He didn't want to talk about the cottage. It would only dredge up the past. It was hard enough with all of the memories slowly bubbling to the surface because she stood in his home. *Home*? He could never view this place as home.

'Do you have tea?' she asked.

It took a moment for Daniel to refocus, to bring himself back into the room. He dragged himself away from his thoughts. 'I think so,' he said, opening the cupboard above the toaster and peering inside. There was a small bag of teabags lurking in the back. 'You don't drink coffee?' he asked. She used to drink it like there was no tomorrow.

She shook her head. 'I gave it up when looking after Mum. It gave me terrible headaches.'

'I couldn't live without coffee,' he said.

'Oh you could. You'd be surprised about what you could live without,' she uttered with a deep sigh.

He opened his mouth to tell her how sorry he was about her mum, but he decided against it. One look at her face told him she wouldn't welcome or appreciate his pity.

'Sit down. I'll make us a drink,' he said instead. 'Are you warm enough?' She only had on her work polo top. Even though the day had been warm, the cottage felt cold and her top was damp. Hannah nodded. 'I'm fine. The tea will warm me up.'

'I'll go grab you one of my shirts, won't be a minute.'

He pulled a clean shirt from the linen basket in his bedroom. He quickly stripped off his wet shirt and pulled the clean one over his head as he never undid the buttons. Then he found another clean shirt, one with less creases and made his way back to the kitchen.

'It is clean,' he said, smiling as he handed it to her. 'You can change in the bathroom, it's just down the hall.'

'I remember, thanks.'

Of course she knew where the bathroom was.

A few minutes later she returned to the kitchen.

The sight of her wearing his shirt nearly made him drop the kettle. The hem of the shirt reached her knees and it gaped at the neck. Her long blonde hair had been towel dried and hung in waves around her shoulders. For a moment he forgot his own name.

He remembered the first time she'd ever worn one of his shirts. They'd come home after school to work on an English project together. They'd sat at the kitchen table, huddled over exercise books and journals, when he'd noticed she was rubbing her arms, tiny goosebumps emerging. On instinct he'd jumped up from the table, went to his bedroom and brought back a shirt for her to wear. Without a word she'd taken it from him and slipped it over her head, the buttons fastened. The sleeves were far too long and she'd had to roll them up to free her hands to write, but he thought she'd never looked more beautiful. That same feeling burnt in his chest now. With a low growl deep in his throat he tore his eyes away to make the drinks.

Once the storm passed he'd take her home. Rekindling old thoughts and memories and feelings was not a good idea. Water under the bridge and all that. Time to think about something else. Food. They needed to eat something. He still hadn't got round to doing a full shop. As the tea brewed he opened and closed cupboard doors. There were several tins of vegetable soup. 'Would you like some soup?' he asked, passing Hannah her tea.

'Erm, no, that's okay.' She wrapped her hands around the mug. 'I'll make something when I get back.'

'It's no problem. I'm going to have some soup. I mean, it's only heating up a can. Who knows how long this rain will last.' And how long you'll need to stay, he thought. Hopefully it would ease soon and he could get her back home. Get her out of his kitchen. It was becoming increasingly difficult to think coherently. It had been such a long time since he'd been comforted by a woman. He wanted to touch her again. He wanted to hold her hand, to feel that connection he had with her, with their past.

He wanted her to stay. He wanted to tell her about his past, make her understand why he had to go away. He wanted to spill his guts about his marriage. About what a disaster it had been from the moment he placed a ring on her finger. How his entire life had spiralled out of control the moment he'd left Middlefern. How could he have all these feelings, and want to share them with her, while at the same time wanting to move away once again, to draw a line and move on with his life?

'Oh, okay then, well, if it's no trouble thank you, that'd be nice.'

It took him a moment to realise she was referring to the soup. Glad he had something to do with his hands, he switched on the wind-up radio to listen to the local news while he warmed up the soup.

'Is there anything I can do?' she asked.

'No, you're fine. This won't take five minutes.' He emptied the contents of both cans into the saucepan and turned on the hob. The smell of leek and potatoes filled the air. The news anchor kept repeating the same news. The storm had brought disruption to the local area, but for now power was back on. He hoped it stayed that way.

Daniel stirred the pan of soup with a wooden spoon and when hot enough ladled it into two bowls.

'Here you go,' he said, placing the soup down on the table.

'Thanks, it smells delicious.'

'Sorry, I haven't got any bread,' he said. 'I always like to dip chunks of bread in my soup.'

She smiled. 'I think I'll live.'

He watched her tuck a strand of hair behind her ear before picking up the spoon. On the radio they repeated the news that power had been restored to all homes.

'It's good the power is back on,' she said. 'I'm worried about my clients. Most of them live alone.'

'It must be frightening, when you're elderly and something like this happens. I mean, you must feel so vulnerable,' he said before swallowing a mouthful of soup.

Hannah nodded, her spoon in mid air. 'I'll try and give them all a phone once I get back. Make sure they're okay. Just to check in with them, you know.' She blew on the soup to cool it down.

'Everyone?' Daniel asked, unable to hide his surprise.

'Yes, everyone.'

'They'll be fine, they're all at home, safe indoors,' Daniel said, offering her reassurance. 'I wouldn't worry too much.'

'I can't help it. It's hard to explain, but they become a part of your family when you see them nearly every day.'

'I hadn't thought about it like that.' He'd viewed Hannah's job as a home carer, as just that, a job, when in fact it was so much more to her. As he slurped his soup he thought about this. She was a young woman, living alone with no family. She had no uncles, aunties, brothers or sisters. A long time ago, there had been him and his mother. Now, she had no one. So the revelation that these people who she cared for were more like family, really shouldn't surprise him that much.

'What are you thinking about?'

'Sorry?'

'You're thinking about something, I can tell. You get these little frown lines between your eyes.' She pointed between her own brows to explain what she meant.

'Oh, nothing in particular.' He concentrated on eating his soup.

She cocked her head to one side. 'Go on, tell me what's on your mind. I'm interested.' She gestured with her spoon.

He swallowed the soup in his mouth. It was far too hot and scalded his tongue. Oh there was so much mulling around in his head, and he couldn't tell her any of it. 'I was just thinking how nice it is to be back and sat here chatting with you.'

Her eyes narrowed and she pursed her lips before looking away from him. 'Liar,' she said.

'Wh-what?'

'That's not what you're thinking about at all. And before you say, how would I know, well, it's because you're not glad to be back here. Not at all. You're back here because you have to be, and as for *me*, well, I think you'd much rather be here by yourself, eating your soup. Plus'—she held her hand up—'you have a really bad poker face.'

He dropped the spoon into the bowl. 'That's not fair, Hannah.' He liked the way her name sounded tripping off his tongue. He ran his hand through his hair. 'I am glad you're here. The bit about being glad to be back here, well, it's not as simple as being happy, but I am happy that you're here and we're able to talk.' That at least was true.

She shook her head and ate her soup.

He thought it best to say nothing more. They continued eating in silence. Nothing could be heard but the murmur from the radio with its constant updates and announcements. He wished he felt more comfortable, more able to open up his heart and talk about what had happened in this house, what had happened in London, but talking about his feelings had never been his strong point.

When Hannah finished her soup she pushed the bowl away with a contented sigh. 'That was lovely, thank you.'

'No problem.' He leaned back, kicking his legs out. One quick glance out of the window told him that the worst of the storm was over.

'It must be strange to be sitting here in this kitchen again. Living in the cottage you grew up in,' Hannah said.

'Yeah, it is,' he said with a shrug. 'It feels strange, you know, in the way that things can change, but they still feel the same.'

'I know what you mean,' she said. Her fingers tapped the table.

He wanted to reach over and grab them. 'Looks like the worst of the weather is over,' he said, glancing once more out of the window. The wind had died down and they could no longer hear the rain pelting against the glass. 'I forgot to ask,' he said, 'where did you leave your bike?' He hadn't seen it propped up outside the surgery and there was no mistaking her bike. 'I'll pop it in the truck before we set off.'

Hannah picked up her empty bowl, pushed herself up from the table and dropped it into the sink with a splash. 'I'll wash up if you like and then get going,' she said, staring out of the window. 'I think I'll be fine walking home. I don't want to put you to any trouble.'

Why was she talking about walking home?

Daniel's chair scraped against the wooden floor as he moved from the table towards the sink. He placed his bowl and cup on the draining board. 'Leave them, please, I'll do them when I get back from dropping you off. You can't go riding your bike home in this, and pushing it home isn't safe either. It'll take me less than five minutes to drop you off.'

She whirled around, her face only inches from his own. He'd forgotten how stubborn she could be and how those pale grey eyes could change into slate-grey slits. He'd expected to see anger, but there was no trace of that or even impatience. She looked almost apologetic. 'I need to confess something.'

He raised a brow and leaned his hip against the sink. 'Oh and what would that be then?' He kept his tone light, even though she looked as if she had the weight of the world on her shoulders.

'It's a bit embarrassing,' she muttered.

He pressed his lips together, waiting for whatever she had to say.

'It's about the bike.'

'Okay, what about it?' he probed.

'It's not outside.'

'*Okaaay*,' he said again, not quite understanding why she found this so embarrassing. So what, she didn't ride her bike today. 'I don't blame you for leaving it at home,' he said. 'I mean, what with the rain and everything, I'd have done the same.'

She shook her head, picked up the tea towel, and twisted it in her hands. 'I left the bike at home because I haven't fixed it yet.'

Why was she embarrassed about that? 'Do you want me to have a look?' And then he remembered their conversation in the pub. How she'd told him that it was fixed when he'd offered to help her. That's why she stood there, shamefaced.

She blushed. 'I shouldn't have lied, it was just—'

He held up his hands. 'I get it. You didn't want me muscling in and being the hero.' He laughed. 'If you want me to take a look though, I can.'

'Thanks, that'd be great.' She let out a tiny laugh and his chest ached at the sound. He'd missed the sound of her laughter, and with a pang he realised she hadn't laughed much on the few occasions they'd been together since his return. He wanted to hear her laugh more.

'Right, so, how about we try again and I drop you back home.'

'Good idea,' she said, 'and thank you.'

'No problem.' He wasn't sure if she was thanking him for the lift or for not making fun of her about the bike.

Chapter Ten

'Are you sure there's nothing else you want me to do?' Hannah stood on Mrs Barlow's doorstep.

'I'm fine, lovely. There's nothing I need. You get on home now.'

Hannah hesitated. She tried to push down her sense of unease, but it wouldn't budge. 'Well, if you're sure there's nothing else I can do, then I'll see you in a couple of days, Mrs Barlow.' She paused, still feeling guilty about leaving this old woman all alone with her poorly cat. 'If you need anything, you can give me a call. You take care now.' She reluctantly waved goodbye. She wanted to stay but she had no reason to. Her work was done for the day.

'Bye love.' Mrs Barlow closed the door.

Hannah leaned over to unchain her bike from the railing. Dan had found a spare tyre in the boot of his truck. Oh look at that, he'd told her when he pulled it out of the boot like a rabbit from a hat. He didn't even own a bike. Hannah wondered how it had gotten there.

Ted still didn't look too well. She'd managed to coax him into eating a cat biscuit, but he refused to budge from his cat basket. She also thought he'd lost a little more weight. When she'd voiced her concerns, Mrs Barlow just tutted and said he'd be right as rain again in a few days. But Hannah clocked the twitch of her mouth, the slight tremble in her hand. Truth be told, she worried about both of them.

Tinkling her bike bell to say goodbye once more, she headed for home.

A few large puddles remained on the road, but other than that there were very few reminders of the storm from the previous night. Thankfully the electricity had remained on throughout the night and there had been no further disruptions. So as they say, after the storm came the calm, but Hannah didn't feel calm. If anything she felt more agitated and confused.

She'd wanted to forget all about Daniel Jackson. Banish him from her mind. Forget he now lived in the village, was now part of the community. Treat him like nothing but an old friend. An acquaintance. But all of that had flown out of the window the moment they'd found themselves locked in that bloody storeroom and she'd found herself holding his hand.

The memories had flooded back and she couldn't stop them. Not now. Over the years she'd painted a fanciful picture in her mind's eye of who he had become. No longer the sweet, caring and kind young man she'd known and loved, but a man who only cared about himself and what he could gain from others. This was what she'd told herself in the months and years that followed his absence from her life. He'd morphed into a different person. A person she would no longer recognise if she bumped into him on the street. But while sitting in the darkness of the stairwell, and then later at his kitchen table, that image had slowly crumbled. He'd written letters and he still had them. He'd kept them. That had to mean something.

She cycled past the Jackson veterinary clinic and there was the Land Rover. The lights were on inside the building. She slowed down, half wondering if she should call in and see Emily. She needed to tell her about the vacancy that had just become available at the agency. One of the long-time carers had decided to take early retirement. Hannah remembered a recent conversation she'd had with Emily, when she'd mentioned that her cousin, Lisa, was seeking part-time work in the care sector, so the job sounded perfect for her.

She could pop in and tell her now, but the thought of seeing Dan again made her carry on cycling home. She needed to sort out her head first before speaking to him. So many emotions swirled around and she needed to process them, figure out how she felt about him being back and being part of her life once more, whether she liked it or not.

How could she still have feelings for him? They say you never forget your first love, but surely that's all this was. Surely she couldn't be falling for him again? She didn't know him. Not really. It was all a trick of the mind. Falling for the boy he had once been.

She pulled up outside her flat and dismounted. She shrugged the bag from her shoulders and unzipped the front pocket to retrieve the lock key. As she chained the bike to the railings, the click of the lock sent a jolt through her body, the sound of the heavy door locking behind them, the flicker of fear on Dan's face before the lights went out.

His behaviour and the way he'd reacted to being trapped frightened her. At first she'd thought he'd attempted to spook her, his fear an act, but as the minutes ticked by, she knew it was no act. What she witnessed was a panic attack, triggered by the dark. Then she remembered he'd told her about being trapped, that he didn't like confined spaces. What the hell had happened to him in London? It must have been a terrifying experience. Maybe he'd become trapped in a lift?

She checked the lock and that the bike was secure and let herself into the flat. She dropped her rucksack onto the floor and stroked Daisy's head. The loud purr hummed through her body.

'Oh I'm so glad to see you.' Hannah knelt down on the cool hallway tiles and Daisy nudged her head against Hannah's leg. 'Come on then, I'll get you something nice to eat.' She pushed herself up off the floor. Guilt bubbled away inside her. Daisy had been home alone for hours at a time, and although cats differed in their behaviours to dogs, preferring their own company and doing things on their own terms, she still felt bad about leaving Daisy on her own for huge chunks of the day, and evening. It had been late when Dan dropped her back home last night.

She found a box of cat biscuits in the cupboard and poured a handful into the cat bowl. She checked the water bowl and topped that up. She switched on the kettle and dropped a peppermint teabag into her favourite yellow mug. She watched Daisy tucking into the biscuits. Another ripple of guilt washed over her. 'You deserve a treat. We both do,' she sighed.

Hannah opened the fridge and peered inside. There were a few chicken thighs waiting to be eaten. She'd cook them and give one to Daisy. She'd rustle up a quick salad to go with her chicken. She brewed her tea and switched on the oven. A quick glance at the clock on the kitchen wall told her that Emily would be home now. She'd give her a quick call, ask her if Lisa would be interested in working for the care agency.

Emily answered on the first ring. Hannah heard Josh in the background, chatting away to the twins. It sounded like he was telling them a story. Before Hannah could even tell Emily about the job vacancy, Emily told her she'd pop round as she wanted to know everything that had gone on during the storm. She said she hadn't had the time to text or call during her shift and Daniel wasn't giving anything away. On a sigh, Hannah told her she was fine and mentally prepared herself for the onslaught of questions Emily would hurl at her.

Less than ten minutes later Emily sat at the kitchen table with a cup of tea watching Hannah devour a chicken salad. Daisy happily munched her own chicken thigh with the occasional meow thrown in for good measure.

'Were you ever going to tell me?' Emily scowled before blowing on her tea.

'There's nothing to tell.'

'Hmm, I really don't think so,' she said. 'You two were locked in the storeroom for at least an hour and, let me tell you now, I'd have done anything to be a fly on the wall.'

Hannah stopped chewing. How did she know about that? She swallowed.

'Phyllis sees and knows everything.' Emily chuckled. 'More importantly, we have CCTV. It only covers the entrance, reception desk and the corridor. It doesn't cover the inside of the treatment rooms or storeroom. She saw you both go in there, then Sammy as she ran out and then the two of you emerging around an hour later.'

'That was still working? How?' Hannah asked.

'Don't ask me.' Emily shrugged. 'Phyllis told me when I got to work this morning, and then she gave Daniel the third degree when he came in.' She flashed a wicked grin. 'You should have seen his face. He didn't know where to look. Tried to brush it off, but Phyllis wanted to know what had happened and what they needed to do to avoid anything like that happening again. Said it could have been her trapped in there for hours by herself. I suppose she has a point.' She took a moment to slurp her tea. 'Me, on the other hand, well, I'm more interested in what the two of you did in that room.'

Hannah felt the colour rising to her cheeks. 'Nothing happened. What are you insinuating?'

Emily offered her a mock shocked expression before smiling. 'Oh, Hannah, relax. I'm not insinuating anything. I didn't mean to make fun of you.'

Hannah's shoulders sagged. 'I know that.' She speared another piece of chicken with her fork. 'We just sat and talked.' She didn't want to tell Emily about how he'd frozen as soon as the door locked behind them. What had happened was between them. It felt strangely personal and even though Emily was her closest friend, she didn't feel comfortable in exposing what had happened. Her biggest problem was that Emily could read her face like an open book and knew she was hiding something. She chose to state the obvious.

'He told me about his ex-wife.'

'He's mentioned an ex-wife to me, but he hasn't shared any details.' Emily looked at Hannah expectantly.

'Nor with me,' Hannah said, shaking her head. Emily raised a brow. 'All I know is that what happened between them was messy. It's what made him move here.'

Emily shook her head and clicked her tongue. 'I feel so sorry for him. I wonder what she did? Must have been bad to make him leave? Or was it him?'

'It wasn't him.' Hannah speared the rest of her chicken.

'And that's all that happened? You spent your time locked up together talking? Nothing more?' Emily cocked her head to the side, a glint in her eye. Hannah knew she wanted more juicy details, but sadly there were none to share. She wouldn't tell how he'd held her hand so tightly she thought her bones would crack, or about the panic attack she'd witnessed and how he'd be leaving once he'd sold the business and cottage. So she shook her head. 'No, nothing else.'

But it was then, as she picked up her empty plate, that it hit her. She'd assumed he was back in the village because of money. Gerald's money to be precise, gained from the sale of the cottage and business. That's why he'd come back after all these years. But he hadn't come home for the funeral. His mother had, but not him. Why was that? If money was the motive, then surely he would have come back then and sold the business. Learning about the break up of his marriage and the destruction of his friendship and business placed a brand new spin on things. Maybe his move back here wasn't about money after all. Maybe he had no choice but to move back here? But then why choose to sell up? Where would he go?

Something didn't add up; she was missing a piece of the puzzle. He'd never been materialistic. Look at the car he drove! Then she thought about those pale blue eyes, the way they crinkled at the corners when he smiled, and the surge of electricity that had shot up her arm when he grasped her fingers.

'You okay?'

'What?'

'You've been standing there with your hands in the sink, staring out the window for the past minute. You look as if you're in a world of your own.' Emily laughed, dropping her empty cup into the sink. 'You didn't hear a word I said then, did you?'

'No, sorry. What did you say?'

'I just wondered what type of day you had? Was it a good day?'

'It was a busy one.' Hannah paused. 'I'm a little worried about Mrs Barlow.'

'Oh. Why's that then?'

'She seems to be more forgetful, more distracted than usual and I think it's because of Ted.'

'We've done bloods, and I know Daniel called her to try and discuss them—'

'He called her? I thought he would talk to her in the surgery, with Phyllis for moral support.'

'He tried to coax her into the surgery, but she didn't want to leave the flat,' Emily explained. 'He had no choice but to talk to her over the phone. But I know she wouldn't let him tell her the results. Told him she couldn't talk at the moment. She was a bit busy. I'm really sorry but I can't tell you any more than that.'

'I understand that, patient confidentiality and all. I don't want to get you into trouble. It's just that I'm worried about her. I got the impression she was still waiting for results and I had the gut feeling she wasn't telling the truth. I think she's in denial or something. Ted is her world and I get how that feels.'

Emily pressed her lips together before blowing out a huff of breath. 'I'll chat to Daniel about it in the morning.'

'Thanks. I'd appreciate that. I'm just a worrier.'

'I know.' Emily grabbed the tea towel from the countertop and dried her cup.

Daisy sauntered over and pushed her head against Hannah's leg, purring loudly in response.

'You enjoy your chicken?' Emily asked, bending down to rub her head. 'You're a lucky girl.

No, Hannah thought. I'm the lucky one.

Chapter Eleven

Something wasn't right. Hannah sensed it as soon as she entered the kitchen the following morning. A feeling, right there, in the pit of her stomach. Maybe it was how a mother felt when their child was sick in the middle of the night. The flat was too quiet, eerily so. She swallowed her rising panic as she opened the kitchen door.

Daisy lay stretched out in her cat basket, her head lolling over its side, a pool of vomit on the floor. Hannah froze, her breath caught in her chest, before logic kicked in. She strode across the kitchen and knelt down beside Daisy. Her hands shook as she touched the cat's body, checking for warmth, for a heartbeat. She found both, and breathed a sigh of relief. Probably just a tummy upset. 'Oh poor Daisy,' she cooed, gently stroking the cat's head, 'I'll clean this up and get you some water.' She pulled off several sheets of kitchen roll and scooped up the mess. Next she added a liberal squirt of bleach to the floor and gave it a good wipe.

Daisy hadn't moved.

She checked the cat bowl – it still contained the cat biscuits she'd placed there last night, and usually Daisy licked the bowl clean.

Another trickle of fear pricked at her spine. She told herself to keep calm. Cats got sick, just like humans. It happened. Rest and fluids, that's what Daisy needed. She'd been fine last night.

She filled the cat bowl with water and placed it down near the basket. 'Here you go Daisy, have a drink of water for me.' She was concerned Daisy may be dehydrated. She remembered reading something about how easy it was for cats to become dehydrated and that this could then lead to problems with the kidneys, something that older cats suffered from. She crouched down on the floor, placed her hand on Daisy's head, and tried to listen to her breathing. Was she breathing more quickly than usual? She held her breath as she tried to listen. Yes, her breathing did seem a little quicker and perhaps more laboured than usual, but it was hard to tell over the thumping of her own heart and the roar of blood in her ears. She sat back up, wrapping her arms around her body and thought.

What should she do? Keep trying to get her to drink or take her to the vets, which meant taking her to Dan? She rocked backwards and forwards, comforting herself as she went through her options. She pushed the water bowl closer to Daisy, tried her best to coax her to drink, but she was having none of it. She placed her hand on Daisy's head, but there was no response. Her hand trembled. She needed to take her to the vets, right now, she just wasn't sure what time they opened. She didn't know the emergency number. Did this even class as an emergency? She thought it did. How was she going to get there? Obviously she couldn't use the bike. She couldn't phone Emily for a lift because she'd either be already at the surgery or having a rare lie-in. She couldn't phone them at such an early hour. She'd have to walk. It wasn't that far. She could do it.

She found Daisy's favourite blanket and wrapped it around her before placing her in the carrier. She knew then that something was seriously wrong because Daisy hated the cat carrier and normally wriggled out of her arms.

Instead of fighting, she went limp like a ragdoll. All she emitted was a short and pitiful meow that tore through Hannah's crumbling resolve. Biting her bottom lip, she closed the door to the carrier and then carried it into the hallway. She grabbed her rucksack. She didn't want to leave Daisy alone for a minute. She made sure there was a supply of wipes and gloves in the bag, just in case Daisy vomited on their walk.

'Time to go, Daisy,' she said. She picked up the cat carrier.

'Please be in, please be in,' she muttered as she sped down the road. She cursed every time she slowed her steps and stopped to put the cat carrier down and swap hands because the handle dug into her skin. Hopefully he'd be at the surgery, and if not, worst case scenario, he'd be at home. Maybe she should have phoned?

Please be in.

Her pace quickened as she turned the corner and the surgery came into view. She also breathed a sigh of relief when she saw all the lights were on. It was only the weight of the carrier and the fear of stumbling and hurting Daisy that stopped her from running.

She nearly fell through the door as she stumbled towards the reception area.

'What on earth!' Phyllis jumped up from her seat, nearly knocking her cup of coffee flying. She still wore her coat. She rushed over to her. 'Is it Daisy? Whatever's wrong, love?' She reached out and gently took the cat carrier from Hannah's grasp. 'Come with me,' she said, before yelling towards the back, 'Emily, we need you out here.'

‘Where’s Dan?’ Hannah asked, half choked. She needed him. She held on to Phyllis’s arm.

‘He’s out at the farm. Don’t you worry, I’ll give him a call in a minute, once Emily’s settled with Daisy.’

‘Oh my God, Hannah! What happened?’ Emily took the cat carrier and Hannah’s arm, ushering her down the corridor and into the nurse consulting room. Phyllis followed them.

‘I don’t know. She was like this when I woke up. I can’t get her to drink anything.’ Hannah clamped her lips together. She would not cry. Not now. ‘Why is she just lying there?’

‘We don’t know, honey.’ Phyllis shushed her and placed an arm around her shoulder. ‘Let Emily take a look. Come on now, come with me.’

Hannah felt Phyllis’s hand tighten on her shoulder. She didn’t want to leave Daisy. She looked so small and so ill. She watched Emily open the door to the carrier and then gently scoop her up, easing her out and onto the table. With gentle yet swift hands she felt Daisy’s tummy, and pinched her skin. ‘Has she vomited?’

Hannah nodded. ‘Yes, there was vomit on the floor, by the cat basket. I noticed it when I woke up and went into the kitchen.’ Her heart raced. Why weren’t they phoning Dan?

‘What about since you got up? Any more vomiting?’ Emily asked.

‘No.’

‘Okay.’ Emily continued her examination, placing a stethoscope on Daisy’s back. ‘I’m sorry girl,’ she said. ‘It’s a bit cold, I know.’

Hannah stood motionless. She couldn't do a thing and it killed her.

A small frown formed on Emily's face. 'What has she eaten today?'

Hannah's nose scrunched up as she thought. 'She hasn't eaten anything. I mean, her cat bowl looked as full as it did before I went to bed and usually she eats all her cat biscuits.'

'Has she been drinking?' Emily asked, placing the stethoscope around her neck.

Hannah shook her head. Emily looked really worried, even though she was doing her best to wear her professional mask.

'What did she eat last night? She ate chicken, didn't she, with us?'

Hannah nodded, swallowing. 'Yes.' Panic rose in her throat.

'Mm-hmm.'

'The chicken's made her ill? But then I'd be ill because I had the same chicken. And I cooked it properly. I know I did.'

'I don't know if it is the chicken, Han, but it could be.' She turned her attention to Phyllis. 'Phone Daniel now and tell him I'm setting up a saline drip.'

'Come on now, love,' Phyllis said, a little firmer this time.

'Emily,' Hannah croaked, 'is it really bad?'

Emily's eyes were round and full of pity. 'I'm not sure Han, we need Daniel.'

Hannah managed to tear her gaze away from Daisy with a whispered, 'Look after her for me,' before following Phyllis into the waiting area. 'He's at the farm, so he won't be long. I'll phone him now.'

Hannah couldn't speak. Fear ripped at her vocal chords. It was bad. Really bad. She'd seen it in Emily's eyes.

'Sit yourself down before you fall down,' Phyllis told her, picking up the phone.

She was far too restless to sit and do nothing. She paced up and down, in front of the reception desk.

'Becky will be here any minute. She'll sit with you, love. Try not to worry. I'll make you a cup of tea once I've spoken to Daniel.'

What good would tea do? She said thank you anyway. Fully aware that everyone was bending over backwards to help her and Daisy.

'Hello Daniel, are you still at the farm?'

Hannah heard the low murmur of his voice through the receiver.

She wanted to snatch the phone out of Phyllis's hand and tell him to hurry, that Daisy was very ill and that her world would fall apart without her.

'Hannah is here with Daisy … an emergency … Emily's already setting up a saline drip … five minutes … okay.'

'He'll be here in five minutes, love. Just try to relax. Your Daisy is in good hands.'

How on earth could she relax?

Hurry Dan, please hurry.

Daniel stifled a yawn and gratefully took the mug of coffee from Chris. 'Thanks,' he said. The smell alone helped to revive him. He hadn't slept well and had woken at four, unable to get back to sleep.

'No problem, thanks again for popping by so quickly.' He lifted his own mug of coffee, one emblazoned with *World's Best Farmer*. Daniel had no idea who'd bought it for him. He swallowed a large mouthful.

The coffee was black and bitter and just what Daniel needed. Chris had apologised profusely for any inconvenience when he'd phoned Daniel at home, asking if he could come and take a look at one of the cows. Daniel found him waiting for him outside the farmhouse as he pulled up in his Landy. He'd apologised once more when Daniel jumped out.

The cow in question clearly had trouble walking and on closer inspection, on one foot in particular. Daniel had quickly found the reason: a cracked hoof. He'd reassured Chris it wasn't too serious and could be dealt with fairly easily. It just needed to be bandaged. The hardest part had been applying the bandage.

Chris slurped his coffee, rubbing a hand over his face. 'Do you know much about Hannah?' he asked.

'Hannah?' The question appeared to come out of nowhere. Why was he asking about Hannah? 'I went to school with her.' He didn't want to tell him that they'd dated. He wouldn't share with him that at that time she'd been the most important person in his world, or that she was slowly creeping back into his life and heart.

'Right, I thought you had,' Chris said. He paused to have another slurp of coffee. 'Do you know if she's dating?'

Daniel did his best not to goggle at him. Was he hinting at what he thought he was hinting at? 'Not that I know of,' he said carefully, avoiding eye contact.

'Right, okay, that's what I thought.'

Daniel sipped his coffee. Was Chris thinking about asking her out? Why did that bother him so much? He'd enjoyed their evening together – if *enjoy* was the right word. He'd told her things he hadn't told anyone else. He'd never confided in Sally about what had happened to him as a child. He'd kept that part of his past hidden from her, not wanting it to sully her or their relationship. Now, with hindsight, he realised he should have told her. But sitting in that stairwell with Hannah had made him realise two things. Not only had the years ebbed away, making him feel like they were both fifteen again, but more importantly that he trusted her and that given time, she'd get to hear the whole sorry story about his childhood.

'You think it's a bad idea?' Chris asked.

'Sorry?'

Chris gave him a sideways look. 'Asking her out. You think she'll say yes?'

Daniel hadn't a clue what she'd say. It was none of his business. 'I have no idea.' He followed this with a slight chuckle, and handed the empty cup back to him. 'I best be off,' he said.

'Thanks again for helping me out.'

Daniel opened his mouth to reply when his phone vibrated in his pocket. He quickly said goodbye and pulled out his phone as he strode towards the Landy. Sammy's head poked out of the window in greeting.

'Hello, Daniel Jackson speaking.'

He pulled open the door, listening to Phyllis's quick words. Concise and professional, but he heard the worry in her voice.

'Ask Emily to set up a drip for me … ah okay, I'll be there in less than five minutes.' He ended the call. It looked like his day was about to get a hell of a lot busier and of course, it had to revolve around Hannah.

Phyllis had told her five minutes, but it felt more like an hour. Becky had arrived for work and been deployed to help Emily until Daniel arrived. The young woman had surprised Hannah by giving her a quick hug before disappearing down the corridor. She wanted to follow her, see what they were doing to Daisy. She wanted to cry but couldn't cry. If she started she wouldn't be able to stop. Everyone could be with Daisy, apart from her.

Daniel pushed through the main door exactly four minutes after the phone call. Hannah jumped to her feet and ran to him. He grabbed her shoulders. 'Come with me,' he said, ignoring the look of shock on Phyllis's face. He took her hand and it felt like the most natural act in the world.

'Let's go take a look at her,' he said.

Hannah's throat felt thick with tears, all she could do was nod.

'What have we got here then?' he asked. Emily moved aside to let him take a look. An intravenous infusion was all set up, ready and waiting. Hannah watched him palpate Daisy's stomach. 'Any more vomiting?' he asked Emily.

'No, nothing.'

He directed his attention to Hannah. 'What has she eaten today?'

'Her bowl was still full of biscuits when I got home,' she said, blinking to stop the tears.

'What did she eat last night?' he asked.

'Chicken,' she said, forcing the word out of her mouth.

'I think it's a bone.'

'A bone? There were no bones,' Hannah said, her face now ashen. She'd been so careful, had meticulously checked for any small bones. But perhaps she'd missed one? If so, this was all her fault.

'I think there may be a small one lodged in the bowel,' he said.

'Oh my God!' Hannah felt faint. She gripped the examination table with both hands.

'Emily, take Hannah outside, get her a drink and something to eat,' Daniel said.

'I'm fine, I don't need anything.' She desperately needed to stay. Daisy needed her more than ever.

'Listen,' Daniel said, touching her lightly on the arm, his eyes urging her to look at him. They were so full of warmth and empathy that she wanted to cry. 'I need to operate on her bowel. So you can't be here,' he said. 'Try not to worry,' he added quickly, in response to her panicked expression. 'Becky will sit with you, Emily will assist me.'

'I want to stay,' Hannah whispered, knowing full well she sounded like a sulky child, but she wanted to stay with her cat. Did that make her pathetic?

'You need to go, Han,' Emily told her gently. 'You can't be in the theatre with us. Please …' she added for emphasis when Hannah shook her head.

‘Hannah, look at me.’ Daniel crouched down to look directly into her eyes. He spoke slowly and calmly. ‘I will look after Daisy. I’ll do my best. But you need to leave.’

Tears trickled down her cheeks. She couldn’t stop them, nor the sob that erupted from her chest. ‘Promise me,’ she gulped out in a half prayer half demand.

‘I promise,’ he said, not allowing her to finish her thought out loud.

Becky placed an arm around her shoulder. ‘Come on, let’s go get you that cup of tea.’

Chapter Twelve

The surgery lasted an agonising two hours. During this time Becky made endless cups of tea which remained untouched. Hannah told herself she was being silly, Daisy was a cat and animals got sick and died, but sitting in the staffroom reminded her of the relatives room she had sat in for endless hours during her mother's last few months on earth. The sterility, the microwave, the shushed silence of the space. She knew it was silly to compare this staffroom with what had happened to her mother, she knew that, but she couldn't help her feelings.

Becky did her best to engage her in conversation, trying to take her mind off what was happening in the operating theatre, but all she could do was offer a tight smile. She wouldn't relax until Dan told her that Daisy was okay, that she had got through surgery and her bowel was undamaged.

It was all her fault.

If she hadn't felt guilty about leaving Daisy alone for most of the day, and the previous evening, then she wouldn't have given her the chicken thigh that had caused this problem.

Stupid, stupid, stupid.

'She'll be fine, you wait and see.' Becky's voice sounded calm and reassuring but it bounced off the armour that Hannah now wore. Those words, no matter how heartfelt, meant absolutely nothing to her. Platitudes meant nothing. She knew that much from bitter experience.

Becky sat by her patiently for a little while before telling her she needed to check in with Phyllis and then she'd be right back. The girl meant well, but honestly, Hannah would have preferred to sit by herself, alone with her thoughts. That way she'd only have her own feelings to consider.

She heard the click of the staffroom door and exhaled. She'd have a few precious moments to herself.

The door reopened and Hannah didn't bother looking up because she assumed it would be Becky.

'Hannah.' Daniel stood in the doorway, wearing scrubs. A sterile mask hung loosely from his neck. She jumped to her feet. 'How is she? Is she okay?'

Please let her be okay.

A smile broke out across his face which told her everything she needed to know. She ran to him, flung her arms around his neck, pressed her face into his chest. He felt solid and safe and warm. 'Thank you, thank you,' she muttered.

Slowly his arms gently held her, just as she'd wanted him to. He stroked her hair as he spoke. She felt his breath on her hair. He spoke so quietly, so gently, as if to add further reassurance that everything really would be okay. 'Surgery went well. I found the bone, a small one, but it had become lodged, which is what I feared. Anyway, she's still sedated and we have the drip up still, but she should be fine by tomorrow. You'll just have the stitches to worry about.'

'Thank you,' she said again.

He released her with a gentle pat on the back. She looked into his eyes and for a fleeting moment thought about reaching up and kissing him. The urge was so primal, so powerful, that she had to physically take a step back from stopping herself doing just that. Instead she reached up and touched his cheek with her fingertips. She felt his muscles tense under her skin. 'Can I go see her?'

Daniel swallowed. 'Sure you can.' He smiled. 'Come on, let's go see how she's doing.'

The sight that greeted Hannah was a most pitiful one. Daisy was attached to a drip, her left leg splinted and bandaged to secure the snake of plastic tubing. Her abdomen was also covered with a large surgical pad. Hannah watched Emily inject something into the port of the IV bag.

'It looks worse than it is,' Daniel said.

Hannah walked over to the table, reached out her hand to touch Daisy's head, but stopped, turning to Daniel for permission.

'You can touch her,' he said. 'She's a bit groggy still, just as we would be after an operation, but she's pain free. Emily has added antibiotics and pain relief to the drip, so she'll remain comfortable.'

Hannah touched Daisy's head with gentle fingers. She didn't want to wake her, or cause her any more pain. Her other hand flew to her mouth to stop herself from crying. Emily gave her a heart-warming look. 'She's fine. She'll sleep through the rest of the day, and night more than likely, and she'll be back to her usual self in no time.'

'How long?' Hannah sucked in her breath. 'How long will she need to be here? I'm off work today, so I can look after her, I can stay,' she said.

Emily looked at Daniel who answered the question. 'She'll need to stay here and be observed for the rest of the day and overnight and then hopefully you'll be able to take her home tomorrow, if she eats and passes a stool. But we'll see.'

Hannah removed her hand from Daisy's head. 'Can I stay with her?' She directed the question towards Daniel who scratched his chin. He cocked his head to one side.

'We'll move her to the hospital, and we only allow staff in there. But,' he sighed deeply, 'if you want to stay overnight, then you can.'

'Thank you,' she said.

'Strictly speaking it should be a no, but as I'm the boss and we have no other patients I'll say yes, just this once.'

Emily spun around to face him and Hannah was alarmed by the fire in her eyes. 'Daniel, I really don't think—'

'Go home, Hannah, get some rest and come back this evening, say around seven,' he said. He looked at Emily. 'I'll do the night shift,' he said.

'But it's my turn. I'm on the rota,' Emily protested.

'You're going to stay all night?' Hannah asked. The look of shock on her face mirrored Emily's expression.

He shrugged, heaving out another sigh. 'Why the hell not. I've not got anything better to do. Right I'll leave you in Emily's capable hands and I'll be back in a bit to help you move her to the hospital.'

Hannah was too stunned to say anything until he'd left the room. 'Is that usual? You know, for a vet to stay the night?'

Emily pursed her lips, her eyes wide and shining. She shook her head before breaking out into the broadest grin. 'No, it's not usual. It should be me staying the night.'

'Is that why you're smiling?' Hannah asked. 'Because you don't have to stay on a Saturday night?'

'Oh Hannah,' Emily said, programming the IV machine, 'you just don't get it, do you?'

'Get what?'

All she heard was a huff as Emily ignored her.

'Have I upset you?' Hannah asked.

Emily whirled on her. She couldn't quite read her friend's expression. 'Sometimes you are just too slow for your own damn good.'

'What do you mean by that?' Hannah asked, genuinely confused.

Emily placed both hands on her hips. 'I should be staying tonight. It is the nurse's role to monitor any animals post-operatively. *My role,* but Daniel has offered to stay and do my job.' She raised a hand to prevent Hannah from saying anything. 'He is also letting you stay overnight, which is never *ever* allowed.' So you tell me what that means.'

Emily stared her out, waiting for an answer.

Hannah knew only too well what it meant. Of course she did, but she couldn't voice those thoughts out loud.

Emily's face softened. She set the IV pump to run and then drew Hannah towards her for a hug. 'Daisy will be fine. Rest and fluids and she'll bounce back to her normal, happy self.' She stroked her hair. 'But promise me something.'

Hannah tried to swallow, but there was a lump in her throat.

'Have a good chat with him won't you, for me? Clear the air for good. He cares about you. You know that, right?'

Hannah offered a watery smile. It's all she could do.

Hannah returned to the surgery just before seven p.m. Daniel was waiting for her behind the reception desk. 'Hi,' he said, 'Daisy's fine. No change. Come on, let's go see her.'

She followed him down the corridor and into the hospital room.

Emily hugged Hannah tightly before letting go and telling her she'd see her in the morning. 'Get some sleep,' she mouthed before closing the door behind her.

'I'd tell you to go home and get some sleep after a busy day, but as I'm not a vet and can't operate that drip you'll have to stay,' Hannah said with a smile.

Daniel smiled back as he checked on Daisy's vitals and repositioned the catheter. 'I'm glad you're here though, as how would I have my endless cups of coffee.' His lips pressed together suppressing a smile, but Hannah caught the gleam in his eye. The small dimple that appeared in the hollow of his cheek.

She wanted to touch him. Her fingertips burned with the desire to feel his skin. What was happening to her? She was full of raging hormones when her cat had just had major surgery. She shuddered at the truth right in front of her. She couldn't hide from it any more. She was still in love with him. Had never really fallen out of love with him, and even if nothing happened between them, and nothing could happen, he would still break her heart all over again when he left her behind for the second time.

'You okay?' Daniel asked, now looking directly at her. 'Daisy's going to be absolutely fine, and I'm only joking about the coffee … well half joking.' He smiled.

'I'm fine. Just tired,' she said, glad he couldn't read her mind. She'd be in a whole heap of trouble if he could.

'She'll sleep for most of the night.'

'Okay, that's good,' she said.

'You should try and get some sleep too if you can,' he said.

'I won't be able to sleep, I might as well keep you company.'

Daniel gave her a long look before emitting a soft sigh. 'I'd like that.'

Before she could respond he cleared his throat. 'I brought us some supplies.' He picked up a bag from the corner of the room. She hadn't seen him bring it in. He started to empty the contents. There were bread rolls, slices of cheese, apples, tangerines, breadsticks, olives, chocolate bars and bottles of flavoured water. 'When did you go shopping?' she asked.

He scratched his neck. 'I just popped to the corner shop during lunch.'

'You didn't have to do that,' she said. He'd gone and bought her food.

'I need to eat as well, you know,' he said, followed by a chuckle. 'It's no big deal.'

But it was a big deal. They both knew it.

'Make yourself comfy, the sofa actually pulls out into a sofa bed and under the seat you'll find blankets. It can get a bit chilly in here during the night, even in the summer.'

'You need to sleep,' she said. 'You have work tomorrow.'

Daniel laughed. 'I need to stay awake, that's why I'm here. I'll have a nap in the morning. I'll be fine. We only see emergencies on a Sunday. Hopefully, it'll be quiet. Are you working tomorrow?'

She shook her head. 'No, day off tomorrow. Two days off in a row. It doesn't happen very often, especially not over a weekend. I'm just glad my rota's worked out that way this week.'

'I bet you are,' he said. 'Ah, well then, you can help to keep me awake.'

'By making coffee?' she asked with a small smile.

He mirrored her smile. 'Yes, with coffee.'

'Well then, I'll go make you one. Is it okay if I make myself a peppermint tea?'

'Of course it is, although I'm not sure we have any.'

'I have some in my bag.'

'Of course you do.' He laughed.

'Do you have sugar? Milk?'

'No, black's just fine,' he said.

Just how he used to drink it.

She made her way to the kitchen and quickly made the drinks, all the time thinking how strange it was that they were together, alone, yet again.

As the drinks brewed she quickly washed up the few cups and plates that had been left soaking in the sink. She picked up the mugs and made her way back to the hospital room, making a list of topics that they could talk about with every step. She'd ask how to care for Daisy's stitches and what she should eat. She'd ask him if he'd settled back into village life. The question she really wanted to ask was why he never made contact with her once he'd left for London? Why write letters and not send them? If an opportunity arose then she would be brave, seize the moment, bite down any embarrassment she might be feeling and just ask him.

Daniel leant over Daisy, a stethoscope pressed to her back when she pushed open the door with her elbow.

Daniel looked up, removed the stethoscope from his ears, placed it around his neck, and took the cup. 'Thanks,' he said.

'How is she doing?'

'Good, all good. She'll be fine.' His eyes softened as he said this. 'You really should try and get some sleep, or, even better, go home. You'll sleep much better there.'

'No, I'd be too restless. Wondering how she was. At least here, I know …'

'I get it. It'd be hard to switch off. People don't understand sometimes, how it is when you have a pet, but they become part of the family, don't they.'

'Yes, exactly that. Daisy – she's important to me. After Mum passed away, she's the closest thing …' Her words trailed away, uncertainty gripping her throat. She didn't know quite how to finish that sentence.

Daniel surprised her by slowly sitting down next to her. 'I understand what you're saying. I think for those who haven't undergone trauma or great change in their life, then it's difficult to understand the importance of a pet. How they can completely change your life.'

She stared at him, the hot cup beginning to burn her hand as she'd forgotten she was gripping it so tightly. She placed it down on the table. What the hell had happened to him? She saw a flicker of something in his eyes, something she couldn't quite reach. Something had happened to him and she had a feeling that Sammy was not a replacement for his ex-wife.

'And before you say anything, Sammy is not a substitute for a wife.'

She burst out laughing, glad she hadn't touched her tea, as she would have spat a mouthful all over him. 'Who is Sammy a replacement for then?' The words were out of her mouth before she had time to fully process them. Heat flooded her face. 'I'm sorry, I shouldn't have blurted that out.' She picked up her tea and slurped it, so he wouldn't see her face. It scalded her mouth. Served her right.

He gripped his coffee cup as he spoke. He gave her a half smile, that dimple trying to make an appearance. 'Sammy isn't a replacement for anyone or anything. Not really. I just went from living with someone and working full-time surrounded by people, to living alone in a one bed ground-floor flat and not seeing a soul for days. She needed a home and so I gave her one. Truth be told, she saved me.' He laughed, an attempt to lighten the mood.

'I feel exactly the same way about Daisy,' she said, wanting to make him feel he wasn't being stupid. She understood completely. 'Speaking of Sammy, where is she?' She hadn't seen her in reception.

'She's back at the cottage. She'll be fine,' he added, when he saw Hannah's look of scepticism. 'I'll pop my head in later on.'

They sipped their drinks. The only sound to be heard was the ticking of the clock and the hum of the IV pump.

There it was again. The elephant in the room.

She couldn't ignore the nagging heaviness of it any more. It was cloying. 'Why didn't you come back?' she asked, trying her best to keep the tone light. 'Why didn't you post your letters?'

Why did you abandon me?

Daniel plonked his cup on the coffee table. His hand rested for a moment on its handle before placing his hands in his lap. He looked directly at her as he spoke.

'I wanted to come back.' He shook his head as if shaking his thoughts to the surface, rearranging what he had to say. 'I wanted so badly to post those letters.'

'But not to visit?' Hannah asked.

Daniel's jaw tensed and he swept a hand through his hair. 'Things were difficult back then. It's difficult to explain to you now what life was like in *that* house, but I had to get away.'

That house? Not his mother, Hannah thought. He left with her. He was talking about Gerald. What had Gerald done?

'Gerald, and me, we just didn't get along. Things would have gotten worse, much worse, without Mum there.'

Hannah chose her words carefully. 'Things were that bad between you?'

'As I said, it was complicated.'

Hannah racked her brain trying to think back to how things had been. Had things really been that bad between them? She hadn't noticed, but then how would she? She'd been so young.

'So you left to get away from Gerald …' It wasn't really a question. She wanted to see his reaction.

He looked down at his lap.

This at least made sense. It was why he hadn't made it back to the funeral, why he never came back to the village. But then for him to react in that way it must have been something pretty awful. So why hadn't he told her? Why hadn't he confided in her? They'd been friends.

Her heart beat faster as a range of scenarios entered her head. Please God no. She couldn't ask him. He would have to tell her. She searched his face for the answers, but he gave nothing away. This time she gave way to the urge to touch him. What had Gerald done to the boy she'd loved? She rested her hand on his face and felt his jaw clench.

'I still care about you,' he said, his voice gruff.

She stroked his cheek, ran her hand up towards his brow. He lowered his head and as if it was the most natural thing in the world, as if the past fifteen years had never existed, he kissed her.

Her hands fisted in his hair as his tongue parted her lips. She found herself lost in the sensations, the taste, there was only him. How could she have forgotten this? How they had been together? How they were two halves of the same puzzle piece. His hands trailed downwards, along her spine, before moving up her body and resting on her shoulder, before stroking her hair.

The loud beep of the IV pump made them jump apart. Her heart thumped wildly in her chest as she gasped for breath. Daniel half walked half stumbled over to silence it. He pressed buttons and adjusted the plastic tubing. 'Just a kink, nothing to worry about.' His voice was now clipped and professional. Hannah wondered if his heart was beating as fast as hers.

She ran a hand through her hair and laughed to cover her embarrassment. What was she thinking? Why had she kissed him? Or had he kissed her? She was the one who touched him. She'd instigated it.

Daniel fiddled with the machine for another minute before speaking. 'I'm sorry, I didn't mean to …'

Hannah's cheeks burned. She couldn't look at him.

'I'm sorry, I shouldn't have … We're both tired and you've had a terrible shock,' he said.

She tried to smile, to show him it was no big deal, but her throat stung and the smile faded.

Daniel rubbed the back of his neck. 'She'll be fine for a few minutes, while I make us a fresh brew.'

Hannah began to tell him that she'd make the drinks, but he silenced her by saying he needed to stretch his legs.

More likely he needed to get away from her for a few minutes, Hannah mused.

As soon as the door closed she pulled out the sofa bed and found the spare blankets. She did feel dog-tired. She'd rest her eyes for a few minutes until he got back. Best not think about the kiss.

Daniel cursed under his breath as he waited for the tea to steep. He'd acted unprofessionally. He could get in real trouble for that.

How she could drink mint flavoured hot water was beyond him. He rubbed a hand over his face. He needed to take a step back, rewind. Best to not talk about the kiss. Best to forget it had ever happened. No good would come of it. He couldn't grow close to her again, not when he'd be leaving again. But by God, his feelings towards her hadn't changed one bit. He pinched the bridge of his nose, while he collected his thoughts and then exhaled.

He needed to get back to check on Daisy. He should have allowed Emily to stay after all, that way he could have kept his distance, kept it professional. The old version of him could have stayed locked away, but now the shadow of who he had once been had slowly emerged.

It had been on the cards ever since he'd set foot back in the village.

Fishing the teabag out of the cup, he dropped it into the small bowl on the draining board, and picked up the cups and strode back to the hospital room, an excuse playing in his mind, about how it was best that she go home. He'd book her a taxi. But when he pushed the door open the excuse died on his lips.

He quietly placed the cups down on the table and crouched over her for a moment, checking she really was asleep. He turned his attention to Daisy; all was well there too.

He pulled the blanket up over her shoulders and settled himself into the armchair, placing his feet up on the stool. His eyes lingered on her sleeping body. Would it be so bad after all? To make a go of things, here in the village? He wasn't so sure. He'd been so adamant when he'd left London and Sally and his cheating ex-best friend.

Move to Middlefern, do up the cottage, work at the surgery while doing so, then sell up and move on when he'd managed to find a permanent vet. That was the plan. But the village was slowly sinking its claws into him, making him plant tiny roots that would mature over time, making it more difficult for him to leave his childhood home. And one of those complications lay fast asleep.

He'd very nearly told her what had happened, but he couldn't find the right words. He still felt too ashamed. And it was in the past. What did it matter now? He didn't want her to know because she would go back in time and blame herself for not knowing, for not helping him, when the blame was Gerald's, no one else's. God damn it, he should have stood up to the man, but he never did.

With sudden clarity, he knew why he had kissed her. He could tell himself that he'd kissed her to stop her from talking about Gerald, about the past, but who the hell was he kidding? He'd wanted to kiss her from the moment he'd rescued her from the side of the road. He couldn't resist the pull of her and the kiss had been – amazing, better than amazing, it had rocked his core completely, taking him back to the time when he'd first kissed her. He'd been nervous then, not entirely sure of what to do and they'd both fumbled, laughing about it afterwards. But this kiss, it had been from his heart and soul. Hell, he wanted to kiss her again and that put a huge dent in his carefully thought out plan to leave the village for good.

Chapter Thirteen

Hannah's eyes snapped open. The light was too bright. Had she forgotten to close the blinds? And what was that noise? She moved her arm to find her phone on the bedside table, but all she was met with was air. She eased herself up onto her elbows and took in the space around her. Of course, she wasn't at home, she was in the surgery.

Daisy, where was Daisy?

'I wondered when you'd wake up. I'm amazed you could fall asleep here. Daniel told me you slept all night.' Emily said all this while wiping down the examination table with a yellow cloth.

'What are you doing here and where's Daisy?' Hannah's heart was now in her mouth. Had something happened to her?

'I know it's Sunday but I offered to come in and work for a few hours and Daisy's fine. Daniel moved her to one of the clinic rooms so you could get some sleep. She's had some water and we'll try her with some food in a bit.'

Dan moved her so she could get some sleep? Where was he?

'There's a cup of tea there for you and some toast.'

Hannah glanced down at the coffee table. 'Thank you, but you've enough to do,' she said, lifting the cup and sniffing the mint. Emily must have found the teabags in the kitchen. Suddenly conscious that she wasn't at home, but in a place of work, she placed the cup down and swung her legs down onto the floor. She needed to see Daisy. She couldn't believe she'd slept all night.

'Oh don't thank me,' Emily said with a wry smile.

Hannah stopped folding the blanket, her head still a little fuzzy. 'Well it was still kind of you when I'm not even supposed to be here,' she said.

'No, what I meant is that you shouldn't thank me. Daniel made the tea.'

'Daniel?'

Emily tutted and placed a hand on her hip. 'He made you the tea and toast before he left for the farm.'

'The farm? Oh.'

'Oh, exactly.' She smiled and it lit up her whole face. 'Did you have a nice evening?'

'He was working.' Hannah rolled her eyes.

'I know that! But you had a nice evening anyway. The two of you?'

The memory of the kiss bubbled up to the surface, along with a rather erotic dream she'd had. 'Yes,' was all she could trust herself to say.

Emily eyed her silently, as if wondering whether to say what was on her mind. She picked up the blanket and hugged it to her chest. 'Drink your tea and then come out to reception and I'll take you to see Daisy.'

Hannah smiled. 'Thanks.'

'No problem.' Emily reached the door when she turned around. 'And just so you know, I think you and Daniel – whatever's going on between you – it's a good thing.'

Emily closed the door behind her before Hannah could think of a suitable response.

She rubbed the sleep from her eyes, thankful she had another day off. She bit into the now cold toast, but was thankful to have something to eat. She washed it down with the warm mint tea. Time to find Emily and check in on Daisy. She ran her fingers through the matted blonde curls. She'd need a shower and a change of clothes. Thank goodness Dan couldn't see her now. She cupped a hand to her mouth and blew out a breath. Yep, morning breath despite the mint tea.

She placed a finger to her lips and briefly closed her eyes, savouring the memory of his lips. Could they try again? She wasn't sure if it was possible to go back in time and rebuild on what they had been, what they had shared. The kiss meant something to her. Did it mean something to him, even though he'd tried to shrug it off? She was falling for him, how could she not? She now knew monetary greed was no longer the motive for his return. He'd returned to Middlefern because he had nowhere else to go and the surgery needed a vet. It all made perfect sense. But that kiss. It had meant something to him, she had sensed it the moment his lips touched hers. But she couldn't allow herself to be weak with him again. The man was unreliable – she still didn't know why he had stayed away from the village all these years, why he hadn't phoned. But damn him, he'd kept her letters. Her and Daniel again? Nothing but pure fantasy. She couldn't trust him. Time to go and check on Daisy.

'How are you, love?' Phyllis leaned over the reception desk, her eyes wide and enquiring.

'I'm fine,' Hannah said, aware of how dishevelled she must look.

'What are you doing here?' It was Sunday, wasn't it? Surely Phyllis didn't work on a Sunday?

I thought I'd call in and see how you and Daisy were doing before church. I'm not working today, if that's what you think.'

Hannah blew out a relieved breath. She was already the reason why Emily was working on a Sunday. She didn't want to be a nuisance.

'Daniel told me to leave you sleeping. Said you didn't have work today and anyway, we don't need the room.'

'I feel terrible about falling asleep,' Hannah said. 'I only meant to close my eyes for a few minutes.'

Phyllis laughed and walked around the desk. 'Well, I wouldn't worry too much about that, you obviously needed it. You'd had a terrible shock after all, and by the looks of things it's done you good.'

Hannah uttered a small sigh of relief. Maybe she didn't look so dishevelled after all, or Phyllis was being kind.

'She's doing well, is your little Daisy,' Phyllis said with a warm smile.

'Could I see her?' Hannah asked. 'Emily said to tell you and she'd come get me.'

'Yes, of course. I'll go and find her for you. See if you can go and see her now.'

'Thank you.'

Hannah leant against the reception desk while Phyllis went to find Emily. She glanced at the walls, at the photographs of animals that had been recent patients. She'd never looked at them properly before. One photograph in particular caught her eye. It was the only print in sepia. Hannah moved closer to the wall to get a better look. In the centre of the image stood Gerald as a younger man. His shirt sleeves rolled up and a smile on his face. Next to him was a younger woman, who Hannah recognised as Daniel's mother, and there kneeling down on the ground next to a large dog was Daniel. Hannah thought he looked around three or four years old. His brown hair was much lighter and had been combed back from his face and his knees were scuffed, a scab visible on the left knee. He looked directly at the camera, a broad smile on his face. Why hadn't she noticed this photograph before? She focussed on Daniel's face. Something didn't sit right. She looked closer, and then it came to her. The eyes. The smile didn't reach the eyes.

'You can come and see Daisy now if you like. She's in the consulting room,' Phyllis said as she eased herself back behind the reception desk. She followed Hannah's gaze. 'Ah, that's such a lovely photograph. I found it in a box of old pictures in the back and thought it would be nice to hang it up here. You know, a photograph of Gerald and Daniel together.'

That explained why Hannah hadn't noticed it before. She wondered if Daniel knew about it? Surely he must have given permission.

'You know the way don't you, love?' Phyllis asked.

'Yeah, thanks,' she said.

'Well, I'll be off then. I'll catch up with you later. I'm so glad all's gone well.'

Daisy meowed the moment Hannah stepped into the room.

'Someone's happy to see you,' Emily said. She applied some tape to the bandage on Daisy's stomach. It looked new.

Hannah nuzzled her head into the soft fur and Daisy rewarded her with a loud purr.

'She's had something to drink and a few biscuits. We'll need to wait for her to have a bowel motion, and Daniel will need to give the all-clear, but I think you'll be able to take her home later on today.'

Relief flooded Hannah's bones. 'Thank you so much.'

'No problem.'

Hannah knew Emily hated praise of any kind.

'It's Daniel you need to thank, not me,' Emily said.

'Do you know when he'll be back?'

'No, he may be a few more hours as he's up at the farm, but he shouldn't be too long.'

'I'll pop home for a shower and something to eat, but I'll be back at lunch to see him. Are you staying?'

'Yep. I'm here until he gets back.'

'Thank you. It's your Sunday off and oh—' Hannah gasped. 'It's your wedding anniversary. You shouldn't be here!'

'We celebrated last night,' Emily said with a wink, followed by a laugh. 'Don't worry. Josh is enjoying some quality time with the boys.'

'Thank you. You'll tell Dan I'll be back soon?' Hannah asked.

'I'll let him know,' Emily said. She opened her mouth as if to say more but she pressed her lips together.

'What is it?' Hannah asked.

'Oh, it's nothing.' She removed the IV tube from Daisy's leg and wound it around and around into a tight ball.

Hannah placed a hand on Emily's shoulder. 'Tell me.'

'Well, it's just – you probably don't remember – but Josh booked a table at that new restaurant in town and …'

'Oh my God.' Hannah's hand flew to her open mouth. 'I promised to babysit,' she stammered. 'I mean, I will babysit the boys. What time is the table booked for?'

Emily shook her head. 'No, it's okay, I only mentioned it because I know you won't be able to watch the boys now because of Daisy, and not to worry—'

'No, no, no,' Hannah uttered. If she didn't babysit then there was no one else who could and that meant Emily and Josh couldn't have their date. Emily's mother was unavailable this week, which was why Emily had asked in the first place. 'I can babysit the boys. I'll just bring Daisy round in the carrier. That'll be okay won't it?'

'You probably want to be at home tonight,' Emily said.

'I'll sit and watch a film at your house, no different to being at mine, so it's no bother. What time do you need me?'

'Would seven be okay? The table's booked for seven-thirty, so ...'

'Course it is. You two need to go out and have some time together, just the two of you. I'll always babysit for you, you know that. All you need to do is ask.'

'I know,' Emily said. 'Hopefully I can do the same for you one day.' Emily wiggled her eyebrow.

Hannah very much doubted that.

'I wasn't going to say anything, but you look rough, mate,' Chris said, in his no-nonsense way.

Daniel rubbed at his eyes and yawned. It had been a long night. 'Had an emergency patient overnight. A cat needed monitoring after bowel surgery, so I didn't get much sleep.'

'Sorry to hear that. Was it a chicken bone? It's always a chicken bone,' he muttered.

'Yep,' Daniel said. 'Anyway, the bandage seems to have done the job. He looked at the cow whose foot he'd bandaged only yesterday. 'I'd give it another couple of days and then I can remove it.'

'That's good news,' Chris said. 'You sure you don't want that coffee?'

'I'm fine thanks, I need to be making tracks.'

'Ah, okay, well, thanks again for popping by, especially when you've had a rough night.'

'It wasn't so bad. I just needed to monitor Daisy.'

'Daisy? Who's Daisy?'

'A cat, Hannah's cat.'

'Hannah's cat?' Chris's expression changed quick as a flash. 'How is Hannah? Is she okay? Does she need anything?'

'What? No, no she's fine.' Daniel bit back his frustration, wondering why he felt jealous all of a sudden. 'Hannah wasn't the patient you know, Daisy was.' His laugh was short and flat.

'I know that, mate,' Chris said, wearing a puzzled expression. 'I just know how much she loves that cat and if anything happened to Daisy …'

'Daisy is fine, so is Hannah,' Daniel snapped. He raked a hand through his hair. He felt cranky because he hadn't slept. He took a breath. 'Hannah and Daisy are both fine. Hannah at least got some sleep.' He chuckled. The memory of her curled up on the sofa with her blonde hair tumbling over the pillow quickened his pulse. She'd mumbled in her sleep, the odd incoherent word here and there. It hadn't escaped his attention she'd said his name several times and he liked how it sounded on her lips.

'So, what do you think then?'

'Sorry?' Daniel asked. He hadn't heard a word Chris just said.

'I was saying that I'm going to ask Hannah out for a drink.'

'Oh right, well, that's good.' He didn't think it was good at all.

'And you think she'll say yes?' Chris asked, waiting for an answer.

Hadn't they already had this conversation? Daniel felt a wave of déjà vu. A bitter taste formed in his mouth. He hoped she would say no. 'No idea mate, you should just ask her.' He forced a smile.

Chris flashed a quick grin, all teeth. 'Thanks mate. Thanks for the advice.'

Chapter Fourteen

Hannah breathed a welcome sigh of relief as she flopped down onto the sofa. Emily had been fretting, as usual. A bemused looking Josh had finally persuaded her to leave the house, telling her that nothing bad would happen while they were out for a few hours. Hannah couldn't quite fathom how he kept so calm, but then, she supposed working full-time and having twins under the age of five probably helped you keep a calm head. Hannah had also reassured her, telling her she'd babysat many times and that the boys would soon be asleep. She'd sit with Daisy and watch a box set.

All was good in the world.

Eventually they had left the house with promises they wouldn't be back too late as it was school tomorrow.

Hannah knelt down on the thick carpet next to the cat carrier to check on Daisy, who lay curled up inside on a cushion. Hannah felt mean leaving her in the cat carrier.

Hannah popped a Malteser into her mouth, savouring the crunch of honeycomb. Emily behaved exactly the same, every time Hannah babysat. She always triple-checked that Hannah had the phone number of the restaurant. Then she had to check the back door was locked. Tonight Emily asked, just as Josh grabbed the car keys, if she was overdressed? Hannah watched in silence as Josh took her hand, kissed her on the cheek and led her slowly to the car.

Oh what it must feel like to be loved like that?

Hannah rested her hand on Daisy's head and was rewarded with the gentle rumble of a purr. Oh how the boys had fussed over her when she carried her in, throwing questions at her, worried with concern. Hannah had reassured them, telling them she'd be back to her usual playful self soon. They'd forgotten their worries when she handed them a huge bag of chocolate buttons each. Now, all was quiet and she could relax into her evening.

An evening spent like every other.

Her mind drifted back to the previous evening, to thoughts of Dan. How he had been so kind to her, how he had treated Daisy and how he had pulled up the blanket to cover her shoulders, thinking she was asleep. She'd felt his hands, gentle yet strong as they touched her shoulders, as he'd whispered, "sleep tight", not knowing she would hear his words. It had felt so strange, to be sharing the same room, the same space, the same air as him. When she'd finally drifted off to sleep, the rhythmic beeping of the IV machine and Dan's breathing lulled her to sleep. She'd slept well, and slept deeply. She hadn't meant to sleep for so long. Only an hour or two, she'd told herself. She wondered what plans Dan had tonight? She imagined he'd be in the cottage, resting, eating a ready meal for one. Was he as lonely as her?

When she heard the knock on the door she flinched and looked at her watch. Emily and Josh had only been gone half an hour. Surely they couldn't be back so soon, and anyway, why would they knock? She ignored it, thinking it would be a cold caller. She lowered the volume on the television and listened, hoping whoever it was would go away.

Knock knock knock.

She heard the letterbox flap lifting. She held her breath while pulling her mobile from her pocket.

'Emily, let me in.'

Hannah jumped to her feet. Why was Dan here?

She ran quickly to answer the door, not wanting him to wake the children. She flung open the door. Daniel looked up at her from his crouching position.

'Why are you shouting through the letterbox and what are you doing here?' she hissed through clenched teeth. If the boys woke up he'd get an earbashing.

He straightened up, but rather than looking sheepish, he appeared somewhat annoyed. He peered over her shoulder, down the long hallway, before eyeballing her. 'What do you mean? What am I doing here? I'm here to babysit – Emily asked me this afternoon.'

Hannah couldn't hide her surprise. She stared at him. Emily asked him to babysit the boys, knowing full well he wasn't needed. This was no misunderstanding or case of crossed wires. Emily had been busy playing matchmaker. Emily would get a tongue-lashing when she got back home, wedding anniversary or no wedding anniversary.

One look at Daniel, and Hannah's words stuck in her throat.

He shoved his hands in his pockets, offering a nervous laugh. 'Ah, I'm clearly not needed …' His shoulders sagged as he turned to go.

'No, don't go,' Hannah cried, making him stop in his tracks and turn back around. 'You're here now, so you might as well come in and have a cup of coffee.' She stepped back, pulling the door wider.

Daniel hesitated for a beat before slowly stepping into the hallway.

Hannah ushered him through to the kitchen where she quickly filled the kettle. She raided the cupboards, emptying packets of crisps into bowls, along with cubes of cheese and crackers. Emily owed her big time. Daniel looked on bemused from the kitchen table. She had to keep busy while thinking of what to say to him. She tried to push their kiss out of her mind. She felt his eyes on her, watching her every move. She very nearly splashed boiling water on her hand as she made his coffee. 'I think Emily has a bottle of wine in the fridge,' she'd told him earlier, but he'd shook his head. 'I'm too tired for wine, and anyway, I need to keep a clear head in case I'm needed.'

'I can't believe she asked you to babysit,' Hannah said. Anger forced the words out of her mouth. Emily knew full well he'd been at the surgery all night and day. How could she do this to him? To her. What the hell had she been thinking?

He shot her a look. 'I don't mind that she asked me.' He rubbed a hand over his face, which told her an entirely different story, 'but I'm a little confused as to why you're here.'

Hannah sank down onto the chair opposite him. Surely he wasn't that dim. She tilted her head to the side. 'Really?'

'Really,' he said, mimicking her tone.

Heat flushed her cheeks making her look away from him.

The silence hung between them, loaded and heavy.

She heard him sigh. 'I guess she wanted us to spend some time together. You know, asking you to babysit and then asking me.' He shrugged off his explanation. 'It can't mean anything else, can it?'

'No.' Hannah's mouth formed a straight, hard line, unsure why she felt mad at him all of a sudden and not Emily. To her surprise his face broke out into a heart-stopping smile.

'It's not funny,' she said through gritted teeth, but there was no bite to it. She couldn't help it; she smiled back at him. 'Let's go sit in the living room,' she said. 'Grab the bowls and I'll take the drinks.'

'How's Daisy doing?' he asked. He set the bowls down on the coffee table. 'You want me to take a look at her stitches?' He crouched down in front of where Daisy lay, curled up and asleep on the cushion.

Hannah shook her head. 'No, you're off duty, remember, and she's fine. I'll bring her in as promised for her scheduled appointment in two days' time.'

'Twelve-thirty.'

'Yes,' Hannah said, surprised that he knew her appointment time.

He eased himself back up off the floor and sat down next to her on the couch. His thigh brushed hers as the seat sagged beneath his weight. He reached forward for his coffee. 'Well, this is nice,' he said.

Her eyes flickered over his face. There was no trace, no hint of sarcasm. She smiled. 'Yes, it is,' and she meant every word. As she leaned forwards to pluck a cracker out of the bowl, she changed her mind and her hand rested on his. She did it quickly, before she could change her mind. It was a light stroke at first, almost implying it was an accident, fully alert to how Daniel would react, but she felt no flinch from him. Instead he lifted his thumb and their fingers entwined.

Yes this is nice, she thought.

'I have someone from the estate agents calling round tomorrow evening,' he said.

'What?' Had she heard him correctly?

'Someone from the estate agents is calling round to value the cottage.'

'You're serious then? About selling up and moving away?' The words came out of her mouth, but they didn't sound like her own. She'd naively thought he'd want to stay longer than his planned six months. She snatched her hand away. He told her he would be staying for a while. The odds were always there, that he would move on, that he might not stay, but it had only been a week and he was already getting the cottage valued.

She should have seen it coming.

Daniel shifted his weight so he could turn and look at her. His brow furrowed. She wanted to touch the dimple in his cheek.

'I need to get it valued for when I sell up,' he said.

Her heart plummeted. So he would be leaving. The slim thread of hope had been cut. 'I thought you were going to see how things went?' she said because she couldn't help it. She wanted him to stay in this village, to never leave again but she had no right to ask him to stay.

'I'm not going anywhere soon, not for at least six months or so. I told you that,' he said. 'But the long-term plan is to move on.'

He studied her for a beat. His eyes soft and warm. She wasn't sure if she wanted to kiss him or punch him.

So, there it was in black and white. He couldn't be any clearer. He wasn't going to hang around here. Not for her, not for anyone. Being here was a matter of convenience, a stopgap while he had no home. A reaction to his broken marriage. She should have seen this coming. The wanderer returns.

'This is about your wife. Isn't it?' she said. 'Moving back here but not wanting to stay, to lay down roots. Sort of like a midlife crisis.'

'I'm thirty,' Daniel spluttered. 'And no, it's not because of what happened with Sally, well, not the whole reason anyway.'

So nothing to do with his ex-wife then?

'What happened between you and Gerald then?' She couldn't help it. If it wasn't the ex-wife then it had to be something that happened with Gerald. He'd already hinted that something had happened between them.

At first she thought he wouldn't answer her, as his lips were pressed together in a thin line. But then they relaxed as he let out a long sigh. 'It's not easy to explain,' he said.

'You've already told me that,' she said, remembering their conversation in the dark storeroom.

'I did?' He raised an eyebrow.

'Mm-hmm.'

'Well, it's the truth and a very long story,' he said with a shrug.

'I'm a good listener.'

His eyes locked on hers, as if searching for acceptance. He opened his mouth to speak.

The loud thumping on the door made them jump apart.

'Shit,' Daniel shouted, as he spilled coffee into his lap. He jumped up, knocking over the coffee table.

Hannah shoved past him to get to the front door. 'Probably Emily and Josh. I bet she forgot her key.'

But when she opened the door it wasn't Emily or Josh. Another reminder that she really needed to check who was on the other side before opening the door.

'Really sorry to bother you love, but I need to get a hold of Daniel and I knew he'd be here.'

Hannah ushered Phyllis into the hallway.

Daniel was busy wiping a damp tea towel over his coffee-stained trouser legs.

'There you are,' Phyllis exclaimed. 'There's a problem up at the farm. Chris told me to tell you it's not the cow you tended to the other day, but one who's just given birth.'

'Oh, okay.' Daniel scratched his head. 'Why didn't he just call me?' he asked, fishing his phone out of his pocket.

'It'd help if it was switched on, love,' Phyllis scolded.

'Shi—' He cleared his throat. 'I am so sorry,' he said, 'making you come out to tell me.'

'Oh, it was no bother, I was out having a drink in the pub and was on my way home anyway.'

'Chris was in the pub?' Hannah and Daniel asked in unison.

Phyllis shook her head and looked at them as if they were both idiots. 'He phoned me, once he couldn't get through to you,' she said, her gaze aimed at Daniel.

'Right, well, I'd best be off.' He pulled his Landy's keys from his back pocket. 'You need a lift?' he asked Phyllis.

'No, love. I'm fine. See you tomorrow, and I hope Daisy is doing well?'

'She is,' Hannah said as Phyllis smiled and made her way back through the open door.

'I can't believe my phone was off,' he muttered.

'It happens to the best of us.'

'Not when I'm meant to be on call.' He winced. 'So, I'll be off to Chris's then,' he said from the doorway.

'Okay.' Hannah wondered why he wasn't moving. Was he about to kiss her again? 'Okay then, see you soon,' she added when the silence had dragged out far too long.

'Yeah,' he said, the word sounding like a breath. 'See you soon.' He moved towards her, stopped and then rocked backwards on his heels. 'Bye,' he called out over his shoulder as he lunged down the path.

Hannah closed the door and rested her head against the cold panel of frosted glass. Once again she felt as if she were losing him, but he had never been hers to begin with.

Chapter Fifteen

Daniel pulled up outside Mrs Barlow's house and cut the engine. He wasn't sure if this was such a good idea or not, but he didn't know what else to do. He'd tried calling her several times, but she hadn't answered the phone after their last and very brief call. It was also the type of conversation he really didn't want to have over the phone. It was the kind of conversation he needed to have face to face, so he could read her expression, offer some kind of comfort, a caring touch. You couldn't do that over the phone. She was also an elderly lady who lived alone. He really didn't want to deliver bad news over the telephone.

His eyes swept the narrow street, as he observed the local residents going about their everyday lives. Elderly people carried bulging shopping bags, heads bowed and shoulders slumped with the weight under the summer heat. Young people's feet pounded on the pavement as they ran to the beat that thumped through their headphones, clamped to their ears. Older men walked their dogs, flat caps pulled down low over their foreheads, even in the heat.

Daniel thought he recognised the old man who walked the golden Labrador, who tipped his cap at him as he passed the Landy. Daniel raised a hand to him, mouthing hello. As much as he hated to admit it, even to himself, he had missed this sleepy and claustrophobic village, and even though he'd only been back a week, he already felt its tight grip on his heart and soul, pulling him in.

Life here in the village differed to that of London. It was a slower pace of life, with fewer cars, less pollution and so much greenery. He briefly wondered why he'd loved London so much. But the answer was obvious. Complete anonymity and the chance to reinvent himself. But he had changed, his life had evolved, and it appeared, while sitting in his Landy in the middle of the day, that Middlefern had remained solidly in the past. And by God, he was thankful for that. He'd missed the green grass of home. The surgery in London had been in the centre of a concrete jungle. So why was he in such a rush to have the cottage valued?

Telling Hannah about the estate agent had been a test. He'd wanted to see her reaction to him selling up. Maybe he should sit on it, consider his options. Maybe he could settle and live in this village? He'd dismissed this option far too quickly because of Gerald. Every decision he had ever made came back to that man. Perhaps it was time to look at his situation from a completely different angle. One in which Gerald's ghost no longer existed to him.

With hindsight he should never have told Hannah about the estate agent. She didn't need to know about any of that. He'd felt the wall come up between them as soon as the words were out of his mouth and this only increased his suspicions that she probably thought he was all about the money, which couldn't be further from the truth.

He undid his seat belt and opened the Land Rover's door.

He hadn't done anything wrong. It would be good to know the value of the cottage. He didn't need to sell up, not if he didn't want to. He was merely keeping his options open. No harm in that.

For a moment he completely forgot that Sammy wasn't with him, as he waited for her to bounce out through the open door. He'd left her with Phyllis back at the surgery. 'Leave her here with me,' Phyllis told him. 'She's good company.' He couldn't argue with that, and anyway, he wasn't too sure Mrs Barlow liked dogs, or even if she'd allow Sammy into the flat, not with a poorly cat.

He locked the door. As a vet, he hated being the bearer of bad news. He wished he could save every animal, make them immortal, but life simply didn't work that way. He couldn't save them all. Bodies broke, grew cancerous cells and bled, and even though he did everything in his power to save those animals, he wasn't God.

He rang the bell and stepped back, dragging a hand through his hair while sucking in a deep breath. This never got any easier.

A few beats passed. No one came to the door. He pressed the bell again. He could have sworn that Hannah told him Mrs Barlow very rarely went out. He took a chance and peered through the frosted glass in the door. The hallway was far too dark to see anything.

He stood motionless for a moment, wondering what to do, before turning round and heading back to the Landy. He pulled his phone from his back pocket. He'd phone. The shattered screen mocked him; it was a miracle it still worked. He really needed to replace it.

He didn't feel comfortable walking away without trying to make contact. He sat in the driver's seat, found her mobile phone number and hit the call button. She answered on the third ring. After a brief introduction and telling her he needed to discuss Ted's care with her, and that he was very sorry, but it wasn't good news, she agreed to a house call the following afternoon. It would be easier than taking Ted to the surgery. She was out at a friend's house, she told him. He ended the call, feeling like a weight had been lifted from his shoulders. He'd half wondered if she'd fallen inside the house and couldn't make it to the phone. He dreaded telling her the news. It was the worst part of his job.

His fingers drummed the steering wheel as he pondered what to do next.

A long hour stretched ahead of him before his next clinic, and there weren't many animals booked in. He should probably be getting back, grab some lunch, but a part of him wanted to stay in the comfort of the Landy and watch the world go slowly by. Sometimes doing nothing was just the tonic.

With a shake of his head he turned the ignition and pulled away from the curb. He'd been on the brink of telling her about the cellar. About what had happened down there. Maybe sharing that part of his past with her would help mend the problems of the past. Maybe honesty could save him and help them both to move on.

He indicated right, towards the farms and the hills. He needed some fresh air and to be away from people for half an hour. Cool air blasted through the open passenger side window. He turned up the radio and a familiar song from his youth filled the space. A song he had shared with Hannah. He swore under his breath. Why did everything remind him of Hannah?

In the short time he'd spent in the village, he realised that most of his waking hours had been spent with her. Kissing her had been a terrible mistake. But he'd felt that old connection with her, the one they'd shared as kids. It was still there. He wondered if she still felt something for him, and he could no longer pretend that his feelings were dead and buried. Even though he'd been tricked into babysitting with her, he'd wanted to stay and chat. If it hadn't been for Chris and his blasted cows, then the night might have ended very differently. He didn't like spending his evenings alone in the cottage. He still couldn't bring himself to go down into the cellar.

Without really knowing why, he found himself turning down the road towards Chris's farm. He'd carry on for a while, past the farm, see where the road led, before turning back around towards the practice. It had been a while since he'd enjoyed a leisurely drive.

He wondered if Chris had asked her out for that drink yet?

She hadn't said anything to him about Chris asking her out, but then why the hell would she tell him? She didn't have to share that part of her life with him. She didn't have to share anything with him. Not now, but once they had shared everything. She had been everything to him. He'd held the whole world in his arms and even though it had killed him to say goodbye, to turn his back on her, he had done just that, because there had been no other way. In fleeing the village and his grandfather he'd had to sever all ties with her. She'd been his best friend and soulmate and he believed what they said about first love. You never forget and he never had. What confused him when he'd told her about the estate agent was her reaction. He'd seen the anger in her eyes, but there had also been a flicker of sadness. Did she want him to stay?

Best think about something else.

He cranked the radio up another notch, tried to clear his thoughts, to just savour the sensation of driving through the green hills and to enjoy the sheer beauty of it all.

He slowed and pulled up into a passing place, rendered speechless at the stunning vista in front of him. Could he really bring himself to leave it all behind once again? And what for exactly? What did he have to go back to?

Aware of the time, he decided to check in with Phyllis, to make sure there were no problems. Phyllis answered on the first ring.

'Anything I should know about?' he asked.

'No love,' came Phyllis's quick reply. 'How did it go with Mrs Barlow?'

'She wasn't in,' he told her. 'I managed to get in touch with her on the phone. I'm going to call around to see her tomorrow afternoon. There's no one booked in then is there?'

'No, you're free all tomorrow afternoon.'

'Is Sammy behaving?' he asked.

'Oh she's no trouble at all. She's such a good dog. Aren't you?'

Daniel heard the squeak of Phyllis's chair as she bent over, presumably, to stroke Sammy's fur.

'Okay, well I won't be too much longer.'

'No rush here, we'll see you when we see you.'

Daniel ended the call. He needed to stretch his legs for a little bit.

He walked over to the low dry stone wall. His eyes swept the hills and valleys beyond. There were miles and miles of untouched land out here. It was a wonder that developers hadn't got their hands on it. If they had he'd be looking out on sprawling housing estates or worse, vast trading estates. There'd be a market for it here. Money to be made.

Not for the first time he wondered what he was doing with his life. Yes he was a vet, a good one, but what else? He'd always wanted a family, kids, but would that ever happen? He'd been a good husband. Faithful. He hadn't been the one to cheat and lie. He rubbed at his face, feeling the stubble along his jaw. Sally's shrill voice rang in his head, telling him he needed to shave. What she thought no longer concerned him.

He kicked a toe against the wall. He needed to get back. Being out here, all alone with his thoughts, wasn't good for him. He took one last look at the vista and got back into the Landy.

He turned around and headed back towards the surgery. Chris's farm became a blur in the rear-view mirror as he hummed along to the radio. He passed the top of Hannah's road and almost turned into it before deciding that turning up on her doorstep probably wasn't the brightest of ideas, even with the pretence of checking in on Daisy. Anyway, she'd probably be at work.

He carried on his way and that's when he spotted her, walking down the road towards her flat. He slowed, his eyes on her. Her rucksack was slung over one shoulder as she pushed her battered bike down the road towards home. She really needed to get a better bike. She hadn't spotted him. Her eyes were fixed straight ahead, her free arm swinging, propelling her forwards. Such a measured and exact movement. Her back ramrod straight. Like a dancer. He smiled. She was the most uncoordinated person he knew. Two left feet, but he'd longed to dance with her, and for the leavers' prom he'd got his way. He remembered telling her she wasn't a bad dancer at all. He'd have danced with her all night long. In fact, he hadn't danced with anyone else.

Finally she looked up, saw him. For a moment he thought she wouldn't stop.

He cut the engine. 'Hi, how's Daisy?' he asked through the open window.

The moment he clocked her reaction, he knew his mistake. He should have asked how she was, and not enquired about her cat.

'She's fine. Eating a bit more today.'

'And the dressing, that's okay, is it?' he asked. Why did he sound so formal? He turned the radio down.

Hannah nodded. 'It looks fine. I've kept it dry as you suggested.'

Now it was his turn to nod.

She stared at him, before looking back down the road. Her shoulders slumped before turning back around to face him. 'Been out on a house call?' she asked.

Daniel shook his head. 'I tried to visit Mrs Barlow, but she wasn't at home.'

'No, she's out visiting a friend today.'

'Yeah, I got through to her on her mobile. I'm going to call in and see her tomorrow afternoon.' He paused before adding, 'It's about Ted.'

'From the look on your face it's not good news then,' Hannah asked.

'No, it's not good.'

'I could be there when you tell her,' Hannah suggested, taking a step closer to him. 'What time are you planning on seeing her?'

'Around two-ish. Would that work for you?' he asked.

She pondered this for a moment before answering. 'It's perfect timing, as I usually call around in the afternoon anyway. I just think it would be good for me to be there.' She sighed before adding, 'I just don't know what she'll do without Ted in her life.'

'I wish I could do something for him, but there's nothing I can do.'

Hannah surprised him by placing her hand on his arm. He felt the heat of her skin through his checked shirt. She gave him a gentle squeeze. 'I know that none of this is your fault,' she said.

His breath hitched. He opened his mouth to ask if she wanted to join him for a late lunch, but she spoke first.

'Anyway, I won't keep you.' She removed her hand.

Keep me from what, Daniel thought.

She must have read his puzzled expression as she added with a scowl, 'You know, your meeting with the estate agent.'

'That's not until this evening,' he said.

'Oh, right well. I need to get back to work anyway. I'll see you tomorrow.'

'Tomorrow? Oh yeah, and Mrs Barlow's.' Why was he finding it so hard to form a coherent sentence?

She lost the scowl. 'I'm popping in with Daisy, so you can check on her progress. You hadn't forgotten, had you?'

He rubbed his jaw. 'Yeah, of course not.' As a matter of fact, the date and time were etched into his memory. 'Well, I'll see you then,' he said. He couldn't ask her out for lunch now.

‘You will. See you tomorrow.’ She flashed him the briefest of smiles before making her way down the road, towards her flat.

He turned the ignition, allowed the engine to idle as he silently watched her walk down the short garden path and then rummage in her bag for her door key. She disappeared inside. With nothing else left for him to do, he pulled out into the road and headed back to the safety of the surgery.

Chapter Sixteen

Hannah entered the Jackson Veterinary Practice the following lunchtime and wondered why it was so quiet. She'd expected to see at least another soul waiting to see Dan, but as she approached the reception desk carrying Daisy in her cat carrier, she noted she was the only person there.

'Hello, Hannah,' Phyllis said with her usual bright and breezy smile. Today she wore a bright purple dress that matched the exact colour of her hair. 'You can take Daisy straight through to the back. Daniel's waiting for you.'

'Thanks,' Hannah replied, wondering if Emily would be with him. She still felt a little bitter about how her friend had tried to trick her over the babysitting incident. She didn't like being played for a fool and that's exactly what she told her on her return from the restaurant. She hadn't seen her since.

Phyllis walked around the reception desk to get a better look at Daisy. 'Oh she looks so much better doesn't she.'

'Yes, she seems to be on the mend.' Hannah waited while Phyllis continued to peer inside the carrier.

'Do you have time for a cuppa?' Phyllis asked, touching Hannah lightly on the arm, her bright red nails glinting under the ceiling spotlights.

Taken aback, Hannah's response was a little slow. 'I'm working this afternoon, but I could stay for a quick drink I suppose.'

Phyllis clapped her hands. 'Oh that's fantastic love. Just come find me out here when you've finished with Daniel and I'll have a drink waiting for you. We can sit here and have a little chat as no one else is due in until later on.'

'Okay,' Hannah slowly said, not quite understanding why Phyllis wanted to have a quick cuppa with her and why she was so giddy with excitement. 'See you in a bit then,' she said.

Daniel opened the door before Hannah had a chance to knock. He flashed a quick smile at her before lowering his head to peer inside the cat carrier. 'Hello Daisy,' he said before directing his gaze once more at Hannah. This time his smile was slow and lazy. He took the carrier from her. 'Come on in and let's see how this wound's healing.'

Hannah followed him into the room and stood by the examination table as Daniel pulled on a pair of latex gloves. 'Could you take her out of the carrier for me please and place her on the table,' Daniel asked.

Hannah did so, stroking Daisy's head as Daniel felt the cat's abdomen. 'I'm just going to remove the dressing and check her stitches.'

Hannah watched him closely as he worked. His hands moved slowly, yet efficiently with tenderness and care. A surgeon's hands, she thought.

'The wound looks good,' he said. 'It's healing well. I'll be able to take the stitches out in ten days. I'll apply a new waterproof dressing now and you just need to carry on as you were, so do your best to keep the dressing clean and dry. Have you still got spare dressings at home?'

'Yes, I've only used one.'

'Okay, you should have enough then.'

Hannah watched as he cleaned the wound with saline and then applied a clean dressing. It was only as he was doing this that she wondered where Emily and Becky were? Surely this is what they did? She'd seen Emily apply dressings before. 'Are you all by yourself today then?' she asked, doing her best to keep her tone light and breezy.

He shook his head as he removed his gloves and dropped them into the bin. 'No, well, at the moment I am, but they'll both be in soon.' He didn't make eye contact.

Hannah processed this information for a beat. Then she understood. 'Hang on,' she said, 'you haven't worked through your lunch break for me, have you?'

'Only by half an hour,' he said, his tone now defensive and accompanying a shrug of the shoulders.

'You didn't have to do that.'

'Do what?' he asked.

'Work through your lunch.' *Give me special treatment.* She didn't want to be treated any differently than anyone else.

He heaved out a deep sigh and rubbed his jaw. 'I live here, it's no big deal, Han. I knew you were at work all day today.'

Han. For a moment she forgot how to breathe. 'I appreciate it,' she said, scooping Daisy back into her arms, feeling her vibrating ribcage. 'I appreciate what you've done for her and me.' She buried her face in Daisy's fur. Why was he looking at her like that?

'It's no problem at all. I'm just glad she's doing so well.'

Hannah stood cuddling Daisy, suddenly unsure of what to do or say.

Daniel cleared his throat. 'Right then. If you ask Phyllis to book you in for ten days' time, I'll see you then.' He laughed. 'Actually I'll see you before then, won't I, at Mrs Barlow's this afternoon.'

Hannah nodded, as she plopped Daisy into the carrier and closed the small metal door. 'I'll be there until at least three.'

'I'll be there at two,' he said.

She picked up the cat carrier. 'I'm just going to have a quick chat with Phyllis and a cuppa, then I'll be off.'

'Oh.' Daniel's smile slipped a little as he stepped back behind the table, and Hannah swore she saw a flash of disappointment in his eyes.

'Bye,' she said, closing the door behind her, with the uneasy feeling that she'd done something wrong.

'Here you go love, a mint tea for you,' Phyllis said, passing Hannah a huge mug. 'That's right, isn't it?'

'Yes,' Hannah said, surprised that Phyllis had remembered. 'Thank you.'

Phyllis patted the seat next to her behind the desk. 'Put Daisy down here and sit down for five minutes. I just wanted to have a quick chat while you were here. I know you're busy with your work and whatnot, so I won't keep you.'

Hannah placed the cat carrier on the floor and then wrapped her hands around the mug. 'Is something bothering you?' Hannah asked, wondering if Phyllis had a medical matter that she wanted to discuss with her. She often found people felt comfortable sharing their troubles or worries with her, because of the type of job she did. 'Are you ill?'

Phyllis's mouth formed a large and round O. She shook her head. 'Nothing like that, love. Oh, I didn't mean to worry you. I'm sorry. Nothing's wrong with me. I'm as fit as a fiddle.'

'That's good to hear,' Hannah said with a smile. 'Sorry, it's just that's what most people want to chat about with me.' Their health worries and other troubles. With a pang, Hannah realised she didn't often receive the same courtesy. Who could she talk to, confide in? She had Emily of course, and in recent days, even though she hated to admit it, she had Daniel.

Phyllis leaned in a little closer and lowered her voice. 'I wanted to have a little chat with you about Daniel.'

'Daniel?' Surely Phyllis couldn't read her mind?

'I'm a little worried about him. I don't know, I just have the feeling that something's going on with him. Call it an old woman's intuition.' She offered a small smile, in an attempt to lighten the mood, but Hannah's heart hammered against her ribcage. She couldn't bring herself to drink the tea.

'Could you keep an eye on him? Oh I know he's an adult and doesn't need looking after, but I'm only asking because I know you were friends when you were younger and you've been spending a lot of time together.'

Hannah's eyes nearly popped out of her head. How did Phyllis know all of this?

'Maybe he'll talk to you?'

Hannah nearly laughed out loud. Talk to her? She very much doubted that, but she nodded anyway. 'I think it's just taking him time to settle back into country life,' Hannah said, hoping that would be the end of the conversation.

‘Maybe. You’re a good girl, Hannah. Your mother would be so proud of you,’ Phyllis said, patting Hannah’s hand.

Hannah sighed. It was her biggest problem. She was always a good girl.

‘What time did you say the vet is calling in?’ Mrs Barlow asked from the comfort of her cosy armchair. Ted lay curled up in her lap. He hadn’t moved much since Hannah arrived.

Hannah bent down to stroke him as she answered. ‘Daniel said he’d get here at two’—she looked at her watch—’so in about fifteen minutes.’

‘Okay, thanks, I thought that’s what he’d said on the phone, but my hearing, it’s not always that good on the phone.’

‘Tell you what,’ Hannah said as she straightened up. ‘I’ll just go and give the bedroom a quick tidy and put the laundry away, and then I’ll pop the kettle on for when he gets here.’

‘Thank you.’ Mrs Barlow’s eyes never left Ted’s body.

Ted’s breathing was much shallower than usual and this worried Hannah. She retreated to the stillness of the bedroom and closed the door behind her. She just needed a minute to compose her face. The air was thick with a sadness she could taste and there was nothing she could do about it. She closed her eyes and pinched the bridge of her nose. She had to stay strong for Mrs Barlow. She couldn’t lose it now. The poor woman had no one else.

She needed to keep busy until Dan arrived.

She retrieved the cleaning products from the basket she'd placed on the floor and began to methodically wipe down all of the hard surfaces. She couldn't think about Ted and Mrs Barlow's grief. Not just yet.

She found the laundry basket and put the clothes away. She glanced at her watch.

She couldn't hide any more, so ventured back into the kitchen to boil the kettle in readiness for Dan's arrival. 'He should be here soon,' she said.

And then the doorbell rang.

'Would you prefer Ted to be put to sleep here? It doesn't need to be at the surgery,' Daniel said gently. Mrs Barlow sat opposite him at the kitchen table with Hannah perched at her side, holding her hand. Ted had been placed back onto his cushion in the living room.

Mrs Barlow nodded, then plucked a tissue from the sleeve of her cardigan and dabbed at her eyes. 'I'd prefer it if he was here, at home. He belongs here,' she said.

'Would ten o'clock be okay for you?' he asked gently.

Mrs Barlow nodded once again.

His eyes met Hannah's.

A shared understanding.

She squeezed Mrs Barlow's hand.

'Well then,' Daniel said, 'I'd best be off.' He stood up, resisting the sudden urge to touch Mrs Barlow's shoulder. To offer a sign of comfort. 'If you need to chat to me about anything else, anything at all,' he added, 'then please don't hesitate to contact me, even if it's in the middle of the night.'

Mrs Barlow looked up at him then, her eyes tinged red and with such sadness that he had to look away. 'Right then, I'll see myself out. See you tomorrow.'

As he passed by Ted on his way to the front door he crouched down to touch him on the head. 'See you tomorrow pal,' he whispered, not quite sure why he felt the need to say something.

He closed the door quietly behind him. Then, standing on the step he rubbed a hand over his face and let out a large ragged breath. That poor woman, he thought. What was going to happen to her without Ted? He'd seen older people quickly deteriorate after the death of a beloved cat or dog, not only physically, but mentally. These animals were their entire world. She would need support of some kind in the following days. At least she had Hannah looking out for her, he supposed. He'd also have a chat with Emily and find out what support there was locally for bereaved owners. There must be some kind of support network. There were numerous charities and support groups that he'd accessed in London. He had a sneaky feeling that many of the support networks available in the village would be found by word of mouth only, so Emily, or Phyllis, were the people to ask. He pulled his phone out of his pocket to check there were no new messages. There were none.

Shoving the phone back into his pocket, he turned away from the house and strode down the hill towards the surgery. He'd decided to walk as opposed to driving, as the day was dry and warm and he needed the exercise. Too much time spent cooped up inside the surgery wasn't good for him. He'd made it halfway down the street when he heard Hannah shouting his name. He turned around and there she was, pushing her bike towards him, a few loose curls framing her face, rucksack on her shoulders. He shoved his hands into his pockets.

'I'm glad I caught you.' She leaned against the bike while she caught her breath.

'What's wrong?' he asked. 'Has Mrs Barlow had second thoughts? Does she want to ask me something?'

'No, nothing like that,' Hannah said. 'I just wanted to say thank you.'

'What for?' Why was she thanking him?

'You were kind. You went to see her,' Hannah explained.

Daniel dismissed her words, her praise. 'It was the least I could do, given the circumstances.'

'And as for offering to put Ted to sleep at home, well that was very kind of you.'

Daniel shrugged his shoulders, as if shrugging off the praise. 'She's an old lady. I didn't want her struggling to the surgery with Ted, it's kinder all round if Ted remains at home.'

'Even so, thank you.'

Why was she making such a big deal about this? He made to step back, to end the conversation. He didn't want to be thanked for simply doing his job. Did she really think he wouldn't want to help an old woman who was about to lose her beloved pet? Anyone could see that her life revolved around Ted.

He should go back to the surgery. Standing so close to her, with the scent of her perfume wafting towards him in the light breeze, combined with the way she was looking at him made him want to wrap his arms around her and never let her go.

Without warning, she stood on tiptoes and lightly brushed her lips against his cheek.

This slight movement ignited a fire within him. He closed his eyes and turned his head to meet her lips. The years vanished away. Once again he was that fifteen-year-old boy kissing the girl he loved. The kiss was deep and long. He wanted to take his time, not rush it, but he felt her quick and needy response to his touch. The way she had always reacted to his touch, his kisses. His hands fisted in her hair as he dragged her closer to him. Her tongue swirled with his as her hands gripped his shoulders. He tried to take his time, not wanting the kiss to end. He desperately wanted to make new memories. He pushed aside all coherent thoughts about how wrong it was, what it meant and what would happen as a result of his actions. He simply didn't care. All that mattered was the here and now. This very moment.

A low moan escaped her mouth and he bit back a growl deep in his throat. It was only when he felt her hands on his chest that he was sucked back into reality. He pulled back, his breathing quick and erratic. 'I'm sorry,' he heaved as he shoved his shaking hands into his pockets. What the hell had he done? All she'd done was kiss his cheek and he'd practically jumped on her. 'I'm so sorry.'

Hannah's eyes were wide, the pupils huge black orbs. Daniel couldn't quite tell if this was because of fear or something else. 'That's the second time you've apologised for kissing me,' she said, her voice breathless.

Anger. She looked angry. Shit. He'd gone too far, thinking only of his own needs and what he wanted.

'I'm sorry.'

‘Stop it,’ she yelled. ‘Just stop. I don’t want to hear how sorry you are … and you know what. It’s okay because I’m sorry too … Oh it doesn’t matter!’ she yelled again. Her face, now a bright red, whipped away from him as she reached for the bike’s handlebars. ‘I know you’re sorry. You don’t have to keep telling me.’

Daniel could barely make out her words as she retreated back up the hill and away from him. He desperately tried to process what had just happened. The primal need that had overtaken him. He’d meant to be gentle. He wanted to yell after her that he wasn’t sorry at all, why should he be? But he couldn’t find the right words.

Chapter Seventeen

'Do you want me to nip to the shop?' Emily asked, her sleeves rolled up, hands plunged into soapy suds as she washed up the cups. 'Becky's busy helping Phyllis with some filing, so I don't mind going instead,' she said.

'No, I'll go. I could do with the fresh air.' It had been a long, slow morning and Daniel needed the distraction.

Emily took her time drying her hands on the tea towel before speaking. 'Have I done something wrong?' she asked, not quite meeting his eye.

'No, of course not.' Daniel's reply came quickly. 'Why would you ever think that?' It was true that he'd felt a little low, mainly because of having to deal with a very upset Mrs Barlow after putting Ted to sleep. It had been a horribly distressing situation that now weighed heavily on his mind. But it wasn't just Mrs Barlow, there was Hannah too. He'd done his best not to think about Hannah and her reaction to him kissing her. He mustn't have hidden his feelings, or emotions, as well as he'd thought he had.

Emily's nose scrunched up as she considered her next remark. The tea towel twisted in her hands. 'You've been walking around like a bear with a sore head all morning, and that's before going to see Mrs Barlow. Something's obviously bothering you, but at least I now know it's not me.' She cocked her head to the side, inviting him to speak.

'I'm just thinking about Mrs Barlow, that's all,' he said.

'Nothing else?' Her eyes bored into his.

'No,' he barked. He did not need to explain his behaviour to Emily or anyone else for that matter.

'Humph,' Emily remarked. 'Well, I don't believe you.'

'What's that supposed to mean?'

'Just what I said. There's something else bothering you.' She left the comment hovering in the air between them, waiting for him to take the bait. He didn't.

'If you want to talk about it, about what's actually bothering you,' she continued, 'then you can talk to me. I'm a good listener.'

'Thanks, but I'm okay,' he said. 'Really, I'm fine.'

Emily continued to scrutinise him as she folded up the tea towel and placed it on the countertop. 'Your mood doesn't have anything to do with Hannah does it?'

'Wh-what?'

'Hannah. You know, your new best friend.'

'My mood has nothing to do with Hannah.'

Could she read his mind?

Emily arched a perfectly groomed eyebrow and threw her hands up in the air. 'If you need to talk you know where I am. I'm going to make a start on tidying up the surgical trolley. Is it okay if I place a few orders? I noticed we're running low on bandages and suture kits.'

'Yeah, of course it is. Thank you.'

Daniel heard the door shut behind her.

He'd gone and made a mess of things, once again, with his *new best friend.*

He shouldn't have kissed her like that in the middle of the street. He'd thought of nothing else since. The way she'd felt in his arms, the touch of her skin, her smell was all so familiar to him. Kissing her had felt as natural as breathing. Her lips felt the same, her taste just as he remembered it and that response to his touch – dear God, she still ignited a spark in him, one that had never been fully extinguished.

He dragged a hand over his face. What should he say when he next bumped into her? He couldn't avoid her. Hell, he wanted to kiss her again, while his more rational brain told him it was a very bad idea. It wasn't fair on her. He needed to sort out his own feelings, his emotions, that were all tied up to this village, and to his past. He needed to follow his head, not his heart. Look what happened last time? He couldn't just waltz back into the village and into her life like nothing had happened. Especially when he hadn't told her his reasons for moving away.

Maybe she'd be better off without him. He'd acted selfishly, thinking only of his own needs when he'd grabbed her in the street. She'd only meant to kiss his cheek. She'd be better off with someone like Chris, but the thought of the two of them together made his stomach lurch.

Why was he even thinking about her with another man? He was quickly losing his mind.

One thing at a time. He needed to be more rational. Think things through one step at a time.

He'd wanted to stay in Middlefern. He'd told the estate agent as much, and they hadn't been too happy. Obviously they'd lost the opportunity for a big sale.

He'd made a few friends in the short time he'd been back. He could settle afresh into country life. He knew it suited him. He'd loved living in Middlefern.

He could make a real go of it at the practice. Why not? It had been Gerald's, but now it was *his* and he was at the helm, running things his way. Why give that up just because of how he'd treated him as a boy? Surely staying and making a go of things was the best way to tackle head on what had happened between them. Running away to London hadn't banished his demons. They were still very much alive and kicking.

He'd stay. It was just that living in the cottage wouldn't be easy, not with all of those bad memories. He'd keep clear of the cellar for now, but he knew that this couldn't go on forever. At some point he'd need to go down there and face his fears.

He rubbed a hand over his face. He'd need help. He'd known that for a long time. He wasn't stupid, conquering his past demons and those fears could not be easily swatted away by simply opening up that cellar door, and going down those steps. The last few times he'd tried he couldn't even get so much as a foot through the door.

No, he would need to seek help and professional help. He'd have to talk to someone, dredge up the past to be able to move on with the rest of his life. To reconnect with Hannah.

Maybe she could help him? Maybe talking to her about what had happened to him in that cellar could help him? Would she be willing to help him? He hoped so.

Mind you, that was if she'd ever give him the time of day again. How could they ever be friends again if she never truly forgave him? And he couldn't blame her for not forgiving him, hell, he could hardly forgive himself.

With a disgruntled growl he stormed out of the staffroom, and passed a bewildered looking Phyllis who asked if he could bring back some chocolate digestives please?

'Come on Sammy, let's go for a walk,' he shouted. She barked and ran up to him, her tail swishing in delight at the chance of freedom. Daniel snapped on her lead, which had its own special hook by the reception desk, all the while fully aware that eyes were on him. 'I'll get the biscuits,' he shouted over his shoulder. They stepped outside, he sucked in the warm fresh air.

'Let's go and grab a few things from the shop, eh, girl,' Daniel said, bending down to ruffle Sammy's head. Sammy answered with a bark. They crossed the road and headed down the hill towards the corner shop. Daniel nodded to the people he passed by, recognising a few faces, but most of them paid more attention to Sammy than to him. One of the biggest benefits in owning a dog was that you were never the centre of attention.

'I'll have to leave you outside here while I go in,' Daniel said, looping the lead to the railings outside the corner shop. 'I'll just be a few minutes, and then tell you what, we'll go over to the field for a bit so you can have a run about.' The day was warm and dry and he was in no rush to go back any time soon. He needed to make the most of any free time while he could. He crouched down, rubbed Sammy's head. 'How does that sound?'

Sammy licked his face in approval.

The bell tinkled as he pushed open the door. Pat looked up from behind the counter where she was serving an elderly man. She paused mid conversation to shout hello. Daniel raised a hand in greeting and wandered over to look at what biscuits were on offer. God help him if he forgot the chocolate digestives.

Standing there, in the middle of Pat's corner shop he found himself suddenly sucked back in time. The shop had barely changed and neither had Pat. The sights and smells that greeted him, those of powdered sugar, washing powder and the rumble of the coffee machine, dredged up memories of his youth. The experience was almost visceral as he rocked on his heels momentarily, gathering his thoughts.

Memories of being sent to the shop as a child for Gerald's Sunday paper and of how he loved to spend his pocket money on chocolate mice and fizzy coca cola bottles, taking his time to suck the bitter sugar tang. As he grew older and reached his teenage years, he'd pop into the shop after school for a can of diet coke and a packet of salt and vinegar crisps. How the years had passed by so quickly. Standing in the corner shop he now thought about how he'd come full circle.

He picked up two packets of chocolate digestives, a packet of custard creams and just because he liked them, a packet of Jammie Dodgers. He then wandered down the aisle and found the teabags and coffee. Why hadn't he picked up a basket on his way in? Shuffling back down the aisle, trying his best not to drop the biscuits, he scooped everything into the basket and headed over to the fridge for a litre of milk. Did Becky usually buy anything else? He didn't think so.

He placed the basket down on the counter.

Pat peered inside. 'Becky usually buys washing-up liquid as well. Do you need any?'

Saying that yes, he did, he walked quickly back down the aisle to fetch some Fairy liquid, feeling like a chastised child.

'So, what brings you out here today, then?' Pat asked. 'Is Becky ill?'

'I needed a walk,' Daniel said. He leant against the counter.

'It's just that it's unusual to see the vet in here buying the staff tea and coffee, you know.'

No, he didn't know. He used to do the coffee run back in London, they all did. He let the comment slide.

'But you're not anything like that miserable old Dr Jeffries, so it shouldn't surprise me. He never stepped foot in here, not once.'

Daniel flashed her a grin.

'Where's Sammy today then?' Pat asked, scanning the box of teabags.

'She's outside.'

'Oh you could have brought her in here, I wouldn't have minded. She's such a good dog.'

'The sign says no dogs allowed, apart from guide dogs,' he said. It had always said, no dogs allowed.

Pat tutted and gave him a look, as if to say, *I thought you were an intelligent man.* 'I'll make an exception for you, being the vet and all,' she said. 'Anyway, how's Hannah doing?'

'Hannah? She's …' He had no idea how to answer that question. Why was she even asking him about Hannah? 'She's fine, I think.'

Pat tutted as she placed the box of teabags into a carrier bag. 'I worry about that girl. Ever since she lost her mum'—she sighed—'she seems to be a little lost herself.'

Daniel turned around in confusion, thinking she must be talking to someone else. There was no one else in the shop. He heaved out a breath. He'd have to say something. 'I saw her yesterday, she seemed okay to me.' He wouldn't mention he'd kissed her and how angry she had been. The way she couldn't get away from him quickly enough.

'Just keep an eye on her for me. I know you've been spending some time together.'

Daniel wondered how Pat knew this? He took the carrier bag and his change. He chose to ignore her remark. What he did and who he spent time with was none of her business. That's the problem with rural life, he mused. Everyone knew your business.

'And how's Daisy doing? I heard she got a chicken bone stuck in her gut. Poor little mite. Hannah loves that cat.'

'Daisy is doing well, she'll be as right as rain in no time.'

'That's good to hear.'

Daniel pocketed the change, about to say goodbye and escape Pat's inquisitive and astute tongue when she interrupted him.

'You should ask her out. I think you'd be good for each other.'

'I don't think so,' he mumbled with a shake of his head.

'Why ever not? You two were thick as thieves when you were kids,' she said.

'When we were kids, Pat,' he said, hoping to put an end to it.

'Even so, people don't change that much.'

Daniel opened his mouth to say that, yes they do, but thought better of it. He said goodbye instead.

People did change. Nothing remained static.

Sammy's tail wagged energetically when Daniel emerged from the shop doorway. He unhooked the lead, and as promised, they crossed over the road towards the open fields where Sammy could have a run around for ten minutes.

To get to the field they needed to walk past The Middlefern Arms. Daniel stopped for a moment to look through the large bay window. Inside, customers crowded around tables, deep in laughter and conversation. It was pretty full for a weekday lunchtime. The smell of bacon drifted towards him on the breeze. His stomach grumbled.

The pub door swung open with a bang. 'Oh hello, Daniel,' Brenda said, very nearly colliding with Sammy as she stepped out onto the pavement. She wafted her hands about her face in an attempt to create a cool breeze. Her cheeks were bright red and her breathing was somewhat laboured.

'Are you all right, Brenda?' he asked, reaching out an arm to steady her, hoping she wasn't about to collapse, right there and then in front of him.

'Oh, it's just too hot in there at the moment,' she said, dismissing his concern. 'We need to get the air conditioning fixed. Went on the blink last night. I just needed some fresh air for a while, that's all.' She laughed. 'Don't look so worried, I'll be fine in a minute.'

'I could give you the number of the firm we use, if that's any help to you?' he offered.

'Ooh, that would be helpful, thank you.'

'I'll root it out when I get back to the surgery and I'll give you a call.'

'Thanks love. Will I be seeing you in here again soon with Hannah? It was lovely to see you both the other evening.'

'I don't think so,' he said. It was kinder than saying a simple *no*. What was it about the older women in this village? Putting their noses into other people's business. It had always been that way, even when he was a kid. The older generation gossiping and wanting to know what everyone else was up to. Surely what he and Hannah got up to in their spare time wasn't that interesting? And anyway, had she forgotten that Emily and Chris had been with them that night?

'Ah well, don't be a stranger. I'd love to see the two of you cosied up in that snug of mine. You need a woman who'll treat you right. Who'll look after you and not run off with your best friend.'

'Bye, see you later,' Daniel quickly said, waving a hand and moving as quickly as he could away from Brenda before she could see how flustered he felt. His face burned with both shame and indignation. How many other people in this damn village knew his wife had run off with his best friend? The only person he'd told was Hannah, and he refused to believe she'd spread gossip in that way.

'See you soon love,' Brenda shouted after him.

He waved a hand towards her retreating back, not looking back, Sammy beside him on the hot pavement.

Three women, and all of them had mentioned Hannah to him.

How they made a lovely couple. How they would do each other good.

Could these three women all be wrong? He sighed, bending down to unclip Sammy's leash.

Surely they all couldn't be wrong?

He watched Sammy bounce away, happy and free.

Chapter Eighteen

Hannah thought about Mrs Barlow all morning. She was incredibly thankful to have such a busy morning, but at ten a.m. she was tempted to call in and see her during a quick break between clients to support the older woman. But she quickly dismissed this thought as Emily would be there, and Dan was more than capable of looking after her; she'd seen it yesterday in the flat. Mrs Barlow was last on her list today, and she'd make sure she had something hot to eat, while offering a listening ear. It was too soon to call in now anyway because she'd need a few hours to herself, to grieve.

With her morning duties finished, she had an hour before her next client. The thought of eating her lunch at home, all alone, was simply not an option. Before she could change her mind, she hopped on her bike and rode quickly down the hill towards the surgery. She needed company and she needed to have a chat with Emily to put her mind at rest.

Emily was working a twelve-hour shift today, and normally took her lunch break at twelve-thirty. As the surgery came into view, the thought of seeing Dan and the memory of their shared kiss made her stomach flip. The years had slipped away when his lips had touched hers. For a fleeting moment she'd been that carefree fifteen-year-old girl once again. Kissing him had felt like coming home.

He might be sorry that he kissed her and want to forget all about it, but if she was being honest with herself, she wasn't sorry. Why should she be? It was a great kiss. The first time it happened, she'd assumed it was a sympathy kiss, a heat of the moment thing that neither of them had been prepared for. But the second kiss, that was a whole different kettle of fish. That had been a deliberate move on his part. He'd wanted to kiss her. She'd felt his heart and soul in that kiss, just as she had when they were teenagers.

So why lie about it? Why lie and apologize for kissing her? Hannah could only draw one conclusion: the kiss had been disappointing to him. He hadn't felt anything, no emotional connection or desire or longing. Nothing. It meant nothing and therefore she meant nothing.

Well, she wouldn't give him the satisfaction of mentioning to him again what had happened between them. She would be polite, but nothing more. To hell with him, she muttered, as she pedalled onwards towards the front entrance. She'd coped without him perfectly well for the past fifteen years and she certainly didn't need him in her life now. He'd made it perfectly clear that he didn't want her and that was fine by her. Let him crawl back to where he'd come from in London.

She didn't care any more.

The man was more trouble than he was worth.

To hell with him she muttered again under her breath as she dismounted the bike and then placed it against the surgery wall. With a deep breath she pushed open the door, hoping and praying that Daniel would be out on his rounds.

'Hello, love,' Phyllis shouted from behind the reception desk. Her smile quickly faded when she peered more closely at Hannah's stern expression. 'Is something wrong with Daisy?' she asked, rising to her feet.

'No, Daisy is fine,' Hannah said as she approached the desk. 'She's doing really well.'

Phyllis heaved a sigh of relief and slowly sank back down into her chair.

'No, I just thought I'd come and have lunch with Emily. That is if she's still here?' Hannah asked.

'Yes, she's in the staffroom if you want to go on through,' Phyllis said. 'She's only just gone on her lunch break, so you're in luck.'

'Brilliant, thanks.' Hannah made her way down the corridor and peered into the staffroom; the door had been propped open with a wooden wedge. 'Hello,' Hannah said as Emily looked up, holding what looked like a cheese sandwich in her hand.

'What are you doing here?' Emily gasped. Her face then broke out into the warmest smile. 'It's lovely to see you.' The smile stopped, replaced by a frown. 'Is Daisy okay? Nothing's wrong is it?' Small worry lines appeared on her forehead.

'Daisy's absolutely fine. I've come to have my lunch with you, that's all. I felt like some company today.' She shrugged off the bag from her shoulders. 'I fancied a catch-up.'

Emily patted the seat next to her. 'What's the matter?' she asked.

Hannah plonked herself down on the couch and unzipped her bag. Damn Emily and her astuteness. She could always tell when something wasn't quite right.

Hannah sucked in a deep breath, hoping she didn't sound pathetic. 'I keep thinking about Mrs Barlow. It's just so, so …' She searched for the right word. *Sad*, just didn't seem to do it justice. The situation was so much more than sad. 'How did it go?' she asked instead.

'It was horrible and very upsetting, but I think she'll be okay.'

'I'm not sure how she's going to cope without Ted in her life.'

Emily pursed her lips together before replying. 'I think she's more resilient than you give her credit for. Yes, this is a tough time,' she said quickly, interrupting Hannah's look of concern, 'but I really do think she'll be okay.'

Hannah reached down into her bag and pulled out a lunch box. 'Maybe,' she said, setting the box down on the coffee table. Mrs Barlow was a resilient lady, but losing Ted must be like losing a limb.

'When will you be seeing her again?' Emily asked.

'Later on today. She's my last client, so at least I won't need to rush off to my next job. I can sit with her for a little while at least. Have a good chat.'

'That's good,' Emily said. 'Now, eat.' She pointed towards the lunch box. 'Anything nice in there apart from carrot sticks and a muesli bar?' she asked.

Hannah smiled and whacked her playfully on the arm. 'Nothing wrong with carrot sticks. No muesli bar today but I have a salad wrap and your crisps.' She dipped her hand into the open bag of salt and vinegar crisps and shoved a couple into her mouth.

Emily made an exaggerated surprised face before bursting out laughing. 'When did you start eating crisps?'

'Just now.' Hannah pulled a face, wishing she hadn't eaten them. She popped a carrot stick in her mouth to take the taste away. '

Emily opened her mouth to say something, but whatever she was about to say was silenced with the opening of the staffroom door.

A large wedge of salad wrap she'd just bitten into stuck in Hannah's throat.

Daniel stood in the doorway. His hip rested against the door frame. He wore a blue and white checked shirt, the top two buttons left open, shirt sleeves rolled up. Hannah's eyes travelled down his body and up again before resting on his face. She knew that face so well, and she wished she didn't. She managed to tear her gaze away, swallowing down the chunk of wrap and salad that had turned to a ball of glue in her mouth.

After a beat, he cleared his throat and walked quickly over to the kettle. 'Just making a quick coffee, then I'll be out of your way,' he mumbled.

Emily looked at Daniel before turning her attention to Hannah, her eyes wide with a silent question.

Hannah ignored the look, ignored the unanswered question and took another bite of salad wrap.

'Do you want a coffee?' Daniel aimed the question towards Emily who shook her head while lifting her full mug of coffee mid-air. 'I'm good, thanks,' she said.'

'Hannah?' Daniel asked.

Hannah dry swallowed. She loved the way he said her name. Shaking her head she quickly looked away. 'No thanks, I'm not staying long.'

Emily shot her another questioning look which Hannah chose to ignore.

The rumble of the boiling kettle and the clatter of the teaspoon in the coffee jar were the only sounds to be heard.

'Will you be seeing Mrs Barlow today?' Daniel asked, as he spooned instant coffee into his cup.

Hannah nodded, then realising he couldn't see her as he stooped over the countertop, she said, 'I'm calling in to see her later on this afternoon.'

Daniel turned to face her, cup in hand. 'I'm a bit worried about her,' he said.

For a moment, Hannah thawed a little. He seemed genuinely concerned about Mrs Barlow's welfare, and he had been so kind to her. 'To be honest, I'm also a little worried about her too,' she said.

'But as I've already told Hannah,' Emily interrupted, 'I think she'll be fine. She's tougher than you think.'

Daniel placed one hand on his hip, the other clutched his cup. 'Let's hope you're right.' He sipped his coffee. 'Hannah, please pass on my best wishes to her and tell her if she needs anything she just needs to ask. If I get the time, I'll pop in and see her tomorrow.'

'Oh there's no need to do that,' Hannah said, wondering why he was still hovering by the sink. She'd never seen him looking so awkward before. Part of her wanted to jump up, grab his hand and drag him down to sit next to her, while the other part wanted him to leave. It was too painful, being in the same room as him, knowing he didn't want her.

'Right, well, anyway, I'd best be off,' he said, his eyes darting from Hannah's face to the open door before his gaze landed once more on her. Their eyes locked. The air hummed.

She found it hard to breathe.

He opened his mouth, closed it, coughed and still gripping his cup, swiftly left the room.

Hannah watched him go, open-mouthed.

What just happened?

Emily rolled her eyes, and heaved out a long sigh, in what appeared to Hannah as a sign of despair. 'What's happened now between the two of you?'

'Nothing's happened.' She wasn't prepared to have this conversation, especially not with Emily. 'Where's Becky today?' she asked.

'It's her day off,' she huffed. 'And stop trying to change the subject. Seriously,' she said, 'what's gone on with him? Something's happened.' Emily jabbed a finger, pushing her point home. 'Come on, spill.' She shot her a wicked grin. 'Come on, you know you can't keep anything a secret from me. Well, not for long anyway.'

'We kissed,' Hannah hissed through gritted teeth, 'but it was nothing. It meant *nothing*. We've both forgotten about it.'

'Ob-vi-ous-ly,' Emily drew out every syllable with another roll of her eyes.

Hannah picked up her wrap, which now looked rather limp, and dropped it back into her lunch box.

'Well, by the looks on his face, and yours,' Emily said pointing a finger at her, 'I would say that neither of you have forgotten about it and that it meant something to both of you.'

Hannah let out a small laugh, the puff of air lifting her fringe up off her forehead. 'I really don't think so.'

'So nothing else happened then?'

Hannah's eyes nearly popped out of her head. 'Anything else?'

'So you didn't sleep with him then?' Emily asked, seemingly unaware of Hannah's unease.

'What!'

'It's not that much of a jump,' Emily protested. 'You've known him for half your life.'

'He's been gone for the other half,' Hannah said.

Emily waved a hand in dismissal. 'That's by the by now, as he's back here.'

'But …' Hannah began before clamping her lips together. There were so many thoughts in her mind she didn't know where to begin.

'But what?' Emily asked.

Hannah took a deep breath. 'We haven't slept together and I have no plans to sleep with the man,' she snapped in reply.

Emily couldn't suppress her snort of laughter. 'Yeah, right and pigs might fly.'

Hannah swallowed down her sarcastic response. There was no point in arguing with Emily when she was in this type of mood. She shoved the lunch box into her rucksack and zipped it up.

'Oh don't be like that,' Emily said, her tone now much softer, the playfulness all but gone.

'No, it's okay, I need to get going anyway.' Hannah looked directly at her friend. 'The thing is, it should never have gone this far. I should never have kissed him.'

'What are you on about? You're both free agents, both adults, there's no harm in kissing, Hannah.'

But that's where Hannah knew Emily was wrong. There was much harm in what they had done.

'My God Hannah, it was one kiss, that's all.'

Hannah said nothing.

'Hang on a minute? It's happened more than once!'

'Twice, but the first time doesn't count as it was a sympathy kiss.'

'A what?' Emily stared at her incredulously.

'Daisy had just come out of surgery. He felt sorry for me.'

Emily blinked several times before speaking. 'Why would you say something like that? Why put yourself down?'

'He told me he was sorry when he kissed me,' Hannah said. 'Both times he said he was sorry.'

'He said that? That he was sorry?'

Hannah nodded, wishing she hadn't said anything.

'Maybe he was simply caught off guard? A reflex?'

'I don't think so,' she said. She picked up her bag. 'And don't forget I haven't forgiven you yet for trying to set me up with him.'

'Someone had to try and do something,' Emily huffed.

'You don't need to do anything. I can make my own decisions,' Hannah said with a finality that she hoped would see an end to the conversation.

Emily obviously had other plans.

'He's still crazy about you, you do know that, don't you.'

Hannah's cheeks flooded with heat. Emily was way off the mark on that one. 'Nope, you're wrong.'

Emily opened her mouth to say something, but one look at Hannah's face must have stopped her.

'We were so young,' Hannah said, almost to herself.

'You're not kids now, Hannah. For God's sake, don't you think you deserve some happiness. A relationship?'

'I am happy.' Hannah spat the words out. She ignored the remark about having a relationship. She needed to go, now, before she said something she'd regret. She swung the bag onto her back.

'What's stopping you?' Emily asked.

Hannah froze, hand holding the shoulder strap.

Emily lowered her voice and placed a hand on Hannah's arm. 'What's stopping you from having a relationship with him?' she repeated.

Hannah made a quick decision. Emily needed to know the truth about Daniel and what was going to happen to the practice. 'He's going to sell up and move on,' she said, all in one breath.

'No he's not,' Emily said, her tone self-assured.

'He told me an estate agent is lined up to take a viewing.'

'Oh that, no, he cancelled that. I think that was his initial plan when he moved here, but it's not any more. He's here for the long term. Believe you me, Hannah, that man's not going anywhere.'

Hannah's mouth opened and closed like a goldfish. Had he really changed his mind? Was he going to stay? 'I have to go,' she mumbled. 'I'll see you later.'

'Are you all right, Han?' Emily asked softly.

'I'm fine.' She forced a smile. She needed fresh air. She needed to think.

'I'll give you a phone later on.'

'Okay,' Hannah said, pushing the door open and then stumbling her way past reception. Thankfully, there was no sign of Phyllis.

Fresh air greeted her like a friend. She sucked in the air through her teeth as she shut her eyes, trying in vain to clear her thoughts. With a shake of her head she told herself to get a grip, she had work to do, people who depended on her. There was no time for moping or feeling sorry for herself. It was time to pull up her big girl pants and get on with it. Adjusting the straps on her shoulders, so that the bag felt more comfortable on her back, she swung her leg up and over the bike seat. She had to get away from here. Away from Daniel and Emily and their prying eyes.

She pushed away from the ground and the bike slowly propelled itself forwards. The breeze rushing through her hair felt good. She felt good as she pedalled down the lane, on the way to her next job.

Why couldn't life be simple? Why did she have to go and make a mess of everything? She gritted her teeth. Dan obviously thought she wasn't good enough. Emily was wrong when she said he had feelings for her and she was also wrong about him not wanting to move on. She bet her life he'd tried to cover up his selling the practice and moving on. After all, he wouldn't want Emily, or the rest of the team, knowing about those plans, It would throw everything up in the air.

He was sorry he'd kissed her. That much was true.

Meaning he wished it had never happened. Well, that made two of them. No more time would be wasted thinking about him and what could have been. She was done.

Far better to remain single, carefree and happy. But even as Hannah was telling herself this she knew she didn't believe it. Single she may be, but carefree and happy?

She cycled along the lane that led towards the farm.

She couldn't remember the last time she had felt truly happy. She was happy in her own skin and in her own company. But happy with life? Maybe. Happy in love? No. She had never let anyone in, fearful of what could go wrong, of having her heart broken. Again.

And then she had a deeper, much darker feeling, the knowledge that Dan had been the one true love of her life. It sounded daft to her own ears, but it was true. No one had come close to being him. But then again, she hadn't really been looking to start a relationship, especially during the last few years of nursing her mother. Her time had been taken up with round the clock care. Even on the rare night off, all she'd wanted to do was to curl up and go to sleep. Dinner with a man, let alone sex, simply hadn't been an option.

As she made her way past the last few houses on the council estate, the road began to narrow and within a few minutes all that could be seen were endless fields and trees and hills. Hannah slowed her pedalling feet so she could stop for a while and take in the scenery.

She was so lucky to live here. She must remember that. So bloody lucky. She had a good job, food in the cupboard, a place of her own and stunning views. Her eyes scanned the vista that sprawled ahead of her. She didn't live in a concrete jungle. Didn't have to fight her way through crowded streets, or push her way through throngs of people on the tube on her way to an office job. She didn't have to endure hours spent in front of a laptop. She preferred to be with people. To be working with her hands, and that's exactly what she did every day. She lived a privileged life and she needed to remind herself of this fact while pushing away negative thoughts about Dan and what might have been …

She was not good enough.

She wasn’t enough to make him stay. Then and now.

Chapter Nineteen

Daniel had been on his feet all morning. He hadn't sat down or had a break, not even for a quick cup of coffee. Phyllis had made him one, as usual, on the dot of ten-thirty, but sadly it had sat cooling, untouched in the staffroom. In normal times he would hate having no time for a brew break, but these were not normal times. Being busy was his salvation. It helped him focus on the job at hand, rather than thinking about Hannah, which if he was being completely honest with himself, was becoming increasingly difficult with every passing day.

So far he'd tended to a dog with a dry skin condition. The owner had been close to tears, telling Daniel with a straight face that they thought their beloved Jackie would scratch their skin off. He'd resolved the issue with a quick consult, a prescription and some comforting words.

Then he saw a rabbit who'd cut its leg on some barbed wire. The distraught owner had no idea where or how this could have happened. Daniel had done his best to reassure them that it wasn't their fault that these things happened, but the owner remained upset, telling him they would be buying a much better cage. This had been followed by a regular blood test on a dog he was keeping tabs on, a dog he was a little worried about, and then finally the last patient of the morning had been a young mum who'd brought in her son's guinea pig because it had stopped squeaking. Daniel had had to clamp his lips together to stop himself from smiling. The guinea pig was absolutely fine, he'd reassured her, just having a quiet day. He hadn't dared look at Emily because he knew the two of them would have burst out laughing.

It had been impossible for him to think about Hannah and those smokey grey eyes.

Until now.

'Here, I've made you a fresh brew,' Phyllis said, handing him a large mug of coffee.

'Thanks,' he said with a smile. His throat felt like sandpaper.

'The afternoon seems a little quieter. No one's booked in until two,' Phyllis said, scanning the computer screen, 'so I'd make the best of it if I were you, and go grab some lunch.'

Daniel slurped his coffee. 'Will do.'

'Emily and Becky are out on some house calls. There aren't that many, but they won't be back until afternoon surgery.'

'Yeah, I told them to take half an hour when they get back. I'll be fine by myself for the first couple of consults. Tell you what, why don't you go grab some lunch while I watch the desk for you.' Daniel gulped another mouthful of coffee.

Phyllis's jaw dropped for a second. 'Oh no, I couldn't ask you to do that.'

'Why not?' Daniel asked, already making his way behind the reception desk.

'Well, you're the vet, you know, and I'm the receptionist,' she said. When Daniel didn't respond she added, 'You're my boss.'

Daniel raised an eyebrow and offered her a lazy smile. 'I need to sit down and drink my coffee, so I might as well sit here and drink it. But while we're on the subject of me being the boss …' He pointed at the photograph on the wall, the one of him as a young boy with his mother and *him.* 'Where did you find that?' He kept the lazy smile on his face, not wanting Phyllis to see the edge of anger bubbling under the surface. It was a photograph he had never set eyes on before, but he remembered that day like it was yesterday. He remembered what had happened the night before it had been taken, while his mother was out working.

'Oh isn't it just lovely?' Phyllis beamed, and Daniel realised she meant every word. 'I found it out in the back, tucked in amongst some old files. I thought it was such a shame to leave it hidden away.' She lost her smile. 'You don't mind, do you? I suppose I should have asked you about it first, but I thought it'd be okay. You know, it being a photo of your grandfather and you.'

He did mind. He wanted to rip it off the wall, but he knew that doing so would hurt Phyllis's feelings, and he didn't want to do that, so he bit down on his anger and resentment. After all it was just a photo. He'd replace it with another one given time. So he simply said, 'I don't mind, but next time you want to hang a photo or anything else, please ask me first.' He sighed. 'Go take your lunch break. I'll grab something when you get back.'

Phyllis looked as if she was about to protest yet again, but smiled. 'Okay then, you're the boss,' she said.

'Yes I am,' Daniel said with a flash of a smile. 'Shoo, go on.'

'I'll be half an hour. Do you need anything from the shop?'

'Nope,' Daniel said, picking up his cup.

He watched as she disappeared through the door, then he exhaled. Nothing but blissful silence.

He jumped when the telephone rang.

'Hello, Jackson Veterinary Practice, Dr Jackson speaking. How can I help you?'

An elderly lady sounded incredibly concerned about her granddaughter's rabbit. 'I'm house-sitting, you see,' she explained to him, 'and for some reason Benny is hopping around his hutch and he hasn't done that since I've been here, and I've been here three days now.'

Daniel reassured her and explained he'd call to see her at the end of afternoon surgery if that was convenient for her. The lady readily agreed with a huge sigh of relief. Daniel located Phyllis's pad of paper and a pen and jotted down the address and ended the call.

He let out a weary breath and prayed no one else would call. He needed to think.

He pushed himself up and out of Phyllis's chair and began to pace up and down in front of the reception desk. He always did his best thinking when moving.

Maybe he should just cut to the chase? Have it out with Hannah. Act like a man and tell her exactly how he felt about her.

He loved her, he had always been in love with her.

He should spill his guts and confess his plans to stay in the village, that he wanted to build his career, here, a place he had feared as a little boy, but which now was his.

He knew it was time he stopped running. Life had given him a curveball and he needed to grasp it tightly with both hands. But still, something stopped him from opening his mouth and spitting his feelings out. Sometimes the hardest thing was to find the right words.

The stark truth was that he was afraid. He was afraid of making a fool of himself, afraid of being rejected.

As promised, Daniel visited Benny the rabbit and the incredibly anxious grandmother at the end of the day. The elderly woman opened the door even before he'd rung the doorbell. As suspected, Benny was absolutely fine, a healthy and happy two-year-old rabbit. He'd reassured the lady and told her if she had any more concerns she could phone him. He'd crossed his fingers as he'd said this, as he suspected it wouldn't be the last time he'd be seeing Benny.

Daniel emitted a long, low chuckle at the memory as he opened the microwave door and retrieved his tray of chilli con carne. Not his favourite, it had to be said, but the corner shop had offered him that or lentil curry. He didn't like lentils.

He set the plate down on the table and slowly pulled back the plastic film. Steam rose in the air. Having found a fork he pulled out the heavy kitchen chair and sat down.

He stared at his meal for one. He supposed it was a step up from his usual sweet and sour pot noodle.

He began to eat. Muscle memory doing its work, rather than tasting or enjoying the food. Such a shame he mused, when in the past he'd placed great importance on mealtimes and eating together.

As Daniel ate, he tried to think about all the positives in his life. No good thinking about what had been. He needed to look at what was right in front of him. What he had and should be grateful for.

He dropped the fork onto the plate. As he rested back in his chair, his eye caught the letter leaning on the kitchen counter.

The letter had been waiting for him on the mat when he got back from the corner shop. He'd better open it, even though it would most probably be junk mail. The letter wasn't addressed to him by name, but merely by address.

With a sigh he tore open the envelope.

Inside was a single piece of paper: a handwritten note from the post office. They'd left a parcel in the recycling box by the front door as he hadn't been at home. Daniel scratched his chin, wondering why they had done that instead of simply delivering it to the surgery. Oh well, better go find out what they'd delivered.

With the note still in his hand, he made his way outside.

As promised, there was a cardboard box. But instead of it being a huge surprise, he knew exactly where it had come from.

It was the cardboard box he had supposedly sent to his mother. Why on earth had it been returned to him?

He turned the piece of paper over in his hand and there on the back, in black and white, was the reason.

"Return to sender".

He picked up the parcel and placed the lid back on the recycling box. He could see now that the box had been opened and resealed as there was a fresh layer of parcel tape. Why had his mother returned it? When he'd last FaceTime'd her he'd mentioned sending the parcel, but it hadn't yet arrived.

He shuffled back into the hallway, kicking the door closed behind him with the heel of his boot and set the box down on the kitchen table.

He retrieved a pair of kitchen scissors from a drawer and slit open the lid. He pried open the flaps and there on the top was a handwritten note from his mother. It simply said: "I think that was meant for you".

Daniel scratched his chin and cast his mind back to when he'd spotted the box on the desk in Gerald's old study. The day he'd moved back to Middlefern. He closed his eyes. He remembered that the box had his mother's name written on it. With a shake of his head he peered inside. There were stacks of photographs and letters, yellowed with age. He reached in and lifted out several bundles. This would take some time, he thought. The photograph on the top of the first bundle was of an image that made him catch his breath. He dropped the photographs onto the floor.

A moment captured in time, a time he hadn't thought about in a very long time. The photograph must have been taken by his mother, but he couldn't quite recall the memory. Either way, she wasn't in the photo. The image that had been captured forever was of Daniel and Gerald standing on the step of the cottage. Both of them staring into the camera. Daniel with a forced smile on his face and Gerald's arm around his shoulder. Daniel could feel the stiffness of his shoulders and the way in which his jaw had ached from the effort of smiling. As Daniel studied the photo he knew his mother must have been the photographer, as the only reason he would have smiled was for her. To make her happy.

He crouched down and scooped up the photographs. He couldn't look through them, not now. It was as he was about to drop them back into the box that he spotted the small envelope. Unlike the others, it looked to be fairly new. Tentatively he gripped it and plucked it out of the box. In very small, neat writing were the words, "For Daniel Jackson". Gerald's handwriting. So, that was the reason the box had been returned to him.

Should he open the envelope? Or should he simply drop it in the bin and forget it ever existed.

His fingers gripped the envelope. What should he do?

He had vowed that once he moved back to the village, he'd erase all traces of Gerald. Not only from the cottage and the surgery, but also from his memory. He hadn't done a great job of it so far, and now this cardboard box of memories had returned to him. Maybe it was a sign. Maybe it was wrong to shun what had happened in the past.

'Oh what the hell,' he muttered as he tore open the envelope.

Inside were two sheets of paper. Daniel quickly scanned the pages of Gerald's familiar tiny handwriting. Words such as "sorry", "weak" and "coward" were repeated again and again. His hands shook as he stared at words that began to blur.

He'd expected Gerald's usual sneer to be present on the page, but all traces of the man he had lived with for nearly sixteen years had vanished. These words appeared to have been written by a completely different man. Despite everything, his vow to never have anything more to do with Gerald once he moved back to the village, he found himself slowly reading the letter.

He read it twice.

He devoured every word.

Gerald wrote in great detail why he had behaved the way he had towards him. He shared stories of his childhood, of his own brutal and harsh upbringing and of how this had impacted his life. Gerald wrote that he had shared none of these details with another soul. But during his bout of illness, he'd had the chance to sit back and examine his life, to mull over past mistakes and writing this letter was his way of trying to make amends. He ended by writing that he didn't expect Daniel to forgive him. He didn't expect nor need forgiveness when he couldn't forgive himself. There were no excuses.

"You deserve this truth," Gerald wrote. "I just never knew how to tell you."

Daniel carefully placed the piece of paper down on the table. He put his head in his hands and wept.

Chapter Twenty

Hannah woke an hour before the alarm went off. Not only was the sun streaming through the curtains, helping to lift her spirits, but she also had a welcome and very rare day off on a Friday and she was going to make the most of it. She couldn't stay cooped up inside the flat all day, not when the sun was shining. She had no concrete plans other than paying a visit to Mrs Barlow first thing. Usually on a day off she'd call round and see Emily during her lunch break but now, given the situation with Dan, she didn't think that was such a good idea. It'd be far too awkward.

She spooned strawberry yogurt into a bowl and added a sprinkling of Special K. What to do today? She stirred the flakes into the yogurt and padded over in stocking feet to the kitchen table. She could always send Emily a text and ask her to call round to the flat for lunch. But no, on second thoughts that would arouse too much suspicion and endless questions. She'd have to miss having lunch with Emily. She'd tell her she wasn't feeling too well and was going to have a quiet day at home. The thought of lying to her best friend made her gut twist, but it was better than the alternative: telling Emily she couldn't meet her for lunch because Dan would be there.

Hannah quickly ate her cereal and then flipped the kettle on to make a cup of peppermint tea.

She'd go and see Mrs Barlow, check she was doing okay. The flat had seemed eerily quiet without Ted's presence when she'd last visited. Hannah wondered if she should broach the subject of another cat? She just wasn't sure if it was too early, or even if Mrs Barlow would want another cat. Best not mention it just yet.

She scooped the teabag out of the cup and dropped it into the food bin.

Daisy meowed, reminding her to fill the cat bowl.

'Sorry, Daisy, I nearly forgot,' she said. She opened a tin of cat food and emptied it out into the cat bowl. 'There you go.'

Daisy tucked straight in. Hannah was so happy to see Daisy eating well again.

She picked up her cup.

What else could she do to fill her day?

She didn't need to go shopping and the flat was clean, and anyway she needed to get out and grab some summer air. She could always go for a bike ride, she supposed. It would help to blow the cobwebs away. More importantly it would prevent her from dwelling on the huge elephant in the room, or rather village, that was Daniel Jackson.

She sipped her tea, thinking about her last conversation with Emily. Did Daniel plan to stay in the village for good? The only way to find out the truth was to ask him outright, but there was no way she was going to do that. She couldn't ask him because then he would know that she gave a damn and she didn't want him to know that because he didn't give a damn about her, no matter what Emily said.

He was crazy about her! Hah! Emily wasn't often wrong but she was wrong this time. The only person Daniel Jackson cared about was himself, no change there. The man had no feelings for her whatsoever. No serious feelings anyway. Never had, no matter what her gut told her.

The best thing she could do was to lie low for a while. Let whatever was happening between them, and she still wasn't sure exactly what that was, blow over. He'd either soon be gone or find someone else to be crazy about. The man didn't know the meaning of commitment. The fact he had been married still amazed her. What had been so special about Sally? Hannah silently seethed, wondering once again why he hadn't made that type of commitment to her. He'd told her that they'd be together forever. She thought about the letters he had kept all these years. The letters he had written. It was almost as if there were two sides to the man.

Men, Hannah huffed quietly, followed by a deep scowl. They were more trouble than they were worth.

Best not think about Daniel Jackson and his crooked smile and easy nature that could fool anyone into thinking he actually cared about them. No, she wouldn't be taken in by him again. He may have fooled Emily into thinking he was staying and making a go of things in the village. But Hannah knew better. He'd soon grow restless and eventually he would grow tired of her. So there would be no more heart-to-hearts, and definitely no more kisses. And the only way to achieve that was by keeping her distance.

She drained her tea and made a plan. She'd wash the dishes. She hated coming back to the flat after being out and having to wash the dishes. So, she'd wash-up, have a quick shower and then head off to see Mrs Barlow. Then she'd come back to the flat to fetch her bike and she'd go for a bike ride. Perhaps to the next village, even further if she felt like it. She'd ride until her legs felt like lead and her lungs burnt. But first things first, the dishes.

‘How are you feeling?’ Hannah asked as she handed Mrs Barlow a huge mug of steaming tea.

‘Oh, you know. Not too bad really. You just plod on, don’t you.’

Hannah tore open the packet of chocolate digestives she’d brought with her.

Mrs Barlow’s eyes lit up. Hannah wondered if she’d eaten breakfast. She’d found half-empty Tupperware tubs in the fridge, which had to be chucked out. ‘Here, take two,’ Hannah said, before emptying the contents of the packet into the biscuit tin.

‘You not having one?’ Mrs Barlow asked, already dunking her biscuit into her tea.

‘I’ll take one for now,’ Hannah said, noticing the look of relief on Mrs Barlow’s face. She tried not to smile.

Hannah slurped her peppermint tea and thought for the second time that morning, just how quiet the flat was without Ted. He hadn’t been a noisy cat, in fact he had hardly made a sound, other than his deep, vibrating purr and the odd meow, but the flat seemed so much emptier without his presence. As if something was missing. She’d felt it the very moment she’d stepped through the door.

‘What are you doing for the rest of the day then? It’s far too nice to sit in here with me, you know.’

A wry smile appeared on Hannah’s face as she wrapped her hands around her mug of tea. ‘I like visiting you,’ she said.

‘And I like you visiting me, but honestly, you don’t need to worry about me you know. I’m sad, but I’ll be okay.’

‘I know you will, but I’m allowed to worry about you.’

‘Well, there really is no need. Now,’ Mrs Barlow said with a steely glint in her eye that Hannah hadn’t seen in days, ‘what are your plans today then? Meeting up with that handsome young vet I suppose.’

‘Wh-what?’ she managed to stammer all bug-eyed.

A huge grin broke out on Mrs Barlow’s face. ‘Oh I’m sorry. I didn’t mean to embarrass you, love.’

‘I’m not embarrassed,’ Hannah blurted out.

‘But it’s obvious to me,’ Mrs Barlow continued, ‘and probably to everyone else that the two of you are an item.’

‘We’re not an item!’ Hannah stopped herself from shrieking.

‘Oh of course you are.’

What did Mrs Barlow know that she didn’t?

‘Really Mrs Barlow,’ she said, ‘we aren’t.’

Mrs Barlow tutted. ‘Oh you young ones today. You just don’t see what’s under your nose.’

‘We’re just friends,’ Hannah said, not knowing if what she was telling the old woman was true. Were they friends? Hardly, she was avoiding the man.

Mrs Barlow tutted once more before picking up her tea. ‘I remember him as a little boy. It took me a while to realise he was Gerald’s grandson. I didn’t know that when I first met him. Hadn’t put two and two together.’

‘We were friends,’ Hannah said. ‘We went to the same school.’

‘You were friends? Oh how lovely. So you are old friends who are now reunited.’

‘He was my best friend.’ She let the words sit heavy in the air between them. Had she really just said that out loud?

‘So what happened then? Why aren’t you together—?’

Hannah, taken aback by Mrs Barlow's abruptness, made to interrupt her, but Mrs Barlow waved a hand dismissively and carried on talking as if she hadn't been interrupted. 'Really, it's as clear as day. I may be an old woman, but I've had my share of love and I can tell when two people are made to be together.'

Share of love? Hannah had never thought to ask Mrs Barlow about her late husband. Why had she never asked her about him?

'Oh don't look so embarrassed. I'm not going to sit here and give you advice on matters of the heart.' She chuckled.

Hannah uttered a sigh of relief.

'But what I will say is this. If you have any feelings for him, you need to let him know. Because that young man is a good one, and he won't wait around here for you to let him know. The good ones never do.'

Hannah's cheeks flushed bright pink. Could Mrs Barlow read her mind? Surely not.

'You do have feelings for him, don't you? I saw the way you looked at him when he was here the other day. You can't hide true feelings.'

'I can't'—she cleared her throat—'I can't, I mean – I don't think the two of us …' She attempted to find the right words. 'Me and Dan what happened between us is in the past. We're different people now—'

'What are you on about, love?' Mrs Barlow said, her soft voice encouraging Hannah to speak her truth.

'Well, back then we were kids, now—'

'Now you're adults,' Mrs Barlow said with a shake of her head, as if explaining the blindingly obvious. 'Now you know better.'

Hannah wasn't sure how to respond to that comment.

'So what's stopping you?' Mrs Barlow asked after slurping her tea and reaching into the barrel for another biscuit.

'What's stopping me?'

Mrs Barlow nodded.

He left me behind and he could do the same again. 'He's not remotely interested in me,' Hannah blurted out. Why had she said that out loud?

'You young ones, honestly.'

Hannah narrowed her eyes. 'What does that mean exactly?'

'Of course he has feelings for you,' she said.

'Oh, I don't think he does,' Hannah replied quickly.

'Listen here, Hannah.' Mrs Barlow set her cup down on the table. She meant business.

Hannah placed her own mug of tea down on the table too. She had never heard Mrs Barlow use that tone of voice with her before. She sounded deadly serious.

'That man has feelings for you, you better believe it, and the sooner you do something about it the better.'

Hannah wondered how she was meant to respond to that? So she picked up her tea.

Mrs Barlow usually spoke a lot of sense, but she was wrong this time. No matter what Emily said, he'd soon be gone. If it wasn't six months then it would be a year, maybe two. She had seen it in his eyes, the restlessness. He'd soon sell up and he would be long gone, and she'd be just a distant memory. She wouldn't be fooled by him again. Let him and his kisses be damned to hell.

'His mother was a lovely lady.'

Mrs Barlow almost appeared to pluck this comment out of thin air.

'Yes she was, I mean she still is, I think, although I haven't spoken to her in years. She was always very kind to me.'

'She was lovely, but Gerald, well, I never did like him much, something about his eyes.' Mrs Barlow held a warning finger up mid-air. 'And before you say I shouldn't speak ill of the dead, I'm not saying anything that no other bugger around here wouldn't say.'

Hannah sat motionless, reminding herself to breathe. This was the most Mrs Barlow had spoken in all the years she had known her. What had the villagers said about Gerald? She'd heard no rumours about him.

Something shifted inside Hannah. A nagging memory of something said during a conversation she'd had with Dan. He'd started to talk about Gerald. She had the feeling he was about to share something with her but then chose not to do so. Her gut had told her then that something wasn't right, that something had gone on, and she got the same feeling now.

Things would have gotten a lot worse. That's what he said.

What had gone on behind closed doors? Hannah had been so young. She wouldn't have heard any gossip. She opened her mouth to ask more. She wanted to know why Mrs Barlow had never liked Gerald. What had he done to evoke such strong feelings in such a mild-mannered lady? 'What was it about his eyes?' she asked.

Mrs Barlow pursed her lips and for a moment, Hannah thought she wouldn't answer the question. 'His eyes changed when he looked at that boy. He tried to hide it, but anyone could see that it was an act.'

Hannah thought about the photograph in the surgery. The one in sepia where Daniel's smile didn't reach his eyes.

'These are all rumours mind you, and the gut instinct of an old woman, but I have a feeling bad things went on in that house.' She threw her hands up in the air. 'I have no proof, as I say, it was a gut feeling, but others said the same. That the boy was treated differently when the mother wasn't around.'

Hannah wanted to ask more. She needed to know more. What others? But her throat had closed up and nausea swirled in her gut. She'd heard enough, confirming her fears.

Those words again. *Things would have gotten a lot worse.* How bad had things been?

Hannah forced herself to finish her tea and changed the subject. 'Do you need any shopping?'

'No dear, I've enough here to last me a good couple of months. You go out and enjoy yourself.'

Hannah reassured her that she would, but deep down in her soul, she knew it was just another long and lonely day.

Hannah swung the door shut behind her, making sure the door was locked before shouting goodbye to Mrs Barlow and telling her she'd call in first thing in the morning. She no longer felt like going on a bike ride, that boat had sailed, but she didn't want to sit at home with Daisy either, no matter how much she loved her.

Maybe she should take a bus ride to the library? She hadn't been there for a few weeks. While thinking about wandering around the stacks and what gems she might find, she walked slap bang into Chris, who had just stepped out of the corner shop clutching a huge carrier bag. Chris, in his attempt to stop Hannah from stumbling on the uneven pavement, grabbed her arms which meant he dropped the carrier bag. Tins and potatoes and packets of biscuits scattered everywhere.

'Shit.' Chris crouched down to pick up a potato that was attempting to roll into the gutter.

'I am so sorry,' Hannah said, bending down to help him.

'No, I'm sorry, I almost knocked you over.' Chris picked up the remaining tins of soup.

'I think that's everything,' Hannah said, standing up. Sweat pooled at the base of her spine. It was going to be a scorcher of a day.

'Are you okay?' Chris took a step closer, his eyes scrunched up with concern.

'I'm fine.' Hannah chuckled, trying in vain to hide her embarrassment. 'No harm done.'

'No harm done,' Chris repeated, making no attempt to move.

Hannah smiled once more, thinking she'd better be on her way. The situation was slowly becoming more uncomfortable with every passing second.

'Actually, I'm glad I bumped into you,' Chris quickly said.

Hannah raised an eyebrow.

'Well, I didn't mean bumping into you, as in nearly knocking you over, but seeing you.'

'Oh okay.'

'Yes the thing is … I was wondering if you wanted to go out with me tonight?'

Hannah's smile froze on her face. Was he asking her out on a date?

'Just for a drink,' Chris quickly added, presumably because of the look of shock on Hannah's face. 'But only if you want to. No pressure.'

He was asking her out on a date. Why was he asking her out on a date? She'd known him for years and not once had he ever shown any interest in her. So why now? He was a nice guy and all, and he was very attractive, but she didn't have any romantic feelings towards him. She supposed she never would. She knew she should tell the truth. Tell him she thought he was a nice guy and all, but she didn't feel that way towards him. But one look at his expression stopped those words in their tracks. She couldn't be the one to disappoint him. After all, he was only asking her out for a drink. It wasn't a marriage proposal, and she couldn't remember the last time she'd gone on a date with a man. What harm could it do? One drink with a friend? The alternative, sitting at home and seething silently about Daniel bloody Jackson wasn't very appealing.

'That sounds nice,' she heard herself say. 'What time were you thinking about?'

A huge pile of clothes had been dumped on the bed and discarded. Hannah stared in despair at her reflection in the bedroom mirror. Why did she care so much about her appearance when going out for a drink with a man she wasn't remotely interested in? How had she become that person?

Disgusted with herself, she quickly removed the pale green strapless top and replaced it with a discarded dark blue tee shirt. She needed to look casual. She really didn't want to give Chris the wrong impression, even though she knew it was far too late for that. Should she phone and cancel? No, she couldn't do that as she didn't have his number, and anyway, she couldn't stand him up. That wasn't fair. She'd agreed to have a drink with him and that's what she'd do.

She looked once more in the mirror and groaned. Now it looked as if she'd made no effort at all. Her gaze turned once more to the pile of clothes on the bed. What about the long flowery dress? It was simple and could be worn with sandals. She tore off her tee shirt and stepped out of the jeans. She pulled on the dress and examined her reflection once more in the mirror. Yes, much better.

She glanced at her watch. Not yet six and Chris wasn't calling till seven. Her stomach grumbled. She should really eat something, but she couldn't stomach the thought of eating anything. Why was she nervous? Chris was an all right bloke. They were friends meeting for a quick drink. Shaking her head she plodded into the kitchen to make herself a drink. She needed to occupy her time. She closed her eyes and took a deep breath.

The evening was bound to be a disaster. If she hadn't gone to see Mrs Barlow, then she wouldn't have had that conversation about Dan and then she wouldn't have been so distracted and caught off guard when Chris asked her out. Dan was to blame. And the realisation hit her like a punch to the gut. She felt nervous because she didn't want Dan to find out.

She had said yes to Chris because Dan hadn't asked her out.

Dan didn't want her. Chris did.

She buried her head in her hands and sucked in a deep breath. By God this was one huge mess of her own doing. She had only herself to blame.

She poured boiling water into her favourite cup and dunked in the peppermint teabag. If only her life was as simple as making a cup of tea.

She scooped out the bag and dropped it into the bin.

Her phone began to ring and for a split second she thought about ignoring it, before picking up and checking the caller ID. She wished she hadn't looked. She'd have to speak to her.

'Hannah, how are you doing? Are you okay? I've not heard from you all day,' Emily asked without taking a breath.

'I'm fine,' Hannah answered on autopilot. Then she realised her mistake.

Five seconds of silence filled the air before Emily spoke again.

'So you're not feeling poorly any more then?' Every word dripped with sarcasm.

Hannah's heart pounded. Why had she lied? 'I'm feeling fine now,' she said. Maybe Emily would let it go.

'You've been feeling fine all day, haven't you? There's nothing wrong with you. You just didn't want to have lunch with me.'

Of course she wouldn't let it go.

Hannah hated the sound of rejection in Emily's voice. 'You've got it all wrong,' she said. 'Let me explain.'

She heard the huge sigh of exasperation down the line before Emily said, 'Okay then. What's going on with you?'

'I'm so sorry for lying to you, I really am,' Hannah said, 'but I didn't want to see Dan. I couldn't see him.'

'Why ever not?'

'It's just too …' Hannah wasn't sure what word to use. She opted for "embarrassing". It was the best she could come up with.

'Embarrassing? What about?'

Where to start? 'Us, the situation we're in.'

'What situation?'

Was Emily being deliberately dim? 'The kiss, the fact he's not interested in me. It's just best that I keep out of his way.'

'What?' Emily shrieked down the line. 'What! Have you heard yourself?'

'It's just best if—'

'If what exactly?' Emily's huff could be heard loud and clear down the line. 'Hannah, you cannot hide from this man. He is here living and breathing in this village. He is a huge part of village life now and the fact is that if you live here, you will bump into him. There's no denying that.'

'I know—'

'And anyway, what's all this talk about avoiding him? Why would you want to do that?'

'Because he's not interested in me—'

'And why does that matter so much to you, when you've declared so many times that you have no interest in him anyway.'

'I-I mean, I never said that. I didn't mean—'

'Oh Hannah! The two of you need your heads banging together. Honest to God, I could scream.'

'It's just better this way.'

'Why is it better? You like him, and don't try to deny it,' Emily snapped, 'and he likes you. He does before you try and deny it. So I really don't get what's going on here.'

Hannah rubbed her eyes. Truth be told, neither did she. 'It's just best that we remain friends.'

Emily's bark of laughter sounded short and shrill down the line. 'And how is that even possible when you are doing your utmost to avoid him?'

'Well, whatever you think about me and Dan really doesn't matter, as I have a date tonight.'

Hannah heard the surprised intake of breath. 'With Daniel?' Emily squeaked, 'Oh my God!'

'No, no not with Daniel. With Chris.'

'Chris, as in Chris the farmer?' Emily asked, her words slow and calculated. Hannah sensed the uncertainty.

'Yes, with Chris the farmer. Actually, it's not really a date. Just a drink at the pub.'

'Just a drink eh.'

'Yes, just a drink.'

'So not a date after all then?'

'No, it is not a date.'

The line went quiet for several seconds.

'You still there?' Hannah asked.

'Is he picking you up?'

'Yes.' Hannah didn't trust herself to say anything more.

'And what are you wearing?'

'What's that got to do with anything?'

'Ev-er-y-thing,' Emily drawled.

'Clothes,' Hannah said flatly followed by a sigh.

'Very funny. You're wearing a dress aren't you? I can tell.'

'So what if I am?'

'Be careful with him, Han. I know he likes you.'

Hannah closed her eyes and pinched the bridge of her nose. She was a terrible person.

'I'll let him down gently,' she said.

'Let me know how it goes, okay.'

'Will do, speak soon,' Hannah said and ended the call.

She placed the phone face down on the kitchen table, then glugged down her cold tea as she waited for the doorbell to ring.

Chapter Twenty-One

Daniel closed the surgery door after saying goodbye to the last patient of the day and felt his shoulders relax. He turned round to smile at Phyllis who was busy tidying the reception desk.

'You need a hand?' he asked.

Phyllis shook her head. 'I'm fine, won't take me five minutes.'

Daniel shrugged and made his way round the desk to Sammy's bed. Unbeknown to him, Phyllis had gone out a few days earlier and bought a dog bed. It was dark blue with a splattering of white cartoon themed dog bones. Daniel hated it, but apparently Sammy loved it as she lay in it most of the day waiting either for Daniel to take her for a walk or to receive dog treats from Phyllis, when she thought no one was looking. He'd been slightly lost for words when he'd first seen Sammy reclining in her new, and now favourite, dog bed. Phyllis had tried to shrug off any thanks. She liked Sammy and simply told Daniel that the dog was great company.

'Hey girl, how are you?' Daniel rubbed her head and flashed her a grin. She rewarded him with a wag of her tail.

'She's been as good as gold during the afternoon clinic. Wouldn't even know she was here.' Phyllis reached into a jar on the desk, retrieved a dog treat and gave it to Sammy.

Daniel watched silently, choosing not to say anything for now, but he'd have to eventually. He didn't want

Sammy to gain weight, which she would if Phyllis continued to give her dog treats all day.

'Right, well, that's me done for the day,' Phyllis said, lugging her handbag up on her shoulder. 'Did Emily tell you that she'll be in a little later than usual in the morning?'

'Yes, she did.' Emily was going to watch her twins in their first football match. She'd told him repeatedly that Josh was more excited than the boys. It was all he'd heard about all day. Well, that and the fact that Hannah wasn't feeling too well. Apparently she'd phoned and told Emily she couldn't make it for lunch as she was feeling a little under the weather. He'd tried to sound nonchalant when he'd asked if Hannah needed anything. Emily had merely shrugged and told him she'd phone her later on tonight to check on her. Then she'd winked suggestively, making him blush to his roots, declaring he could always give her a phone. Daniel had cleared his throat and mumbled something about needing to see the next patient.

'Are you doing anything nice tonight?' Phyllis asked.

'No, nothing exciting.' He tried to smile to hide his embarrassment. He did have plans but he felt stupid about saying them out loud.

Phyllis raised an eyebrow. 'So you won't be paying Hannah a visit then?'

Daniel scratched his neck. Was this woman psychic? 'I am going to pop round, you know, because she hasn't been feeling well, and she lives alone …'

'Oh you don't need to explain yourself to me.' She patted his arm. 'Give her my love, won't you.'

'I will,' Daniel said, relieved Phyllis wasn't going to dig any deeper.

'Be sure to take flowers,' she said as she grabbed the door handle.

'Flowers?'

'Every woman likes flowers …' She paused, chewing her lip before finally adding, 'And don't leave it much longer.'

'For what?' Daniel asked.

'To tell her how you feel of course.'

He tried to stumble out a response, to tell her she was barking up the wrong tree, but his mouth went dry. 'I erm, well, I'm not entirely sure …'

'You have to make a move, Daniel. Show her how you feel.'

Boy, was it getting hot in here. Make a move? Why hadn't Phyllis left yet?

'Ask her out, why don't you? After all, you have the perfect excuse for calling round with flowers. Checking if she's feeling better.'

'I really don't think that's a good idea,' Daniel stuttered, now beginning to feel uncomfortable with the way this conversation was heading. Wouldn't it look a little predatory if he rocked up on her doorstep with flowers, asking how she was feeling and then proceeded to ask her out on a date?

Phyllis let go of the handle and stepped towards him. 'You two are friends aren't you?'

Daniel's first instinct had been to say he wasn't entirely sure at the moment, as it was perfectly clear she'd been avoiding him and friends generally didn't avoid speaking to each other. But they had been friends, were still friends. At least he hoped they were. 'Yes,' he said, opting for the simple answer.

'Take it from this old lady who's been around the block a few times, that girl would jump at the chance of going on a date with you, and before you say anything, what have you got to lose?'

Hannah would jump at the chance of going out with him? Did she really feel that way about him? Ever since their last kiss she'd been avoiding him. He'd assumed she didn't feel anything towards him, but what if the reason for her avoiding him was down to embarrassment, or simply not knowing how to be around him? It felt strange for him too, after all these years, so obviously she must feel the same way.

Phyllis had hit the nail on the head. What did he have to lose? Absolutely nothing. He needed to tell her and he needed to do it today before he lost his nerve. She needed to know that his heart and soul were here in the village, that he was staying and he wanted her to give him another chance. He'd let her go once before and he couldn't bear it if he lost her again. A huge grin spread across his face now that he'd made his decision, and without thinking he stepped forwards and kissed Phyllis lightly on the cheek. 'Thank you,' he told her.

Phyllis's smile matched his own. 'I only told you what you already know.' Then the smile dropped from her face. 'So what are you doing standing here? Go get her.'

'Ooh, they're a lovely bunch of flowers,' Pat said as she wrapped them in brightly coloured tissue paper.

Daniel had popped into the corner shop on his way to Hannah's hoping that there would still be bunches of flowers for sale. As luck would have it he found several large bunches standing in the bucket by the till.

He fumbled in his pocket for his wallet and pulled out a ten pound note.

'For anyone special?' Pat asked, her focus on wrapping the flowers, not on Daniel's embarrassed expression. He couldn't remember the last time he'd bought flowers for a woman.

Pat looked up at him. 'Rather not say, eh?' She chuckled. 'Don't blame you. It's difficult to keep a secret around here.' She passed him the flowers and took the ten pound note.

The huge bunch consisted of daisies, carnations and tulips. All brightly coloured. He hoped she liked them.

'Here you go,' Pat said, handing him the loose change, 'and tell Hannah hi from me, and I hope she's feeling better soon.'

'How? How did you—?'

'As I just said, it's hard to keep secrets in this village, and anyway, who else would you be buying flowers for?'

Daniel wasn't sure if he should be offended or not. He pocketed the change and said he would pass on her regards. He chose to ignore the exaggerated wink as he turned to leave the shop.

What was it about small village life and the gossip mill? Why couldn't he go into the local corner shop and buy flowers for a friend without the owner knowing every single thing about his life? He really didn't miss London that much, he preferred the fresh country air and quieter pace of life, but by God, he did at times miss the anonymity that city life provided. Nobody cared what you did or where you went. The same could not be said for Middlefern. It should have been named Meddlingfern, he thought as he unhooked Sammy's lead from the railing and strode along the street towards Hannah's flat, the bunch of flowers clenched in one hand. He kept his head down, hoping and praying he wouldn't bump into anyone he knew on his way. He realised much too late that this wasn't a possibility as Brenda stepped out of the pub and onto the pavement at the very moment he tried to sneak his way past without being seen.

'Oh hello, love.'

'Hello,' Daniel mumbled, attempting to sidestep her. She was a lovely lady. She'd always been incredibly kind to him when he was a kid, but by God, the woman loved to talk and he was in a hurry.

No such luck.

'It's hot as hell in there, even with the air con fixed.' She ran the back of her hand over her forehead, the charms on her bracelet jangled as she did so. 'Thanks for the recommendation. They did a grand job of fixing it.'

'No problem,' Daniel said, attempting once more to move on.

'Oh what a beautiful bunch of flowers.' She buried her face into the blooms.

Manners got the better of him. He could spare her a few minutes. He smiled politely. 'How are you?'

'I'm very well my love, and so much the better for seeing you and these lovely flowers.' She dipped her head so that her nose touched the petals and inhaled deeply. 'For someone special are they?'

What was it about the women in this village? 'They're for Hannah, she's not been feeling too well.'

'Oh I heard about that, poor little love.' She bent down to pat Sammy's head. 'Well, I'm sure she'll be thrilled to get these, and over the moon to see you.'

Daniel shuffled his feet. 'Anyway, I'd best be off,' he said.

'Of course, I don't want to keep you. Give her my love won't you.'

Daniel promised that he would as Brenda retreated back into the pub and waved from the step.

Surely he wouldn't bump into anyone else?

Daniel's heart hammered in his chest as he prepared to ring the doorbell. His breath stuttered and his hand shook as he reached towards the bell.

'Am I doing the right thing?' He directed the question towards Sammy and didn't expect an answer, so was surprised when Sammy answered him with a wag of her tail and a short, happy sounding bark. 'Thanks, girl,' he said with a smile. 'I need all the support I can get.'

He could do this, ask her out for a drink. He had to stop making such a big deal out of everything. He needed to—

The door swung open and all thoughts evaporated.

As he gazed into her eyes he had the sudden urge to confess all, to purge himself. He wanted to share his story about growing up with Gerald, about what happened to him. He wanted to show her the box of photographs, the letter. Then she would finally understand why he had to leave and why it had been so incredibly difficult to come back home, here to the village.

'What are you doing here?' she asked.

Daniel held out the bunch of flowers. There was a brief hesitation before she took them.

She didn't look happy to see him. Why didn't she look happy to see him?

‘Thank you, they’re beautiful.’ She turned an inquisitive face towards him. She hadn’t moved from the doorstep. Sammy nudged her face into Hannah’s leg. He heard Hannah’s short peal of laughter as she leant forwards to rub Sammy’s head. ‘Hello girl,’ she said.

Daniel’s jaw clenched, not sure what to do next. She sounded more happy to see his dog than him. He ran a hand through his hair.

‘Are you feeling better?’ he asked.

‘What? Oh, yes, much better, thanks.’ She buried her face into the flowers.

Did she look embarrassed?

‘Emily told me about how you were feeling poorly.’ He shrugged by way of explanation.

‘Of course she did.’

Daniel observed the faintest of smiles.

He narrowed his eyes. She looked remarkably well for someone who had been unwell at lunchtime, and then he took in the bigger picture. Come to think of it, she didn’t look ill. In fact she looked positively radiant in that dress. It looked like she was dressed to go out. She looked so pretty.

He took a step back. This had all been a terrible mistake.

‘Come on girl,’ he said. ‘I’ll leave you to it.’ He turned to go, but Hannah reached out and unexpectedly grabbed his hand. ‘No don’t go, why don’t you come in and have a cup of coffee?’ She stepped back and Sammy pushed past her down the hall, her tail wagging in delight.

‘Oh, okay,’ he said and stepped into the hallway, Sammy having made the decision for him.

Hannah retreated into the kitchen, shouting, 'Just close the door behind you.'

He closed the door and walked into the kitchen where he found Sammy lying on the floor next to Daisy's cat bed. Hannah was busy filling a glass vase with water.

'How's she doing now?' he asked.

Hannah turned to face him. 'Who?'

He wanted to touch the little frown lines that appeared on her forehead.

He swallowed. 'Daisy, how's she been?' It'd been six days since he'd operated. Where'd that week gone? he wondered.

'Oh, she's fine now. No problems.'

'That's good to hear.' He watched her place the flowers into the vase and then to fill the kettle.

'Coffee okay for you?' she asked.

'Sure, but don't go to any trouble if you're going out.'

'It's no trouble. I've got an hour to kill.' She smiled as she spooned instant coffee into a large, red mug. 'You can sit down.' She laughed.

Daniel dragged out the wooden kitchen chair and sat down. 'Are you going anywhere nice?' he asked.

'Just for a drink … with Emily.'

Had he detected the briefest of pauses?

'Oh, that sounds nice.' Emily must have phoned her and persuaded her to go out for a drink.

He studied her silently as she made the coffee.

'Here you go.' She placed the mug on the kitchen table and sat down opposite him.

'You not having a drink?'

'I've just had tea.'

He picked up the mug for something to do with his hands.

'Busy day?' she asked.

'You could say that.' He placed the mug back down on the table.

'You settled into surgery life now then?' Hannah asked. 'And settling into the cottage and village life?'

Daniel rubbed at his cheek. 'Yeah, it's beginning to feel like I never left. Nothing much has changed.'

Was that a flicker of sadness that passed across her eyes? Had he said something wrong? 'I'm getting to know the regulars at the surgery and the cottage feels more like home than ever before.' *As long as he stayed away from the cellar*. Gerald's letter had made him see what he had and what he would miss out on if he gave everything up and walked away. He could never do that now.

Hannah cocked her head to one side, as if trying to read his thoughts. Her face softened and she smiled. 'That's so good to hear. So that means you won't be selling up any time soon then?'

'Selling up? No.' He shook his head. 'It had been a long-term plan, but not now. I cancelled the estate agent. No, I want to stay here.' He looked her directly in the eye. 'I want to stay here in the village, make a go of things. Settle down.'

Hannah jumped up suddenly out of her chair and turned her back on him as she ran the tap, washing up her empty tea cup.

'I wanted to tell you something actually.'

'Oh?' She turned round to face him, her face slightly flushed.

He breathed in deeply, preparing himself to share what he'd found in the cardboard box. 'I want to tell you about Gerald, about growing up with him in the cottage.'

Hannah dried her hands on the tea towel and sat back down.

'He'd left a cardboard box in the cottage. It was in his study, well what had been his study, on the day I moved in.'

Hannah nodded, encouraging him to carry on.

'It was addressed to Mum, so I never opened it, just forwarded it on to her. Anyway, when I finished work yesterday I found a note on the doormat saying that it had been delivered to the cottage. They'd left it in the recycling box.'

Hannah remained silent. Daniel knew he was making a dog's ear of telling this particular story, but he had to ease himself into it. Had to keep talking to get it all out.

'Inside the box were lots of photographs that he'd kept over the years. Pictures of me and him mainly, and a few of Mum.'

'That must be nice, to have those memories. I haven't got many pictures of me and Mum from when I was little.'

'That's so sad.'

Hannah shrugged. 'Did you see something in the photographs then? Something odd? A secret?'

'What? No. This isn't about the photographs.' He leant forward, scratching his chin. 'Well, it is and it isn't.'

'Something else was in the box?'

He slowly nodded. 'Yes, there was.'

Hannah leant towards him, her eyes probing him. 'What was it?'

'A letter.'

'And it upset you?' she asked.

His jaw clenched. 'Let's just say, it explains a lot.'

Hannah rocked back in her chair.

Daniel wished he had something stronger than coffee in his hand.

'Growing up here, in this village, with Mum and him, there was a lot going on.'

'What did your grandfather do?'

'He never deserved the name, Grandfather.' His reply was quick and cutting.

'What happened, Dan?'

He closed his eyes, willing the words to come.

She'd called him Dan. She had always called him Dan.

'He was cruel to me. He never hit me or anything like that, but he made it abundantly clear that he didn't like me living under his roof.'

Hannah's gasp sounded loud and clear in the stillness of the kitchen.

'He used to lock me in the cellar when Mum was working nights. He told me that's where a boy like me, a boy born of sin, deserved to live. He told me I was no better than a pet dog.'

Hannah's hand flew to her mouth and tears sprang to her eyes.

'I spent many a night down in that cellar. I still can't go down there. I've tried, but I can't bring myself to go down the steps.'

'It all makes sense now,' she said after several seconds had ticked by.

'What does?'

'How you reacted in the surgery, when Sammy locked us in the storeroom. Your reaction. I should have guessed.'

'How were you to know?'

'You should have told me.' She reached across the table and touched his hand. He grasped her fingers. He never wanted to let go.

'I couldn't tell you. I felt so ashamed.'

'You were a little boy, none of it was your fault.'

'I'm not a little boy any more. I'm a grown man who is still afraid of the dark.' He tried to laugh off his embarrassment. Hannah's expression didn't change. 'You should have told me. I'd have listened to you.'

'You wouldn't have believed me. Everyone loved Gerald. I've never heard anyone say a bad word about him.'

'Mrs Barlow didn't like him much.'

'What? She said that?'

'Hmm-mm, and I'd say she's a pretty good judge of character. Why tell me all of this now?' Hannah asked. She hadn't let go of his hand.

'I've been wanting to tell you, and reading his letter yesterday, it just puts things into perspective. It made me realise what's important in life. That the past is just that, the past. But I need to make amends with you. I need to be honest with you.'

'Okay, I'm listening.'

'Gerald was the reason I left and never came back. It had nothing to do with you. *Nothing*. I wanted to come back but the thought of having to see him again, just—'

'I get that now. I really do,' Hannah said. 'But why leave it so long? You could have given it six months and then came back, told me what had gone on.'

'Life's never that simple, is it? With hindsight, that's exactly what I should have done. But at the time I was so confused. I just had to get away from him, to not only protect myself, but Mum. She had no idea about what he did to me. I never want her to know. What good would it do now anyway?'

'I understand that, I do, the need you had to protect your mother, yourself, but you didn't need to protect *me*. You should have told me. You should have trusted me.'

'I know that now. I should have told you.'

'I waited for you,' Hannah whispered.

His breath caught in his mouth. 'I'm so sorry. I thought, I just thought you'd forget all about me. Move on with your life. Be happy – without me …'

'You read my letters. You kept my letters.' Her voice came out as barely a whisper. 'You wrote letters back to me. You knew my feelings and in your heart, you never let me go.'

Daniel sucked in a deep breath. 'I thought it was best for everyone. I thought you'd be better off without me.'

'Not for me. It wasn't best for me. I missed you so much.'

'I'm so sorry.' He wished he could turn back time. Wished he'd told her what was happening, but then he'd been frightened and confused, and the solution had been to run.

Hannah let go of his hand and swiped angrily at her tears. 'What was in the letter? What did he write?'

'He explained why he behaved the way he did. What happened to him as a child.'

'I see.'

'It helped to explain his behaviour towards me.'

'There's no excuse though, Dan. There never is.'

'I know, but a part of me …' He searched for the right word. 'I now at least understand why he was so cruel, and that it had nothing to do with me.'

'Of course it didn't. You were a child, and to think I used to call round all the time. He was like a granddad to me, to all the kids in this village.'

'It's a lot to take in, isn't it?'

'You can say that again.'

They sat in silence for a few moments. Better bite the bullet and get this over with, he thought. If he didn't ask her now then he never would. 'Listen, about the last time we kissed, I know—'

'It's okay, you don't need to say anything.'

'I need to explain, you see—'

'It's okay. Really it is. I get it, we don't need to talk about it again.'

'But I want to explain things. I think you've got all of this wrong. You see—'

But his next words were cut off by the ringing and rather persistent doorbell.

Hannah jumped to her feet. A look of pure shock etched on her face. 'Who the hell is that?' she cried.

Daniel stared dumbfounded. 'It'll be Emily,' he grunted. Of course, Emily had to turn up and ruin things.

'Emily?'

'You're going out, remember, for a drink.' Surely she hadn't forgotten? 'Listen. I'll get out of your way. Come on, girl.' He gestured for Sammy to get up and follow him out.

Hannah didn't move.

He shot her a concerned look. 'Really, I'll get going,' he said. 'Get out of your hair.' He bent over, clipped on Sammy's lead and took a deep breath. 'I was actually wondering if you were free for a drink?'

But Hannah had already scurried away towards the front door.

He'd missed his chance.

Hannah flung open the door. Daniel peered over her shoulder.

Why was Chris standing there clutching a large bunch of flowers?

Chris's smile froze when he saw Daniel in the hallway.

Then the penny dropped. She hadn't been waiting for Emily at all, had she. Of course not. She'd been waiting for Chris, who by the looks of it was taking her out on a date.

How had he missed the signs? The pretty dress, God she looked beautiful in that dress.

'Chris, hi, you're early.'

She stepped aside to let him in, but Daniel and Sammy were in the way.

Why didn't she look happy to see him?

'Hi Daniel.'

'Hi Chris. I'm just going. Just came to see if Hannah was feeling better.'

'Oh, are you not feeling well?' Chris asked, the flowers still in his arms.

'I'm fine,' Hannah snapped. 'Nothing wrong with me.'

Daniel stepped out onto the path and nodded at Chris. He noticed he'd gone to a lot of effort. He was wearing a suit and had layered on the aftershave.

'Have a lovely evening,' Daniel said to both of them.

'Thanks,' Chris said, his attention already on Hannah. 'Here, I bought you some flowers.'

Daniel walked away. His footsteps were slow and heavy as he retraced his steps back home.

He'd blown it. He'd missed his chance.

Chapter Twenty-Two

'Hello,' Brenda said from behind the bar. Tonight she wore a fuchsia pink top that clashed glaringly with her green eyeshadow. 'Are you feeling better?' she asked, her concerned eyes on Hannah's face. 'I saw Daniel earlier when he passed by on his way to yours and he told me you hadn't been feeling too well. He looked very worried when I chatted to him.' Brenda didn't pause to take a breath, just carried on talking despite Hannah's attempt to shush her. 'Did you like the flowers? They were a large bunch, weren't they?'

Hannah's cheeks flushed with heat. She felt Chris's shoulders stiffen and the discomfort that radiated from his posture. Had Brenda not seen him? Why was she deliberately ignoring him? It wasn't like her to be so rude.

'I'm feeling a lot better, thank you,' Hannah mumbled. Never again would she tell a white lie. It would only come back to bite her on the bum.

'I bought Hannah flowers too,' Chris said, his tone almost pleading.

The flowers had been placed into the mop bucket and she still felt ashamed about that. She only had one vase.

'That's nice, dear,' Brenda said, reaching for a wine glass. She turned her attention back to Hannah. 'So where is Daniel then? He not joining you?'

Hannah's face became even redder.

'We're on a date,' Chris said slowly. He turned to Hannah. 'What would you like to drink?'

A date? She hadn't used that word and Chris had not said they were going on a date. He'd said they were going for a drink. A drink was not a date. Oh this wasn't going at all well.

'A glass of white wine, love?' Brenda asked, coming to her rescue.

Hannah flashed her a grateful smile. 'Yes please.'

'And a pint for you, Chris?'

'Yeah, thanks,' Chris replied. He dug his wallet out of his jacket pocket.

'I'll pay for my drink,' Hannah said, handing Brenda a note before he could object. 'It's what friends do when going out for a drink.' She picked up her wine glass and hovered self-consciously beside him.

'Right, where would you like to sit?' Chris asked.

'By the window?' Hannah said. It was the least cosiest place to sit and the least private.

Chris nodded and followed her over to the table.

'See you later, love,' Brenda hollered to their retreating backs.

Hannah wanted the ground to swallow her up.

They sat down. Hannah forced a smile.

'Are you sure you're all right?' He cocked his head to one side, his eyes softening and Hannah despised herself for it. She was a terrible, terrible person.

'Honestly, I'm fine. Not sure what it was, maybe a reaction to a rare day off.' She attempted a laugh that sounded hollow. It died in the air.

Chris attempted his own smile, but it didn't reach his eyes. 'I'd love a day off,' he murmured.

'Must be hard, being a farmer,' she said. 'Early hours and always having to attend to the animals.'

‘It’s not too bad,’ he said. ‘I grew up on a farm. It’s in my blood.’ He looked at his pint. ‘I wouldn’t know how to do anything else.’

Hannah nodded in shared understanding. ‘Yeah, I feel that way about being a carer.’

‘That’s a hard job. Harder than farming.’

‘Not harder, different, yes, but I suppose it’s just as rewarding.’

Chris sipped his pint and Hannah took the opportunity to sip her wine, racking her brain for something to talk about next. Her thoughts were firmly fixed on Dan and his revelations about his grandfather. She’d wanted him to stay. She shouldn’t be here, in this pub, on a *date* of all things.

Chris placed his now half-empty pint glass down on the table and leaned back in his chair. ‘Now, don’t take this the wrong way,’ he said slowly, ‘but I really do get the impression you don’t want to be here.’

‘What, oh no, no, of course I do,’ Hannah replied quickly, plastering a smile on her face. ‘Whatever gave you that impression?’

Chris smiled back, and for a fleeting moment, Hannah realised he was a handsome man. Just not the handsome man she wanted in her life. ‘Let’s just finish our drinks eh, and say no more about this. No harm done.’

‘Chris,’ Hannah began, ‘you’re a lovely guy—’

‘But not the right guy for you,’ he finished for her. ‘Really, it’s okay. Honestly, I was surprised you agreed to go out with me in the first place. I mean, you’re well out of my league.’

‘What? No, that’s not true at all. It’s just that …’

Oh where to go with that train of thought?

'It's Daniel, isn't it?'

When she remained quiet he continued. 'There's no way I can compete with him.' He sighed, but there was a smile on his face.

'Is it that obvious?' There was no point in denying it now, was there?

'Yep,' came Chris's curt reply, but there was no sign of malice in his tone. 'Want to talk about it? I'm a good listener.'

'I've known him a long time,' Hannah explained with a smile. 'Well, what I mean is that we were friends years ago, but he moved away with his mum when he was nearly sixteen.'

'Yeah, I heard about that,' Chris said, his fingers drumming the table. 'The rumour mill was rife the week before he turned up back here. Anyone would think he was royalty or something.'

She wished she could tell Dan that he'd been the talk of the village. That people had been excited about his return to village life. Hannah hadn't heard any rumours. 'I think people were just intrigued as to why he'd come back,' Hannah said, herself included.

Chris scowled. 'I thought that would be pretty obvious. I mean, he came back to take over his grandfather's business, didn't he?'

'Yes,' Hannah said, not liking the sarcastic tone. Of course she knew that was the main reason why he returned to his childhood home. 'What I meant was people wanted to know why someone who had lived in the big city and had a life there would move back here when he could have very easily sold the business and the cottage.'

Chris studied his drink while she spoke, then looked up, mulling over her words. 'Yeah, that makes sense. Hard for me to understand that, as I've always lived on farms. Never knew any other kind of life. I don't get why people run away to the city when you can live in a beautiful part of the world like this.'

'We are lucky,' Hannah said.

Chris drained his pint, wiped his mouth with the back of his hand and belched quietly.

Hannah grimaced.

'So he was your first love then?'

Hannah scrutinised him. She didn't think he was making fun of her.

'They say you never forget your first love.' A wistful look crossed his features. Hannah wondered if he was thinking about someone?

'It was more like puppy love to be fair, not real love. We were only fifteen.' *Who was she kidding?*

'But it felt real at the time, right? Emotions don't really change, do they? No matter what age we are.'

'Yeah, you're right. We were young, but I knew how I felt.'

'And still feel,' Chris prompted. 'Those feelings haven't died have they?'

'No, no they haven't changed, but we both have.'

'I need another drink if we're going to have a heart-to-heart like this.'

Hannah laughed, she couldn't help it. 'A heart-to-heart usually involves two people sharing their feelings with each other.'

'Yeah, I know that,' he said with a roll of his eyes, making him appear ten years younger. 'But it's a serious conversation, and I do much better at this type of thing with a drink in my hand.'

Hannah bit her cheek. What was she doing, sitting here with her date of all people, telling him how she was in love with another man? He didn't seem to mind.

'Listen, I'm not embarrassed. I'm just glad to get out of the house for a change and to wear nice clothes.' He laughed. 'Honestly you'd be doing me a favour. I could do with a friend right now, and you could do with a good listening ear.'

'Okay,' Hannah found herself saying. 'Thank you.'

Hannah pushed the door closed with her hip and released a shuddering breath. It hadn't been such a bad night after all and she'd made a new friend and that was such a good feeling. She kicked off her shoes and padded to the kitchen where Daisy greeted her with a purr, wanting to be stroked. 'Hello girl, you had a good evening?' She bent down to rub Daisy's head.

She wobbled slightly as she stood back up, the alcohol having gone to her head. She very rarely drank and the two large glasses of wine had pushed her right to her limit.

Water, she needed to drink some water.

She fetched a glass from the cupboard, ran the tap and filled the glass to the brim. She stood there at the sink and gulped it down in one fell swoop. The last thing she needed was to wake in the morning with a throbbing headache.

A small giggle escaped her lips. Surely she couldn't be drunk? No, just a little tipsy that's all.

Chris had insisted he walk her home, despite Hannah telling him she was a big girl and used to walking alone in the village at night. Chris ignored her protestations, linking his arm through hers, leading the way home. Thankfully there was no awkward doorstep scene where he tried to kiss her goodnight, thanks to their new-found friendship. He simply kissed her chastely on the cheek, told her to have a good night's sleep and that above all else, she really needed to talk to Dan. 'He's a good bloke,' he told her before waving goodbye. 'I've only just met him I know, but I can tell. Give him another chance.'

Those words now rang strong and clear in her head. This was her second chance she'd told herself as she stepped through the doorway. She'd been given this chance with him and she had to take it, didn't she?

She poured dry cat food into Daisy's bowl and topped up her water before slumping on the floor next to her. 'Why is my life so complicated?' she moaned, her head now resting on her knees. 'Why do I make a mess of everything?'

The ringing of the doorbell, followed by a bang on the door made her jump. She squinted at her watch. Who'd be calling round at ten o'clock at night? She stood slowly, the ground only shifting ever so slightly this time as she moved down the hallway. She flung open the door.

'Oh, so you're finally home then!' Emily shrieked.

Hannah opened and closed her mouth.

'You shouldn't open the door without asking who's there,' Emily scolded, her hands on her hips. 'I could have been an axe-wielding serial killer.'

'What?' Hannah slowly shook her head. What was Emily doing here?

Emily stepped towards Hannah and sniffed the air. 'Have you been drinking?' Her voice rose an octave in pitch. It hurt Hannah's ears. She'd been to the pub. Of course she'd had a drink.

Hannah mumbled that yes, she had been drinking and stood aside to let Emily in. 'Is everything okay?' she asked as she filled the kettle. She was acting on autopilot.

'I don't want a drink,' Emily snapped.

Hannah swivelled round to study Emily's face. She sounded mad. Really mad.

'I'm okay, but I'm not sure you are,' she said with a jab of her finger. 'What's going on with you, Hannah? Have you lost your mind!'

'Do you want to sit down?' Hannah asked.

'Yeah, let's sit in the living room.'

Hannah nodded, glad that Emily no longer looked quite so angry with her.

They sat down on opposite ends of the sofa.

'Let's start with why you lied to me?' Emily asked.

'I already told you. I didn't want to bump into Daniel.' Hannah wished she had gone to the surgery at lunchtime. If she had then maybe she'd have spoken to Daniel then and cleared the air. Maybe her date with Chris wouldn't have happened and Emily wouldn't be so angry with her. She hated that Emily was angry with her. 'I'm so sorry I lied to you.'

'Never do that to me again. I mean it, Han.'

'I'm sorry, I really am.' Hannah's lip began to tremble and despite telling herself not to cry, she couldn't help it. Huge, shaking sobs erupted from her mouth and soul as tears trickled down her face. She cried for being a terrible friend. She cried about going on a date with a man she had no intention of dating, and she cried for Dan and what he had been through.

Emily scooted along the sofa and flung an arm around her shoulder. 'This is so unlike you. Whatever is going on, eh? Why did you go on a date with Chris? I don't understand it?'

'Chris asked me out and Dan didn't,' Hannah said. She knew she sounded weak and pathetic.

'Chris asked you out for a drink, you said, not a date!'

'He did. It wasn't a date!'

Emily gave Hannah the evil eye. 'Daniel called round here tonight, didn't he?'

'H-how do you know that?' Hannah stammered.

'I bumped into him at the corner shop. I needed drinks for the boys' lunch boxes for tomorrow, so once Josh got home I popped out and there he was, loitering by the freezer cabinets.'

'And he told you he'd been here, to see me?'

'We got chatting, Hannah. I actually talk to the guy. You should try it sometime.'

Hannah ignored the sarcastic jibe. 'How did he seem?'

'He looked so sad, Han.'

Hannah bit her lip. She didn't want to cry again. 'What did he say exactly?'

Emily sighed. 'He just told me he'd been round to see you, to check how you were and that you were all right. I didn't tell him that I already knew you were fine and well.'

Hannah had never felt more ashamed in her life. 'He brought me flowers,' she blurted out.

Emily's mouth hung open in surprise. 'He brought you flowers!' Her hand swooped to her mouth. 'Oh Hannah, he never told me that.'

'Yep, a huge bunch of flowers. They're so pretty.'

'Oh I have to see them. Are they in the kitchen?'

Before Hannah could answer, Emily jumped up and half walked, half skipped into the kitchen. 'Two bunches. Wow. You are a lucky girl. Josh has never bought me two bunches of flowers.'

'Erm, no, the bunch in the vase is from Daniel.'

'So the bunch in the mop bucket is from Chris?'

'Yes,' Hannah said.

'Good job Daniel didn't see them,' Emily said. 'Now that would have been awkward.'

Hannah looked away. She didn't want to tell Emily the rest of the story.

'Oh for God's sake, don't tell me Daniel was here when Chris rocked up?'

Hannah swallowed. 'Yes, he was here.'

'Well that explains why he looked so sad,' Emily said.

She'd made him feel sad.

'You really shouldn't have gone out with Chris,' Emily said.

Hannah sighed, after all she couldn't argue with that.

'Right, I do think I need that cup of tea and then you can tell me everything that happened tonight. Is it a deal?'

'Yes,' Hannah said with a slight smile, 'it's a deal.'

Chapter Twenty-Three

Daniel locked the cottage door and stood for a moment on the path, his face upturned towards the sky. Even at this early hour on a Saturday morning, the heat hit his skin, making him feel glad to be alive. He rubbed his face. He just needed to get through the next couple of days. Then things would get a lot easier. He'd survived much worse.

He pushed open the surgery door with a deep sigh. Phyllis was already seated behind the reception desk with a cup of coffee and beamed at him.

'Good morning, Daniel,' she said, 'and how was your night?' She raised an arched brow, her eyes twinkling with reversed mischief.

Daniel let out another deep sigh. Here we go, he thought, as he prepared himself to tell Phyllis what had happened the night before. He might as well get it over with.

'I spent it in the usual way, Phyllis, with a microwave meal in front of the telly.' He made a half-hearted attempt to sidestep her, both physically and mentally, hoping to escape from her inquisitive stare, but no such luck.

She grabbed his sleeve and pulled him towards the desk and the vacant chair. 'Sit,' she ordered, her face now stern.

Daniel slumped down on the chair, resigned to his fate.

Daniel dumped his empty coffee mug into the sink and stood for a moment, his forehead resting against the wall cabinet.

'Daniel,' Emily shouted. 'I hoped I'd catch you in here before the clinic started.' She strode over to him and, without another word, grabbed his arm and dragged him down the corridor and into the empty consulting room. She pushed him inside and locked the door.

'What are you doing?' Daniel hissed, spinning round to look her in the eye.

'I need to talk to you,' she said.

'And we can't talk in the staffroom?' Daniel rested against the examination couch.

Emily leaned back against the storage cupboard and folded her arms. 'I don't want us to be disturbed,' she said.

She looked serious, deadly serious. The colour drained from Daniel's face. 'What's the matter? Has something happened to the boys? Has there been a family emergency?' All sorts of upsetting scenarios flashed through his mind. 'Do you need to take some time off, because if you do it's not a problem …'

Emily shook her head. 'No, nothing like that. This isn't about me. But there is something I need to tell you.'

'Okay …' Daniel had no idea where this was leading, but he'd hear her out.

'I saw Hannah last night, after chatting to you in the shop, and the truth is she looked downright miserable.'

'So, was she erm, well, was she home alone?'

'If you don't count Daisy, then, yes, she was home alone.'

'Oh.' Daniel pondered that for a moment. Then an awful thought struck him. 'Chris didn't hurt her, did he?

Did she call you and ask you to call around because he'd done something—'

Emily cut him off with a wave of her hand and a stern expression that could have soured milk.

'Chris couldn't hurt a fly, Daniel,' Emily cried. 'You must know that.'

Daniel sighed. Of course he knew that. Chris was a good bloke. 'But she looked miserable?' He raised an arched brow.

'Don't gloat,' Emily snapped.

'I am *not* gloating.' He lost his smile. He knew he shouldn't ask, but he had to know.

'So, it didn't go well then, her date?' He rubbed his neck.

'I never said that.' Emily pushed herself away from the storage cupboard and joined Daniel on the examination couch. She swung her legs, backwards and forwards.

Daniel's face fell.

'She had a good evening with Chris.' Emily sighed. 'It wasn't a complete disaster by any means.'

So why had Hannah been miserable then? Nothing Emily said made sense. He stretched out his legs and placed his hands on his thighs. He turned to face her. 'Why are we in here again?' he slowly asked. He really didn't want to hear all the gory details about Hannah's date night with Chris, but a part of him yearned to know what happened.

'So I can talk to you without being disturbed.' She flapped her hands, as if the question was a stupid one. 'Becky will be in soon and I don't want her to hear any of this.' She lowered her voice, which Daniel didn't quite understand because there was no one else in the room.

'This is important,' she said, followed by a deep scowl.

'So is the clinic,' Daniel replied sarcastically. Had everyone forgotten that he was the boss. He jumped down. He needed to get to work.

Emily either ignored his comment or hadn't realised he was being sarcastic. 'You need to talk to her.'

He leant against the door, folding his arms. 'Are you going to tell me what happened last night then?'

'That's not for me to tell,' Emily said, surprising him. 'You need to ask Hannah and I'm sure she'll tell you.'

So, she wasn't about to spill the beans after all, Daniel mused. 'Okay, I will.' He lifted up his arms in mock surrender. 'I'll talk to her. Happy now? We need to get to work.' He turned to open the door.

'No.'

'No,' Daniel said, spinning round to face her, hands on hips. His blue eyes now likely a steely shade darker.

'You need to do more than that, Daniel. You need to man up and tell her exactly how you feel. How you *really* feel.'

Daniel lowered his gaze to stare at his feet. 'You have no idea how I really feel.'

'Oh I think I do, you're not a great liar,' she said, reaching out to touch his arm, in a surprisingly tender gesture. He looked up, and met her gaze. 'Has anyone ever told you that you wear your heart on your sleeve?'

He laughed, to cover up his unease and mumbled, 'No, not really.'

'You need to tell her.'

'She doesn't feel the same way about me,' he muttered. 'There's nothing to tell.'

'Oh will you get over yourself,' she cried. 'How do you even know that when you don't talk to her? You two never have a proper conversation.'

She was right. They'd never really shared their feelings.

'She's calling in here to see me at lunchtime,' Emily said with a suggestive wink. 'You should talk to her then.'

Daniel cursed under his breath. 'I won't be here. I have a couple of house calls that I need to do.' He thought for a moment. 'I'll pop round to see her after work.'

'And you'll ask her out on a proper date?' Emily prompted.

'A date?'

'You were going to ask her out last night, weren't you.'

'How do you even know about that?'

A grin appeared on her face. 'Really, as if you need to ask.'

'Okay, okay, I'll ask her out. Will that make you happy?' He opened the door and had one foot out in the corridor.

'Yes, and no,' Emily said.

He turned back round. 'What? What does that mean?'

'You need to do more than that,' she said.

'I'll buy more flowers,' he said.

'Flowers aren't the answer,' she said. She stepped closer. 'Listen, I have an idea.'

Chapter Twenty-Four

'What's the matter, love?' Mrs Barlow's incredibly perceptive eyes scrutinised Hannah. 'I only ask because you don't seem to be your usual cheery self today.'

Hannah removed the yellow rubber gloves and draped them over the kitchen tap. 'I'm fine Mrs Barlow. Oh I don't know, I'm just tired I suppose.'

'Sit down a minute,' Mrs Barlow said as she patted the kitchen chair. 'Come and talk to me. It looks like you could do with a good chat.'

'I've still got to hoover and put the washing away,' Hannah said, thinking she only had half an hour left before she needed to get to Mr and Mrs Billing's and she didn't want to keep them waiting.

'Five minutes, come on, let's have a good gossip, eh, and you can tell me what's on your mind.'

'I'm okay, honestly—'

'Fiddlesticks! I may be old, but I'm not stupid.'

Hannah sat down.

Mrs Barlow pursed her lips together, waiting for Hannah to begin.

'I'm not a very nice person,' she began.

'What nonsense,' Mrs Barlow said, reaching out to pat Hannah's hand. 'You are one of the nicest people I know. No one ever says a bad word about you.'

'I went out with a man, on a date, and I shouldn't have.'

‘And?’ Mrs Barlow asked, utterly perplexed. ‘Why can’t you go out on dates with men? You’re a pretty girl. You’re single. You should be having the time of your life.’

‘This man has feelings for me and I knew that when he asked me out, but I don’t feel the same way about him. I led him on, and that’s not fair.’ Her hands covered her face.

She waited for the disapproval, but Mrs Barlow merely shook her head and laughed. ‘Don’t look so serious, love. These men, well some of them, need to be put in their place. There’s nothing stopping you from going out with whoever you like. Don’t beat yourself up over it. Anyway, how did it go? Not good by the look on your face.’

‘I had a good time,’ Hannah said, ‘once we got over the awkwardness. He’s a nice guy.’

‘Well, there you go then. There’s nothing to feel bad about’—she paused—’unless that’s not the whole story.’ Her eyes narrowed. ‘It’s not the whole story is it? What aren’t you telling me?’

‘I shouldn’t have gone out with this man because’—Hannah took a deep breath—’I’m in love with someone else.’

‘And that man would be Daniel Jackson, wouldn’t it? Please tell me I’m right?’ Mrs Barlow was positively beaming now.

‘Yes,’ Hannah replied in a small voice.

‘And you love this man? Daniel?’

‘Yes.’

‘Well, as far as I can tell, then there’s no problem. There really is no need for a sad face.’

'Last night was horrible. Dan was with me in the flat, when Ch—' Hannah nearly said his name, but she stopped herself. 'When my date called round to take me to the pub. It was very embarrassing.

'Well, that's all it was, dear. A bit embarrassing.' She cleared her throat. 'So I take it that you haven't spoken to Daniel yet?'

'Not yet,' Hannah sighed.

'But you will?'

'Yes. I'm calling round to the surgery to have lunch with Emily, and hopefully I'll see him there.'

'It'll all be all right in the end, you mark my words. I'm sure that in a few years you'll be laughing about it with your grandkids.'

Hannah's face went white as a ghost. *Grandkids*?

Mrs Barlow patted her hand with a low chuckle. 'Just talk to him, love and clear the air. Everything will be fine.'

'I will,' Hannah said.

'And tell him you love him. Men need to hear these things you know, just as us women do.'

Hannah nodded, her throat now thick and tight. She stood up and brushed down her apron, ready to start work again.

'Feeling better now?'

'Yes, thanks, I am,' Hannah said, and she did. Just a few hours to get through as best she could before she could see him, and the moment couldn't come quick enough.

The ride to Jackson Veterinary Practice took less than a minute. Hannah's heart was hammering in her chest and her cheeks were flushed as she pedalled furiously up and down the hills to get there as fast as she could. She came to a screeching halt by the driveway and hopped off the bike. She needed a few minutes to collect her thoughts before walking through the door. She sucked in lungfuls of cool, fresh air in an attempt to slow her beating heart. She placed her left palm against her cheeks; her face felt warm and droplets of sweat pooled along her brow.

She propped the bike against the wall around the side of the building and removed her rucksack so she could get to the bottle of water in the front pocket. After a few deep glugs of warm water, she checked the time on her watch. Emily would be on her lunch break now, and so should Dan, so with any luck she'd be able to chat to him. She didn't know how she'd get through the rest of the day without talking to him. She'd very nearly called round to the cottage before starting work, but had chickened out at the last minute, not knowing what time he got up, or if he had early morning rounds. She also hadn't wanted to surprise him at such an early hour, having no idea how he'd react to her standing on his doorstep.

With a final deep breath she put the bottle back into her bag, zipped it up, shrugged it onto her shoulders and stepped round the corner. Straight into Daniel who was striding towards his Land Rover.

She felt the hardness of his body, the warmth of his skin as his arms reached out to steady her from falling as he pulled her towards him. She swayed for a moment, resisting the urge to lean towards him, to be held, before stepping back. His hands gently, yet firmly, brushed her arms, moving upwards before resting on her shoulders.

'I'm so sorry,' he said, 'are you okay? I wasn't looking where I was going.' His eyes locked on hers as he brushed a stray strand of hair behind her ear.

She held her breath.

His fingers lingered near her neck, his touch hot, sending an electric jolt through her body.

His grip loosened, he stepped back.

'You sure you're okay?' His head tilted to the side as he lowered his voice. 'You look a little peaky.'

'No, no I'm fine,' she managed to say, attempting a breezy tone, feeling her cheeks flush with embarrassment. She swallowed, her throat dry. 'Actually, I was hoping to bump into you.' Her face grew redder. 'What I mean is—'

'I need to talk to you too, but now really isn't a good time.'

'Oh, yes of course. I can tell you're busy.' She looked down at her feet.

She felt his fingers brush her cheek, then her chin, as he tilted her head upwards. She had no option but to look into his eyes.

'I really do want to talk to you,' he said, 'but I'm off on a few house calls now.' He dropped his hand. 'Are you free tonight? Can I call round to see you? That is unless you have other plans?'

Was he blushing?

'Yes,' she managed to croak, while her heart skipped a beat. 'I'll be at home from around five, so anytime after then is fine.'

'Okay,' he said, holding her gaze.

Her breath hitched. Was he going to kiss her? Here, out in the open, where anyone could see them?

He cleared his throat, blinked and the spell broke. He smiled that lopsided smile she loved so much and sighed deeply. 'Right then, I'll see you later on.'

'See you later.' Hannah stepped to the side, giving him room to pass, but instead of moving forwards he hesitated before bending his head to kiss her on the cheek.

She felt his breath, hot and sweet, resisting the urge to turn her face so that their lips could touch.

'See you later,' he repeated, his breath in her ear.

Hannah's hand flew to her cheek as she watched him walk away. She could still feel his heat. She should have told him then that she loved him, but the words had stuck in her throat.

'And oh,' he said as he turned back around. His face broke out into the most dazzling smile that for a moment, she forgot to breathe. 'I have a surprise for you.'

'A surprise?' she asked. 'What kind of surprise?'

He shook his head and carried on walking. 'You'll see,' he called over his shoulder.

She watched him walk away, those familiar long strides of his as he headed to the Landy, then as he pulled out onto the country road, and only then, did she move.

'Oh hello, love,' Phyllis called as Hannah pushed open the surgery door.

'Is Emily in the back?' Hannah replied breathlessly, already running past the reception desk.

'Yes, she is.' Phyllis was now on her feet and tottering after her. Sammy looked up at them from the comfort of her dog bed. 'Whatever is the matter, lovely?' she said, gasping for breath. 'Oh, I'm far too old for this,' she muttered.

Hannah whirled round on the spot while grinning and threw her arms out wide. 'Everything is wonderful,

Phyllis,' she said, before spinning back round and running down the corridor towards the staffroom.

She flung the door open wide and lunged through the gap.

Emily, who'd just bitten into a cheese and pickle sandwich, stared at her.

Becky, who'd just made a cup of tea, nearly dropped the cup on the floor.

Phyllis leaned against the doorframe, panting for breath.

'I've just seen Dan,' Hannah squealed, popping down next to Emily on the couch.

'Daniel, as in our Daniel?' Becky asked quietly.

Phyllis threw her hands in the air. 'Oh that explains everything then.' She chuckled. 'I'll leave you girls to it, come on Becky love, you come with me.'

'But I'm on my lunch break,' Becky whined, most probably thinking she'd miss out on the gossip.

'Well, you can come and keep me company for a change,' Phyllis insisted, opening the door for Becky to pass through. 'Catch up with you later,' she said to Hannah before softly closing the door behind them.

'You want a drink? Emily asked.

'I'll just have water, thanks.' Hannah grabbed a glass from the shelf, filled it with tap water and drained it in a few deep glugs.

'You want to tell me what just happened, then? I take it you saw him in the car park?'

A grin so wide that it hurt, spread across Hannah's face. 'We bumped into each other, or rather, I bumped into him. I wasn't looking where I was going, but then again, neither was he.' She knew she was babbling, but she couldn't stop herself. The words flew from her mouth. 'I didn't see him, and anyway, he stopped and spoke to me.'

'And?' Emily raised an eyebrow and tapped her foot on the floor. 'What did he say?'

'Not much, he was in a rush, he couldn't stop because he's on house calls, but he didn't look mad or angry or sad.' Hannah's face broke out into the widest smile. 'In fact he looked pleased to see me.'

'Of course he looked pleased to see you. Why wouldn't he be?'

'Aren't you having lunch?' Emily asked, biting into her sandwich.

Hannah shook her head. 'I'm not that hungry.'

'What did Daniel say then?'

'He asked if he could call round to see me tonight?' She couldn't help it, she let out a small squeal of delight.

Emily joined in and threw her arms around her, squeezing her as if for dear life.

'He did?' she exclaimed. 'He's calling round to see you tonight?'

'Yeah.' Hannah laughed.

Emily grinned back. 'I am so happy right now,' she exclaimed. 'So bloody happy I could scream!'

Hannah laughed. 'Really, I can't tell.'

'Oh Hannah, I wish I'd known you both as teenagers. You would have made such a cute couple, you two were just made for each other. I really mean that.'

Hannah still felt that a little hard to believe, but at least they were back to talking again. It was a start. 'He told me he has a surprise for me.'

Emily ripped open a packet of crisps. 'Really, he did, did he?' She shoved a crisp into her mouth. Her eyes twinkled.

Hannah's eyes narrowed. 'You know, don't you? Spill the beans.'

'No, no, no, I am sworn to secrecy. He'd kill me if I told you.'

'Please tell me. I hate surprises.' She used her most pleading tones.

'It wouldn't be a surprise then, would it?'

'Is it a good surprise?' Hannah said, after taking a deep breath.

'What do you think?' Emily let out a chuckle.

Hannah didn't know what to think.

'So what are you going to wear?' Emily picked up her mug of tea and kicked off her shoes.

'Erm, my work clothes. I'll have just got in from work,' she said, now flustered at the thought of having to get dressed up. Would he expect her to dress up? But then, this wasn't a date, he was simply calling round to see her.

'Stop, stop those thoughts right now,' Emily said soothingly. 'I know exactly what you're thinking. I was joking. You could wear a potato sack and that man wouldn't care.'

'I think he would.' Hannah attempted a laugh but her throat was so dry with nerves she ended up having a coughing fit.

Emily jumped up and filled a glass with water from the tap. 'Here, drink this.'

Hannah gulped down a few mouthfuls. 'Thanks.'

'There's no need to feel anxious, you know. This is Daniel we're talking about. The kindest man I know.'

‘I’m scared, Emily.’

‘I know, but there’s no reason to be.’

Hannah let out a deep, shuddering sigh. ‘What if we’re making a mistake? What if it’s too soon?’

‘You’ve waited for this man for half your life Han, no one can accuse you of rushing anything.’

‘But what—’

‘There are no buts. It’s time you were happy, that you were both happy.’

Hannah managed the smallest of smiles.

‘I know why you’re afraid. He’s no longer the boy you fell in love with, he’s a living, breathing flesh-and-bones man.’ Emily raised a questioning brow, inviting Hannah to tell her she was wrong.

‘You’re right,’ she whispered. ‘The only long-term relationship I ever had was with him. There’s been no one else in my life, well no one who was important anyway. When he returned I told myself he’d soon be gone, just like last time. I tried to keep my distance from him.’

‘To protect yourself. I get that.’

Hannah’s face flushed with heat. ‘It sounds so silly, but when I saw him he seemed exactly the same and in my heart I knew I was in love with the boy he had been, not the man he is now, because the man standing before me was a stranger.’

‘I get it,’ Emily repeated. ‘But now you do know him, and he is staying here in the village because of you.’

‘Not just because of me, he has the practice here.’

‘Oh believe you me, he’d sell up in a heartbeat. It’s you he’s staying here for and I think that given time, he’ll grow to love the practice and the inhabitants of the village just as much as you.’

‘Has anyone ever told you that you should have been an agony aunt.’

‘I know I’ve missed my vocation in life.’ Emily matched Hannah’s smile. The two women grinned like idiots at each other.

‘It’ll all be all right, won’t it?’ Hannah asked, trying to control the wobble in her voice.

‘Course it will,’ Emily said as she wrapped her arm around Hannah’s shoulder.

‘And you won’t tell me what the surprise is?’ Hannah nudged Emily’s arm with her elbow.

‘Damn right I won’t. You’ll just have to wait and see.’

Chapter Twenty-Five

The clock struck five as a gorgeous Border collie with a sprained ankle left the clinic, with their very relieved owner. What had been a fairly quiet afternoon on paper had actually turned out to be a hectic and busy shift. 'You want a hand tidying up?' Becky asked, interrupting Daniel's thoughts.

'That'd be great, thanks,' he said, already ripping off the paper towel from the examination couch. He scrunched it into a ball and threw it into the waste bin. Ten minutes tops, then he'd be on his way to Hannah's flat.

Hannah with her smokey grey eyes and the kindest soul. A slow smile spread across his face.

'I can tidy up myself, if you like,' Becky said, interrupting his thoughts.

Although tempted to accept her kind offer, he never liked leaving the tidying up at the end of the day to the nurses. It never seemed fair to him, so he always tried to do his fair share. 'It'll be quicker with the two of us,' he said.

Becky remained tight-lipped for a moment before speaking. 'Honestly Dr Jackson, I can tidy up here, so that you can go and see Hannah.' Her face flushed a deep pink.

'Please call me Daniel,' he said, followed by a flash of a smile. 'Emily told you to send me on my way once the clinic finished, didn't she?'

Becky's neck flushed red as she stammered out her response. 'She did, but she didn't say anything about your date with Hannah.'

Daniel just about managed to repress his smile, but his eyes gave him away. 'Let's compromise. I'll stay for five minutes, then make tracks. That way Emily will never know.'

Becky appeared to relax and nodded her approval.

Two minutes passed before the door swung open, revealing a stern-looking Emily. She wore a scowl on her face. 'What are you still doing here?' She demanded before turning her full fierce stare on Becky. 'And as for you, I told you to make sure he didn't hang around here.'

'Hello-oh!' Daniel exclaimed. 'Who is the boss around here?'

For once Emily, stunned by his outburst, remained silent.

'The last time I looked, it was my name above the door so I call the shots.'

'I just don't want you to keep her waiting,' Emily said. 'And technically speaking, your name isn't above the door, as yet.'

With a rumble of laughter he raised his hands upwards. 'Okay, I'm going. You don't need to push me out the door.

'See you in the morning, Becky.'

'See you tomorrow, Daniel.'

'You have a good evening.'

'Get going,' Emily said, now looking more impatient than ever before as she gently pushed him out the door and into the corridor. 'Did you manage to get it?'

'Yes I did, and it's …' His voice trembled a little. 'It's perfect for her.'

Emily let out a tiny squeak as she clasped her hands together. 'I'm not sure who's more excited. Me or you?'

He smiled. There was no way he could explain how nervous he felt. Emily gave him another gentle shove. 'Now get going.

'I'm going,' he said. He couldn't wait to be with Hannah.

Hannah's last client of the day, Mr Bennett, took a little longer than expected and for once wanted to talk to her about a problem concerning his stiff, right knee. Hannah listened attentively, with her usual professional smile and reassured him that she'd escort him to the doctors if he so wished, while thinking that Dan might already be standing waiting for her on the doorstep. With a cheery wave and a promise to check up on him the following day to make sure he'd managed to grab a doctor's appointment, she jumped on her bike only to realise that she wouldn't be going anywhere. A rusty great big nail stuck out of the front tyre.

She slapped the handlebar with her hand, then winced as a jolt of pain surged up her arm. She'd have to walk, yet again, and there was no way of contacting Dan as the phone signal was so patchy out here. She checked her phone anyway, just on the off-chance, and her heart sank a little lower when the words "Emergency calls only" appeared on the screen. With a sigh of resignation she began to push the bike down the hill.

As she passed Chris's farm she slowed to a halt and hovered for a moment by the dry stone wall. Could she ask Chris for a lift, or was that being far too presumptuous? While she pondered this dilemma she heard the rumble of a tractor approaching, on its way down the hill.

A friendly voice called out to her. 'Hello Hannah. What are you doing out here?'

'I've just finished work,' she said, 'but I have a bit of a problem.' She pointed to the front tyre and the rusty nail.

Chris leaned out of the window to get a better look. 'That is a bit of a problem.' He chuckled. 'Right then, you want a lift?'

'Thank you, that would be absolutely wonderful!'

Hannah pulled out the bobby pins that were keeping her bun in place and shook out her hair, allowing the long, blonde tendrils to be free. Her scalp tingled and her skin itched with the heat. Running her fingers through her hair she wondered if she'd have time to change, then quickly dismissed the thought. She simply didn't.

Daisy brushed up against her leg, as if sensing that Hannah needed a little reassurance. She bent down and stroked her arched back, feeling the deep purr reverberate through her fingers. 'You're such a good girl and you're going to see Daniel soon, the nice man who saved your life. What do you think about that?' she asked.

Daisy replied with a bump of her head against Hannah's thigh. 'I think you're just as excited as me.' Hannah laughed, standing up, knowing that what Daisy really needed was food, not chatter.

A nice man, a good man, she thought. A flesh, blood and bones man who was one of the most remarkable men she'd ever known.

The knock on the door jolted her out of her thoughts and a warm glow spread across her skin. She told herself to breathe as she opened the door.

‘Hi.’ Daniel stood there with the widest grin on his face.

For a second, Hannah almost forgot to breathe.

‘Hi,’ she replied in barely a whisper. She cleared her throat. ‘Come on in,’ she said, taking a step back.

‘I can’t,’ he said, his eyes narrowing ever so slightly as his lips twitched.

‘You can’t?’ Hannah’s throat tightened and the words very nearly got stuck. ‘You don’t want to come in?’

‘Oh God no.’ He reached out and took her hand in his and laughed. ‘I can’t come in because you need to come outside with me.’ He pulled her gently towards him and she got a delicious whiff of his aftershave. She tottered for a moment, lost in his eyes and those long eyelashes. She longed to touch his face, to sweep back the damp, brown hair that looked shower fresh and had fallen forward over his brow.

‘Come with me,’ he said again. His fingers intertwined with hers, giving them a gentle squeeze as he led her outside.

‘Where are we going?’ she asked. ‘I’ll need to lock the door.’

‘No need to lock the door,’ he said. Then he pointed to the railings.

Hannah tore her gaze away from his face to the railings opposite her flat. Propped up against them was a bike, and a brand new bike by the looks of it. The bright yellow paintwork gleamed in the evening sun and there wasn’t a patch of rust in sight. A light brown wicker basket adorned the front, as did a large pink bow. Her heart pounded in her chest. She hadn’t let go of his hand, she couldn’t let go.

'Do you like it?' he asked.

The slight hesitation and faint tremble in his voice made her heartbeat quicken. The thought that she wouldn't love this gesture, or the man behind it brought a lump to her throat.

She turned to face him, the uncertainty of her reaction so clearly evident on his face she wanted to cry. She threw her arms around him, there on the street where anyone could see them and buried her face in his neck. His arms encircled her waist and held her close to his body. She could feel the pounding of his heart against her ribs, matching her own. 'I love it. No one has ever done anything so nice for me, never,' she said.

'You deserve nice things.' His mouth, close to her ear, sent tingles shooting down her spine. His hands gently stroked her arms as he stepped backwards, giving her space to turn and look at her shiny new bike once more. 'Did I choose the right colour?'

'Yes.' Her voice was breathy and she found it hard to articulate how she felt. 'I love yellow. It's such a happy colour.'

'I chose yellow because it matches your personality.' His words were slow and deep.

She turned to face him once more, her eyes searching his face for any signs of amusement, but she found none.

'You're such a happy person, Hannah, a ray of sunshine for those in need. You brighten up everyone's day.' He reached out and brushed an index finger along her cheekbone. 'Including mine,' he added softly.

'I brighten up your day?'

'Hm-mm,' he said, his fingers now toying with a strand of hair.

'This is so thoughtful of you,' she said, her heart thumping against her ribs, 'but I'm not sure how long it'll take me to repay you.'

'What? No.' He looked positively offended. 'This is a gift, Hannah. I mean, your old bike is lovely and all, but it really has seen better days, so I just thought—'

She silenced him by pressing a finger to his lips. His hand reached up and clasped her fingers. He kissed them slowly.

She briefly closed her eyes, savouring his touch that was so unexpected.

'I know it's a relic of a bike,' she eventually said, forcing her eyes open. She took a deep breath, preparing for his reaction. 'Actually about that, your timing is pretty much perfect.'

'Oh,' he slowly released her fingers, a lopsided smile appeared on his face and yet again, Hannah wanted to reach up and kiss him. 'My bike is actually in the back of Chris's tractor.'

'Oh', he repeated, this time with a raised eyebrow, 'and what's the story there then? I take it there is a story?'

Hannah smiled, happy in the knowledge that he hadn't reacted badly to the mention of Chris's name. 'I'd been to see Mr Bennett, out near the farm. You'll have to pop in and see him. Have a catch-up. I know he'd love to see you, hear all your stories from the big city. To be honest I do feel a little sorry for him.'

'Hm-mm,' Daniel murmured with a touch of amusement in his eyes.

'Well, anyway,' Hannah continued, now fully aware of her babbling, but she couldn't stop. 'When I hopped on my bike I spotted a rusty great big nail sticking out of the wheel.'

'This sounds vaguely familiar.' Daniel laughed. 'Let me guess, Chris drove past in his tractor and rescued you.'

Hannah scrutinised his face for any tell-tale sign of jealousy, but saw none. Her shoulders relaxed. 'Yes,' she said, 'exactly that.'

'Well, it's a good job he drove past and could help you.'

'He's just a friend,' Hannah blurted out, before she could stop herself. 'We just went for a drink last night, nothing else happened.'

'I know Han,' he said. 'We don't need to talk about that.' He gave a small chuckle and said, 'I nearly forgot. Take a look in the basket.'

The basket? Hannah swivelled around, her eyes falling once more on her new bike.

'Go on, look in the basket,' he said.

Nestled inside was a small brown envelope. She picked it up, sensing that whatever was inside weighed very little. Her fingers reached inside and plucked out a small object. A locket in the shape of half a heart. Her hand flew to her throat. 'You kept it,' she forced out the words. 'All these years.'

Searching her eyes with his he let out a soft sigh. 'I think we got off to a bad start. What with one thing or another, but I'd like to try again. Can we do that? Start again? Me and you?'

She loved the sound of that. Starting over. 'Yes, I'd like nothing better.'

He held out his hand.

She took it.

'My name is Daniel Jackson and I'm in love with you.'

He was still nervous, she thought, as she reached up on her toes to kiss him. Her hands touched his face, feeling his strong jaw and then she ran her fingers through his hair as he wrapped an arm around her waist, pulling her closer towards him. The kiss was deep and sweet and for a fleeting moment she forgot they were standing on the pavement.

With a shuddering sigh and a wry smile, his eyes smouldering with love and desire that made Hannah want to weep, he released his grip and smiled.

'I love you too.' Her words came out in a rush, her heart still racing and the blood in her veins thrumming with the sheer joy of him. 'I love you,' she repeated again, this time slowly before reaching up with shaking hands to undo the clasp of her necklace and pulling free the long silver chain from around her neck that had been tucked into her tunic top, revealing a locket in the shape of half a heart. She pressed the silver chain and locket into the palm of his hand.

'You kept your half too,' he said. 'All these years, you kept it.'

She took the locket from the palm of his hand and joined the two halves together, making one complete heart.

'A perfect match,' he said. His voice shook as he bent down to kiss her once more.

Chapter Twenty-Six

One year later

The sleepy village of Middlefern basked in the heat of the lazy summer sun. There hadn't been a drop of rain all week and the residents were making the most of the unexpected dry spell. Hannah Jackson had just finished her last shift of the day and for the foreseeable future. She waved goodbye to Mrs Barlow, promising she'd call in and see her next week, before riding her yellow bike down the hill and towards the surgery.

'Hello lovely,' Phyllis said from behind the reception desk. 'You're in luck. He's just finished with the last patient of the day.'

'I'll just go on through then,' Hannah said.

'Course you can, lovely.' Phyllis abruptly stood up. 'Oh I nearly forgot, how did your last day go?'

'It was fine, same as usual really.' She forced a smile. It had been like any other day. 'I'll still keep in touch with everyone, so it doesn't feel like the end of things really.'

'Of course it doesn't, but even so, you've worked for Claire for such a long time. It's bound to feel a little strange.'

'I don't think it's sunk in yet, maybe tomorrow it'll hit me.'

'Maybe, oh you've got such exciting things ahead of you now.' Phyllis scooted round the desk and gave Hannah a quick, friendly hug. 'I know your mum would've been so proud of you.'

'I know,' Hannah said.

'There you are!' A gruff, deep and to Hannah's ears, incredibly sexy voice sounded behind her. She turned to find Daniel striding towards her with a smile on his face. 'Well, how was your last day?' He planted a kiss on her cheek.

'Good, it was good,' Hannah said, suddenly feeling weary and just wanting to go home.

'Everything all right?' He touched her shoulder, giving it a gentle squeeze.

'Yeah just a little tired, that's all.' Her smile wobbled.

'Let's go home then,' he said, wrapping an arm around her.

She rested her head on his shoulder. 'Yeah, let's go home.'

Together, they'd ripped the brown wallpaper off, painted the walls, and removed the rust red carpet to make the old cottage their new home. Jugs containing wildflowers adorned window sills and throws covered the hardwood floors. It had taken them six months of hard work to transform the cottage.

It had taken much longer for Daniel to walk down those cellar steps.

At first, he only made it down a few steps before he started gasping for breath and needing the safety of light and space and air. But even though it had taken him nearly a year, he'd done it, he'd forced himself to walk down every single step and stand in that dark, damp cellar with Hannah by his side, holding his hand. He'd only managed it because of Hannah and months of counselling. Hannah had suggested he visit the therapist she had seen following her mother's death. At first, he thought he might conquer his debilitating fear with Hannah's help alone, but she had urged him to see her therapist and he was glad she had persisted, as she'd been right.

He still had a long way to go, it was still early days, but he'd learn to live with his fear and to not allow it to destroy his life. Hannah had plans for the cellar. She wanted to paint it a bright yellow colour and use it as a reading nook. She'd already installed a few bookshelves and it would be the perfect spot to curl up and re-read all of Dan's letters, *love letters*, the ones he had written to her but had never posted. She had read every single one, twice and knew she could never part with them. He had poured his heart and soul into those letters and she'd shed happy tears while reading them.

Dan liked her idea of a reading nook and hoped that one day he'd be able to sit in there and relax with a good book. That together they could make new and happy memories.

One day.

'Just one drink, then back here,' Hannah said with a sigh. She really wasn't in the mood for going to the pub, but Dan insisted she needed to celebrate her new start in life.

'One drink, I promise,' he said, buttoning up his white shirt.

'You're getting dressed up for a pint in the pub.' She laughed.

'And why not?'

'Hm-mm, you look kind of sexy tonight,' she murmured, resting a hand on his chest. She could feel his heart beating through the fabric. 'Couldn't we just stay in?'

Clearing his throat, Daniel rested his hand on top of hers. 'As much as I love the sound of that, no. I'm taking you out, Mrs Jackson.' He quickly squeezed her hand, then reached behind him for a tie.

Hannah smiled, still loving the sound of her new name on her husband's tongue. Instinctively she twisted the gold band around her finger.

'Blue or green?' he asked, holding out two ties.

'Blue,' she said without hesitation. 'Here let me.'

Taking the tie from him she wrapped it around his neck and placed it under the collar.

'Do you think I've made the right decision?' she asked.

'About the tie? Yes, but perhaps the green?' He smiled and asked gently, 'What's brought this on?'

'I don't know, it's such a big change.' She stepped back. 'There you go.'

'Thanks, it is a big change, but sometimes change is good.' He arched his brow. 'I mean, look at us, we're a great example.' He snaked an arm around her waist and pulled her to him. 'You just need to relax and enjoy what's ahead of you.'

'I know, I'm just being silly.' She breathed in the scent of his aftershave, the comforting sense of him.

'No you're not,' he said as he brushed away her fringe and kissed her forehead. 'It's normal to have doubts, but you've always wanted to study English literature and now you can and who knows where that will lead …'

'I'm not too old?'

'Hannah, you're thirty-one.'

'I know, but everyone else will be eighteen.'

'Not everyone, and some will be older than you, you know.'

Hannah sighed in agreement. He was right.

'Right then, I just need to grab my wallet and we're good to go.'

Hannah grabbed her purse and willed herself to smile. She should feel happy, she should be happy, but something troubled her. Why hadn't Claire said thank you for all her years of dedicated service? Not even a text or phone call. She didn't want chocolates or flowers, but a quick thank you would have been nice. She'd been out of the office all day.

'Come on, let me take my beautiful wife out for a drink.' He kissed her cheek. 'Ready?'

'Yeah, let's go.'

The two of them held hands as they walked the short distance to The Middlefern Arms. They didn't pass another soul, which Hannah thought a bit odd on such a lovely Friday summer evening.

As they crossed the road to the pub the evening seemed to become even stranger. 'It looks like the pub's closed,' she said. Maybe she'd get her quiet night in after all.

'It can't be closed on a Friday night.' Daniel peered through the large bay window.

'Let's go home.' Hannah tugged his hand.

'I'll just knock on the door,' he said, 'check Brenda's okay.'

'Oh, I hadn't thought of that.' What if something had happened to her? She was getting on a bit.

Daniel rapped his knuckles against the glass on the door and then pushed to see if it was locked. The door moved. 'Wait here,' he said.

'No way,' Hannah argued. Brenda might be hurt. With her hand on his back to steady her nerves she followed him into the dark pub.

'Hello, Brenda, are you all right?' Daniel shouted. He grabbed Hannah's hand and then all the lights came on.

'Surprise!' A chorus of voices shouted.

Hannah shrieked out in shock before fully processing the scene before her. Daniel's grip tightened.

Brenda stood in the middle of the room surrounded by a chorus of much loved faces. Mrs Barlow sat on a chair and gave Hannah a quick wave before dabbing at her eyes with a tissue. She spied Emily and Josh with the twins, the two small boys jumping up and down in their excitement, and she swore Emily was trying not to cry.

Streamers and bunting hung from the ceiling and the tables that usually dominated the room had been pushed up against the walls to make room for dancing. A row of long trestle tables, covered with white linen cloths, had been placed at the back of the room, on top of which were plates of buffet food. In the centre was an enormous chocolate cake decorated with pale pink flowers. Hannah tried to take this all in as her friends cheered and clapped.

Claire stepped forwards with a huge bouquet of flowers.

Hannah's throat tightened, and to think she'd thought the very worst of her boss.

'This was Claire's idea, to throw a surprise party,' Daniel whispered in her ear. 'So don't go blaming me.' He chuckled.

'This is just a small token to say how much I'm going to miss you.' Claire handed her a gold coloured envelope. 'And hopefully this'll come in handy for your studies.'

Hannah's hands shook as she slipped out the piece of card. A book token. 'Thank you so much, you didn't have to do this,' Hannah said, now with tears in her eyes.

'Oh, yes I did,' Claire said and then after a brief hesitation gave Hannah a quick hug.

Hannah patted her back. She'd always found it slightly ironic that Claire worked in the care industry but didn't like hugs.

'Right, this is all getting a bit too serious for me,' Brenda shouted at the top of her voice. 'Let's get this party started!' As if on cue, the lights dimmed and music began to blare out of the speakers.

Hannah turned to Daniel, the brightest smile on her face.

'Want to dance?' he asked, a wicked glint now in his eyes.

'You hate dancing.' She giggled.

'Here, let me take those for you.' Emily had appeared as if out of nowhere and took the flowers and envelope. 'Go have fun,' she said over the music.

Hannah laughed as she took Daniel's outstretched hand. 'Really, you want to dance?'

'Hm-mm,' he said, his mouth twitching as he stroked her knuckles with his thumb.

Soon everyone was up and dancing. The room swayed with the uptempo beat of the music and echoed with the sounds of laughter and chatter. Daniel held Hannah in his arms, her head on his shoulder as they moved around the room. She felt his love and his strength with every fibre of her being. She wrapped her arms around his neck and together they danced the night away.

* The End *

Thank You

I would like to thank you, the reader, for reading this book. I hope you enjoyed Daniel and Hannah's story as much as I enjoyed writing it.

If you've enjoyed *A Vacancy for a Village Vet* then please do leave a review on the website where you bought the book. Every review helps a new author like me. You can follow me on Twitter and Facebook at @JoBodenAuthor.

Please do get in touch for a chat and all the latest news! I look forward to hearing from you.

Much love, Jo x

About the Author

Joanne Boden lives in Lancashire with her husband and their two sons. When she is not busy writing, she likes to take her boys to the local museums, cafes and for walks in the countryside. Joanne has published four non-fiction works aimed at parenting children on the Autistic spectrum, based upon her experiences as a mother of an autistic son. She has also self published a contemporary romance novel, *Picking up the Pieces*.

Joanne writes contemporary romances with gorgeous heroes.

For more information on Joanne visit:
www.twitter.com/JoBodenAuthor
www.facebook.com/JoBodenAuthor

More Choc Lit
from
Joanne Boden

Escape to Little Bluewater Bay

Start the new year in Little Bluewater Bay ...

New year, new Willow Jenkins? All Willow knows is that she needs an escape. So, she takes an extended break from her PR job and retreats to her grandmother's cosy cottage by the sea in Little Bluewater Bay, where a limitless supply of hot chocolate will soothe her broken heart and a limited wi-fi connection will prevent her workaholic tendencies.

Willow is soon made to feel welcome by the friendly locals – although grumpy artist Noah Atkinson doesn't seem to like her very much. Just what is his problem?

But then Willow is asked by her grandmother to approach Noah with a very special commission, only to discover that he hasn't painted people for a long time – and with good reason. Will he make an exception, and in doing so usher in a hopeful and healing new era for them both?

Visit www.choc-lit.com for more details.
Also available as an audiobook.

Introducing Choc Lit

We're an independent publisher creating a delicious selection of fiction.
Where heroes are like chocolate – irresistible!
Quality stories with a romance at the heart.

See our selection here: **www.choc-lit.com**

We would love to hear how you enjoyed *A Vacancy for a Village Vet*. Please leave a review where you purchased the novel or visit: **www.choc-lit.com** and give your feedback.

Choc Lit novels are selected by genuine readers like yourself. We only publish stories our Choc Lit Tasting Panel want to see in print. Our reviews and awards speak for themselves.

Could you be a Star Selector and join our Tasting Panel?
Would you like to play a role in choosing which novels we decide to publish? Do you enjoy reading romance novels? Then you could be perfect for our Choc Lit Tasting Panel.

Visit here for more details ...
www.choc-lit.com/join-the-choc-lit-tasting-panel

Keep in touch:
Sign up for our newsletter for all the latest news and offers: www.spread.choc-lit.com.
Follow us on:
Twitter: @ChocLituk * Facebook: Choc Lit
& Instagram: ChocLituk